CHARTERS & CALDICOTT

A novel by
STELLA BINGHAM

based on the BBC tv serial by
KEITH WATERHOUSE

PENGUIN BOOKS

PENGUIN BOOKS

Viking Penguin Inc., 40 West 23rd Street,
New York, New York 10010, U.S.A.
Penguin Books Ltd, Harmondsworth,
Middlesex, England
Penguin Books Australia Ltd, Ringwood,
Victoria, Australia
Penguin Books Canada Limited, 2801 John Street,
Markham, Ontario, Canada L3R 1B4
Penguin Books (N.Z.) Ltd, 182–190 Wairau Road,
Auckland 10, New Zealand

First published in Great Britain by the
British Broadcasting Corporation 1985
Published in Penguin Books 1986

LIBRARY OF CONGRESS CATALOGING IN PUBLICATION DATA
Bingham, Stella.
Charters & Caldicott.
I. Charters & Caldicott (Television program)
II. Title.   III. Title: Charters and Caldicott.
PR6052.I777C5   1986   823'.914   85-31976
ISBN 0 14 00.8998 5

The characters of Charters and Caldicott first
appeared in *The Lady Vanishes*, a film made by the
late Alfred Hitchcock for a production company which
became part of The Rank Organisation PLC.

Printed in the United States of America by
Offset Paperback Mfrs., Inc., Dallas, Pennsylvania
Set in Times Roman

CHAPTER 1

It was the first Friday in June. As on all other first Fridays in the calendar, Hugo Charters was listening to Radio News-reel on the World Service of the BBC on his ancient, bakelite wireless while he made ready to leave for Town. His country cottage, complete with beams and diamond-paned windows, was unmistakably Home Counties but his furnishings spoke of years of service in the Far East. Trophies and mementoes from long-free colonies were arranged fussily on the bamboo dressing table and rattan whatnot. On the wall hung a framed and faded photograph of Charters in a white dinner-jacket arm-in-arm with a lady at some outpost-of-the-Empire function long ago. Charters himself, even in retirement, gave the bristly impression that, if called upon, he would have taken command of a small court of inquiry or a large gin sling with equal aplomb.

His toilet complete, Charters, a prudent man, picked up his hat, raincoat and umbrella and went out, double-locking the front door behind him. He walked briskly to the main road and raised his umbrella imperiously, as if to hail a taxi. The approaching Green Line bus came obligingly to a stop.

In his flat in Viceroy Mansions, an imposing Edwardian block near Hyde Park, Giles Caldicott was also tuned in to the World Service. Compared with Charters' neat taste in interior design, the Caldicott residence was bachelorish, almost Bohemian. A clutter of pipe-racks and cricket prints, well-read detective novels and curios from round the world crammed the living room and overflowed into the bedroom where Caldicott was examining himself critically in the mirror. Satisfied that his hair lay smooth and his jacket was entirely free from fluff, he went into the sitting room, filled his cigarette case from an onyx box, collected his hat and brolly, turned off the radio and left the flat. An ancient lift took him down to the lobby where he found the porter polishing the brasswork.

''Morning Grimes.'

'It's a very good morning, Mr Caldicott. If you're walking as far as Niceprice, sir, I'm told they've got teabags on special offer.'

'I think not, Grimes. Besides, this is my first Friday.'

5

''Course it is, sir. With Mr Charters. So you won't be back?'

'Until sixish, thereabouts. Why do you ask?'

'The young lady, sir. If she calls again.'

'Oh, Miss Beevers. Look – if she *does* come back, see if you can't worm a phone number out of her. Better still – if she calls before three and cares to wait, let her into the flat, then ring me at the Club at once.'

'Would that be all right, sir?'

'Good heavens, yes. Known her since she was so high.' Caldicott set his hat on his head at a slightly rakish angle and strode off towards the park.

Charters arrived first in St James's and, to his annoyance, was accosted outside the Club by a pretty young woman selling flags for Petunia Day. He paid up with poor grace and permitted a flag to be pinned to his lapel. Caldicott, coming along shortly afterwards, responded in an altogether sunnier fashion. The flag seller and a young, uniformed chauffeur who had been lounging against the bonnet of a Jaguar reading the racing pages during these transactions both watched, with keen but covert interest, as Caldicott climbed the steps and vanished through the doors. Satisfied that both men were safely inside the Club, the pair behaved in a curious fashion. They threw the chauffeur's cap and the flag seller's collecting tin and tray onto the back seat of the car, climbed into the front and the Jaguar screeched off down the street.

Caldicott came across Charters in the Club cloakroom, a marble and bronze monument to Victorian plumbing.

'There you are. I see they nobbled you, too,' said Charters, looking up from washing his hands.

'What's that, old boy?' Charters indicated the petunia flag. 'Oh, Petunia Day. Good cause, Charters. Nannies out to grass, what?'

'Not the point,' Charters grumbled. 'Petunia Day was last week.'

'So it was. Two bites at the same cherry, eh?'

'As it happens, they don't clash with any other charity but I don't mind telling you, Caldicott, had today been Lifeboat Day I should have declined that petunia. Shall we go in?'

They began their lunch in comfortable, companionable

silence, their small talk exhausted years before. The Club dining room, dark-panelled, high-ceilinged and still fairly empty, was not, in any case, conducive to idle chatter. Only when the meal was ordered and the first course disposed of did Caldicott move on to the business of the day.

'Well, Charters, have you studied the form?'

'Yes. I thought that thing at the Curzon.'

'It's in French,' Caldicott protested.

'Is it? The title's in English.'

'They do that nowadays. That's how they catch out our country cousins.'

Charters was wounded by the slur but before he could come up with a suitable retort a fellow member paused by their table. Although Venables looked every inch the typical clubman, there was something elusively mysterious about him. Little was known about his background and even his occupation was a matter for speculation.

''Morning, Caldicott,' he greeted Charters. 'Charters,' he nodded to Caldicott.

Charters looked peeved. 'No, he's Charters, Venables,' said Caldicott. 'I'm Caldicott.'

'Of course you are,' said Venables amiably and drifted off to his own table.

Charters glared after him then transferred his ire to Caldicott. 'He knows very well which one of us is who. Why do you always rise to the bait?'

'Hardly worth taking issue with the man, old chap. One has to be civil.'

'That's a matter of opinion.'

'Well, back to the agenda. What do you say to that thing at Plaza One?'

'I've already seen it,' said Charters, getting his own back at last. 'At the ABC, Reigate. We're not entirely out of touch in the country, you know, Caldicott.'

While Charters and Caldicott were squabbling over their afternoon's cinema viewing, a taxi drew up outside Viceroy Mansions and decanted an attractive young woman, smartly dressed in a grey suit. As Grimes had half anticipated, Jenny Beevers had called to see Caldicott.

'You've missed him again, I'm sorry to say, Miss,' Grimes told her, not best pleased. 'I believe I *did* mention – his first Friday.'

'First,' said Jenny, dismayed. 'I thought you said third.'

'First. Never misses – noted for it. He *did* say could you leave a number, where you could be contacted, style of thing.'

Jenny Beevers hesitated. 'No – I'm moving about. I'll try to come back. Will you let him know?'

'I'll put a "While You Were Out" slip in his pigeon-hole.' Grimes went behind his desk to scribble the message. 'Shall I say you hope to make contact later?' Jenny nodded. 'I'll see he gets it.' Jenny watched Grimes put the note in Caldicott's pigeon-hole on the wall behind the desk, smiled her thanks and moved off as Grimes's telephone rang.

'Porter. Yes, Mrs Brinovsky . . . Oh, yes? . . . I expect he's after a pigeon, madam – it has been known with cats . . . Yes . . . Yes . . .' Grimes yawned and shifted his weight from one leg to the other, resigned to its being a very long call.

Meanwhile Jenny, pressed against the wall out of sight of Grimes, waited.

Charters and Caldicott eyed their main course critically. 'Two lamb cutlets, you'll notice. It used to be three,' Charters grumbled.

'In days of yore. Say this for 'em – they *are* keeping prices down.'

'Two lamb cutlets for the price of three isn't keeping prices down, Caldicott. It's fifty per cent inflation.'

Caldicott attempted a spot of mental arithmetic. 'How do you make that out?' he asked, giving up.

'It's perfectly obvious. Starting with three lamb cutlets we reduce the quantity by a third while keeping the price constant. Hence a fifty per cent increase in real terms.'

'But fifty per cent is a half, old man. Even I know that.'

'What's that got to do with it?'

'Whereas we've reduced our lamb cutlets by a third. How can a third be the same as a half?'

'I don't think you're getting the hang of it at all, Caldicott,' said Charters, readily donning the mantle of instructor. 'Look, may I?' He reached across to remove one of Caldicott's cutlets and put it on his own plate. 'Here are three lamb cutlets. Now let us say they cost . . .' He rummaged for change. 'Have you a tenpenny piece?' Caldicott, totally baffled, produced one obediently. 'For the sake of simplicity and purely for the purposes of demonstration, let us say they cost thirty pence. Or ten pence each. Are you with me so far?' Charters laid the three coins down on the table.

'Ten pence each,' said Caldicott, adding knowledgeably, 'That's not in real terms, of course.'

'Quite. Now I remove one lamb cutlet . . .' Charters laid it back on Caldicott's plate '. . . while not altering the price. See the coins. The cost is still thirty pence, but for two lamb cutlets instead of three. Thus we are paying fifteen pence per cutlet instead of ten – an increase, in other words, of fifty per cent. Now do you follow me?' Charters slid two of the ten pence pieces into his palm and would have removed the third had not Caldicott pressed his finger firmly on it. 'Ah,' Charters apologised.

Caldicott frowned down at his own plate, then across at Charters'. He was still not satisfied. 'There's just one thing, Charters.'

'Yes?'

'This isn't my cutlet. Do you mind?' To Charters' irritation, Caldicott returned one cutlet to his plate and removed a larger one that he believed to be his own.

'Yes, madam,' said Grimes, yawning again. 'Yes, madam . . . no, madam, I think you'll find cats *don't* fall off balconies as a general rule, Mrs Brinovsky . . . All right, madam, if it makes you happier in your mind . . .' Sighing, Grimes replaced the receiver, pulled down the security grille over the desk and left his cubby-hole, checking that the door was securely locked behind him. When she heard the lift doors close, Jenny emerged from her hiding place, pushed up the grille which Grimes had omitted to lock, hoisted herself up onto the counter and jumped down the other side. She took Caldicott's spare key from the pigeon-hole where she'd seen Grimes leave her note and dropped it into her handbag.

'By the way, I've been meaning to ask you, Charters,' said Caldicott, looking up from the remains of his second lamb cutlet, now unappetising and cold as a result of its contribution to higher mathematics. 'H.L.C.?'

'Come again?'

'Your initials.'

'You know perfectly well they're my initials. Dammit, you saw me carve them on a school desk.'

I meant in *The Times*.'

'Oh, *The Times*!' Charters placed his knife and fork neatly together on his empty plate. 'My little appreciation of Jock Beevers. "H.L.C. writes . . ."'

'Well put, I thought, Charters. Caught the spirit of the man in a few well-chosen phrases.'

'Did you think so, old chap? Thank you. Thank you very much. I value your opinion. One did feel a need to add to the obituary. It didn't quite do justice to the Jock Beevers we knew.'

'Quite. I've been meaning to tell you. I think his daughter came to see me.'

'I didn't know she was in England. What do you mean, you "think" she came to see you?'

'I was out. It does sound like her, though, doesn't it?'

'I wasn't there.'

'Nor was I – but how many Miss Beevers does one know? Presumably she's after Jock's bits and pieces.'

'*I* have those,' Charters pointed out.

'But does Janie know that?'

'Not Janie – Jeannie.'

'Jenny.'

'Jenny. Of course. She must be all of – what? – twenty-five by now?'

'When she turns up again we ought to take her out to dinner.'

'Soho?' said Charters doubtfully.

'Lunch?'

'Tea, I would have thought. More appropriate . . . So you thought my little postscript on Jock hit the right note?'

'Absolutely. Only one minor quibble, old boy.'

'What?'

'On a matter of the tiniest historical detail. I nearly wrote to *The Times* myself but I thought you might take offence.'

'Not at all,' said Charters, offended. 'These things are checked through and through by sub-editors, you know, Caldicott.'

'They missed this one, Charters. In referring to Jock Beevers' cricket accomplishments, you said his school batting average had never been surpassed.'

'Nor has it.'

'By point three runs,' said Caldicott. 'Nineteen seventy-nine. One Thistleton, G.R.W. Now plays for one of the minor counties.'

'Yes, I've heard of him. Promising all-rounder. He wasn't at Grimchester – it would have been in the school rag.'

'Expelled for pot-smoking the same term.'

'I shall need proof of that.'

'Do you doubt my word?'

'My dear fellow, not in the least. I want to see if there's a footnote. Expulsion, especially in the summer term, may mean his average doesn't count.'

Caldicott began to get up. 'Only one way to find out.'

'Would you mind, Caldicott. I haven't had my welsh rarebit yet.'

Jenny Beevers made her way up to Caldicott's flat unchallenged and let herself in. She glanced diffidently round the sitting room, uncertain where to begin. Suddenly she froze, staring in terrified horror through the open bedroom door.

The Club's substantial and well-stocked library was more valued by members for its comfortably upholstered chairs and rule of silence than for its literary riches. But Charters and Caldicott were too early to disturb any post-prandial dozers as they searched the shelves with growing irritation. 'I shall write to the library committee,' said Charters crossly from the top of a set of steps.

'The one Wisden we need to settle the argument,' said Caldicott, glaring at the gap in the row of cricketers' almanacs.

Charters climbed down. 'The notice is there, as plain as the nose of your face. "Rule 43B. No volume to be removed from the library under any circumstance except by arrangement." '

'Nonetheless, removed it has been. Now what's to be done?'

'Ah, that's where *our* rules come in. You lose by default, therefore you owe me a large port. Come along, there's just time.'

'I don't think so, Charters. I don't think so at all! I tell you I can give you chapter and verse for that batting average!'

'Chapter and verse maybe, but first find your volume!'

'I shall. I have Wisden back at the flat going back to the year dot. As you know.'

'You're not suggesting we traipse all the way back to Viceroy Mansions on such a trivial matter, Caldicott?'

'Trivial, Charters?'

'Well, we do have prior commitments, old chap,' Charters mumbled, shamefaced as a bishop caught speaking dismissively of the Bible. 'Thought we'd agreed to see that film at the Empire, Leicester Square.'

'You really should try to be more adaptable, old chap, if you don't mind me saying so. After all, there's such a thing as the Odeon, Kensington High Street.'

Charters accepted defeat.

'Your porter conspicuous by his absence,' he said a little while later as the pair marched briskly across the lobby of Viceroy Mansions, brollies swinging in unison.

'I expect he's round at his osteopath's. He has a slipped disc, you know,' said Caldicott, pressing the button to call the lift.

'Does he?' said Charters, totally uninterested. They stepped into the lift.

'All it needs now, of course, is to find that my Mrs Duggins-what-does has given my 1979 Wisden to the jumble sale,' said Caldicott, letting them into the flat and heading straight for the set of Wisdens in the sitting-room. 'It's precisely the kind of thing she's capable of . . . Hello!'

'She hasn't!'

'No, it's there right enough – it's that door yonder I'm puzzling over. When I went out this morning I made a point of shutting it.'

'Oh really – why?'

'Because otherwise it creaks on its hinges, to the annoyance of the – what does it matter why, Charters? The point is – who opened it?'

'Your Mrs Duggins-what-does?'

'Not her day.'

Charters closed the offending bedroom door. Then he paused, frowning, his hand still on the doorknob while he belatedly registered what he had seen on the bedroom floor. 'Caldicott,' he said finally, 'There's a body in there.'

'No there isn't, old chap.'

'I think you'll find there is, old chap.' Charters opened the door. Caldicott glanced past him, then strode into the bedroom and bent over the body.

'Stabbed,' Charters diagnosed.

'Dead as a doornail.' Caldicott stood up and went to telephone for the police.

Charters heard Caldicott introduce himself over the telephone as he wandered in a bemused fashion over to the bookshelves. He reached instinctively for the 1979 Wisden and sought solace in its statistics.

CHAPTER 2

Inspector Snow took charge of investigations. He was unexpectedly young, immaculately dressed and fastidious to the point of obsessiveness. Leaving his sergeant to take care of the body in the bedroom, Snow concentrated his own inquiries on the activities of Charters and Caldicott. Standing side by side in front of the fireplace, hands behind their backs, ex-military men at ease, the pair watched as Snow laid out his notebook and pen with precise neatness on a side-table, then arranged round them the ashtray, a couple of ornaments and other bits and pieces that lay to hand in an exact, geometric pattern. Satisfied that everything was in order, Snow smoothed down the pages of his notebook, flicked open his ballpoint pen and glanced at his watch before writing his first note in a copperplate hand.

'Two fifty-eight. Mr Caldicott and Mr Charters. Let me just get down what we've established so far. The knife belongs to you, Mr Caldicott.'

'That's correct, Inspector.'

'It's a Malayan kris, you say?'

'Yes.'

'How are you spelling that, Mr Caldicott?'

Caldicott's spelling was no better than his arithmetic. He appealed to Charters who obliged the inspector.

'It's a souvenir of your travels which you now use as a paperknife?' Snow asked.

'That's right.'

'And you keep it sharpened for slitting open envelopes?'

'I don't *keep* it sharpened, Inspector. I mean to say, it's never gone blunt.'

'Now as to the body. You say you knew her, Mr Caldicott. You say you *think* you knew her, Mr Charters.'

'No, *I* said I thought I knew her,' said Caldicott. 'But I'm dashed if I can say from where.'

'*I* may have said I knew her. What I meant was, I recognised her,' said Charters.

'We both did, but we can't place her, d'you see?'

'That's what we meant to say,' said Charters, satisfied they'd made themselves plain.

'That's what you meant to say,' Snow repeated, wearily resigning himself to the prospect of a number of similar

14

exchanges as the case progressed. 'But you don't know who she is?'

Caldicott shook his head. 'It's not even on the tip of my tongue.'

'Nor mine,' said Charters. 'It's someone we've met but we don't know where or when.'

Sergeant Tipper came out of the bedroom and put in front of Snow a plastic bag containing most of the contents of the dead girl's handbag. He handed her papers separately to the inspector who laid them down on the table with great care, touching only the edges. It wasn't the risk of smudging fingerprints that worried him but the fear of loitering germs.

'Jenny Beevers,' Snow read. 'Does that ring a bell?'

'Good God!' and 'Oh no! Poor girl!' Charters and Caldicott exclaimed together, shocked.

'Then you did know her?' Snow asked. Caldicott agreed that they did. 'A moment ago you said you didn't.'

'We said we recognised her but we couldn't place her,' said Charters. 'Not surprisingly – we haven't set eyes on her for, what, twelve years?'

'She was only a schoolgirl last time we saw her,' said Caldicott.

'Twelve or so years ago. Yet you don't seem altogether astonished that the body on your bedroom floor turns out to be her,' said Snow suspiciously.

'Ah, but you see, I knew she was back in London and was trying to get hold of me,' said Caldicott.

'Back in London from where?'

'I don't know where she lives these days. Home base would be her father's place in Hong Kong. He died very recently.'

'What was he doing in Hong Kong?'

'He was in Trade.'

'Shopkeeper?'

'The British Trade Commission,' said Charters severely.

'Your connection with him being what?'

'We were at school together. If you want anything on his background, I did a short appreciation in *The Times* . . .' Charters produced his wallet hopefully and took a cutting from it.

Snow shook his head. 'I'm more interested at the moment in what his daughter was doing in Mr Caldicott's flat.'

'I can answer that, Inspector,' said Charters. 'Her father

15

was due to retire. He sent some of his books and papers for Mr Caldicott to keep in storage against his return.'

'In the event,' said Caldicott, 'I passed them on to Mr Charters. No room here, d'you see.'

'Whereas I have a loft.'

'So no doubt Miss Beevers was interested in reclaiming her late father's effects. Does that answer your question, Inspector Snow?'

'Not really, Mr Caldicott. The question was, what was she doing here? In other words, how did she get in?'

'Oh, I see! The porter, I expect. I'd told him if she came back while I was out and she cared to wait, he was to let her in.'

'Yet when he *does* let her in – always supposing he did – and you find her body, it doesn't even cross your mind who it might be.'

'But you see, I instructed Grimes that if Miss Beevers *did* turn up, he was to ring me at the Club at once. Since he did no such thing, I simply didn't put two and two together.'

'Reliable, is he, this porter?'

'No,' said Charters, bitterly.

'Has Grimes surfaced yet, Sergeant Tipper?' Snow called through to the bedroom.

Tipper appeared in the doorway. 'I've told the man on the door to send him straight up, guv. Due back any minute.'

'From his osteopath's. He has a slipped disc,' said Caldicott.

'I don't think Inspector Snow's interested in that, old chap,' Charters murmured.

'Could I be the judge of that, sir?' said Snow, unwarily encouraging Caldicott to continue, 'It gives him gyp, apparently.'

Snow, in truth as uninterested as Charters in Grimes' health, changed the subject. 'Can we discuss your own movements today, gentlemen? Would anyone have had prior knowledge that you would be vacating the flat at lunchtime, Mr Caldicott?'

'It's conceivable. They'd only have to notice it was the first Friday.'

The inspector looked blank. Charters explained. 'When we have a standing lunch engagement.'

'I see. Returning home generally about what time, Mr Caldicott?'

'Sixish, as a rule.'

'From lunch?' Snow asked, amazed.

'We always go to the cinema. That's the main purpose of the exercise, truth to tell.'

'You see, Inspector, neither of us has a television,' said Charters.

'All right, so you meet on a regular basis and visit a cinema.'

Charters was anxious to avoid any misunderstanding. 'A moment, Inspector. In case there's any doubt in your mind, perhaps I could make it clear that it's the *legitimate* cinema we're talking about.'

'Oh, indeed yes!' said Caldicott. 'None of your Soho junk. Those Agatha Christie films, that's about our mark. In fact, we'd made up our minds today to see that one at the Empire, Leicester Square.'

'I think that should be on record, Inspector,' said Charters.

'Mr Charters, Mr Caldicott – it's no concern of *mine* which cinema you intended to visit. What's more to the point is that whatever film you meant to see, you didn't.'

'No, we had a change of plan and plumped for the Odeon, Kensington High Street,' said Caldicott.

'Calling back at the flat on the way,' said Snow.

'To settle an argument,' said Charters.

Snow pricked up his ears. 'An argument? Who with?'

'Each other,' said Caldicott. 'Well, not so much an argument, more a difference of opinion. As to whether the late Jock Beevers' batting average in his last year at Grimchester still stands as a school record.'

'I'm sure the Inspector doesn't want to concern himself with batting averages,' said Charters pompously.

'I'm concerned with everything for the moment, Mr Charters. So you were discussing the late Mr Beevers?'

'Colonel, actually.'

Inspector Snow, a patient huntsman, had his prey in his sights and was anxious not to startle him. 'You return to the flat and who should you find dead on the bedroom floor but this same Colonel Beevers' daughter, whom you haven't set eyes on for twelve or thirteen years.'

'If it comes to that, we hadn't set eyes on either of . . . Oh, I see what you're driving at,' said Caldicott uneasily. 'Long and fishy arm of coincidence. I thought we'd explained

17

that. Jock Beevers' death being the cause of Jenny Beevers turning up here.'

'What you haven't explained,' said Snow, 'is why you chose to break your routine by coming back to the flat.'

'Wisden,' said Charters, feeling himself to be on firm ground again.

'Come again?'

Caldicott explained. 'That argument or difference of opinion I mentioned. About Jock's batting average. We decided to check our facts with Wisden – er, that's Wisden's Cricketers' Almanack – in the Club library.'

'Only to find that the relevant volume had walked,' said Charters.

'Whereupon, unexpectedly, you came back here to consult your own reference books,' said Snow.

'Precisely,' said Caldicott. 'But too late, unfortunately, to prevent murder being done.'

Charters sighed. 'A few minutes earlier and we might have been in time. You know, Caldicott, I shall regret ordering that welsh rarebit to the end of my days.'

'No point in reproaching yourself on that score, old man. After all, if that Wisden hadn't been missing from the Club library we shouldn't have come back here at all.'

Inspector Snow closed his notebook, placed it precisely in the middle of the table and meticulously squared off its edges. 'Unofficially, now, any theories who might have been responsible?'

The old friends gave the matter their serious consideration. At last Charters said with a sigh, 'One of the members, I regret to say.'

Caldicott nodded. 'I certainly wouldn't point the finger at any of the Club servants without evidence.'

'Oh, no, no, no,' said Charters, adding, for the benefit of Snow who looked puzzled, 'Foreigners, you see.'

'Spanish mainly. No motive,' said Caldicott.

'Quite,' Charters agreed. Then a thought struck him. 'Although. *Although* – what about that relief steward they bring in on Ladies' Night? He's a Pakistani.'

'No, I don't think so, old man.'

'You don't think he's the culprit?'

'I meant, I don't think he's a Pakistani, actually. Korean, I'd say.'

'Then he wouldn't be our man. Koreans don't play cricket.'

'That's what I just said, old man.'

'No, you said you didn't think he was Pakistani, you didn't say he wasn't the culprit.'

'It comes to the same thing. Whoever stole that Wisden must be interested in cricket,' said Caldicott, adding patronisingly to the inspector, 'Not that I'm trying to do your job.'

Snow took a deep breath and may even have counted to ten before saying with heavy irony, 'Excuse my momentary puzzlement, gentlemen. Wrong sense of priorities, I expect. I was thinking not so much of your missing cricket almanac as about the murder.'

'Oh, the murder. Of course,' said Charters with diminished interest.

Just then, the police constable on duty outside the flat opened the front door to admit Grimes. For some reason, the porter was a very worried man. He'd almost outstripped his escort in his anxiety to reach the flat and find out what was going on. Sergeant Tipper took him into the bedroom and lifted up the corner of the blanket that covered the dead girl.

'You're definite this is the lady you admitted to the flat?' Tipper asked.

'Definite,' said Grimes, sweating.

'And you're definite about the time?'

'Three and a half minutes past one,' Grimes said firmly.

'Yet phone call to the Club came there none. Why?' Caldicott demanded.

'Could just one of us ask the questions, Mr Caldicott,' said Snow.

Caldicott apologised. 'Carry on, Sergeant.'

Inspector Snow took over the questioning himself. 'What time have you got now, Mr Grimes?'

'I don't carry a watch, sir.'

Observed by Charters and Caldicott, Snow resumed his seat at the occasional table and repeated the performance with notebook and pencil. 'For the record, it's three-eighteen,' he said, consulting his own watch and making a note. 'And it's Mr Frederick Grimes, correct? Well, Mr Grimes?'

Grimes licked his lips nervously. 'You mean, why am I so sure of the time, sir? The lady told me.'

'You having asked her. Why?'

'Ah well, you see. I had an appointment at the osteopath's.

Only if he doesn't fit me in at half-past one sharp, he can't fit me in at all. So that means leaving ten past one latest.'

'You see, it's her way of expressing herself I find rather puzzling, Mr Grimes. "Three and a half minutes past one." Very precise way of putting it. Wouldn't you say?' His own sense of precision bothering him, Inspector Snow readjusted the position of an ashtray on the table and eyed it critically. 'I mean, if you ask most people the time they tend to give you a round number "Just gone one o'clock." "Nearly five past." Do you see what I mean?'

'Ah, well, I didn't exactly ask her the time, sir.'

'You just said you did,' Snow pointed out. 'Try to be a little more careful what you're saying, would you, Mr Grimes? Now I'm sure there's no great mystery to it – just tell me what took place.'

Grimes took a deep breath. 'I'll tell you just what happened, sir – and I'm sorry for any trouble I've caused, Mr Caldicott. I was due to go out, as I said, at ten minutes past, and my clock downstairs being sometimes that little bit fast it was showing just coming up to ten past as she came through the door. I said, joking like, "You cut it a bit fine there, Miss, you had me worried." And she looks at her watch and says, "Nonsense. You said before ten past and it's not five past yet. In fact, it's exactly three and a half minutes past one."'

Caldicott's bewilderment at Grimes' tale turned to amazement. 'Well, I'm blowed!'

'Do you mind,' said Snow.

'Yes, but this is something you ought to know about, Inspector,' Caldicott insisted. 'Are you saying, Grimes, you let Miss Beevers in by *appointment*?'

The name startled Grimes badly but before he could reply, Snow tapped imperiously with his pen. 'Mr Caldicott! I'm conducting an inquiry here! Any more of that and I shall ask you to wait in the corridor.'

'Sorry.'

'Sorry? Hang it, Caldicott, he can't turn you out of your own flat,' Charters exploded. Then, feeling Snow's eyes on him, he added uncertainly, 'I'm pretty sure of that.'

'Can we get on,' said the inspector. '*Now* you can answer Mr Caldicott's question, Mr Grimes. Did you let Miss Beevers in by arrangement?'

Thoroughly rattled, Grimes looked to Caldicott for guidance, but no help came from that quarter. 'Yes, I'm sorry to say I did,' he admitted.

'She was anxious to get into the flat while Mr Caldicott was safely out of the way?'

'That's about the size of it,' said Grimes even more reluctantly.

'I don't believe it. I simply do not believe it,' said Caldicott indignantly. 'I've known that girl for years, Inspector! She simply wouldn't do such a thing! Now look here, Grimes, I don't know what your game is . . .' His voice tailed off as he remembered the inspector's warning but it was too late.

Inspector Snow had carefully laid down his pen. He completed the adjustment of some of the items on the table to maintain their symmetry before saying with a sigh, 'Sergeant Tipper!'

Hands behind their backs and smartly in step, Charters and Caldicott retreated down the corridor, the picture of wounded dignity. The constable on duty outside Caldicott's flat watched them go and smirked to himself.

'I should complain to the Commissioner, if I were you, Caldicott,' said Charters as they about-turned at the end of the corridor with the formality and precision of Buckingham Palace sentries and began to retrace their steps.

'Oh, I don't know, Charters. The chap's only doing his job.'

'And enjoying every minute of it. Jumped up little pipsqueak! You know what's the trouble with that young man, Caldicott? Too hasty promotion – it's gone to his head.'

'Yes, he *is* rather fresh-faced for an inspector, isn't he? One's always heard one would know one was getting on when the policemen started to look younger, but I never realised it would include senior ranks.'

They continued to pace up and down for a while in silence, mulling over the afternoon's events, then Charters said, 'Bad business this, old chap.'

'Very. Such a pretty little thing she'd grown up to be. Thank God we don't have to break the news to poor old Jock Beevers.'

'That's one mercy of a sort. What's at the bottom of it? Any ideas?'

Caldicott shook his head. 'I can't begin to make head nor tale of it. Why should Grimes want to make up that cock and bull tale about the poor girl wanting to get into the flat?'

'Can we be sure it *was* entirely a cock and bull story?' Charters asked, then, ashamed of his suspicions, he hurried on, 'Yes, of course you're right. She'd never have done such a thing.'

'Of course she wouldn't! Dammit, Charters, we both *knew* the girl. I've never told you this, old man, but had it not been for the fact that Jock didn't want to cause you offence, I should have been her godfather instead of Ginger Lightfoot.'

'No, it was the other way round, old man,' said Charters, after the briefest of pauses.

'What do you mean, old man, it was the other way round?'

'He didn't want to cause *you* offence, old man, otherwise *I* should have been godfather instead of Ginger Lightfoot.'

'Balderdash.'

'I am not in the habit of talking balderdash, Caldicott. I remember it very well – I had a personal note from Jock explaining the position.'

'So had *I* a personal note explaining the position.'

Growing irritation had driven their steps to a most proficient quick march. Now they came to an abrupt halt and stared at each other, each considering the implications of what the other had said. Charters broke the silence. 'Caldicott, did it ever occur to you at the time that he could easily have asked us both to be godfathers?'

'It did cross my mind,' said Caldicott. 'I took it to be Jock's tactful way of saying he didn't consider you godfather material.'

'That's what I took him to be saying about you.'

'I should have made a dashed sight better godfather than Ginger Lightfoot.'

'So should I.'

'Do you know what, Charters? He was a bit of an old slyboots on the quiet, our Jock – God rest his soul.' Thoughtfully, Charters and Caldicott resumed their pacing.

Inspector Snow completed his interrogation of Grimes. 'Nothing else you want to say to me?' he asked, tidily closing his notebook.

'No, I don't think so.'

'Don't want to change your story at all – about how you let the girl in by arrangement?'

'Not at all.'

'Well, not for the moment, let's put it that way.' Snow

poked fastidiously with his pen inside the plastic bag containing the dead girl's belongings until he found what he was looking for.

Charters and Caldicott had tired of walking up and down and were lounging against the corridor walls smoking, like two theatre-goers waiting for the performance to resume. Eager for any distraction, Charters nudged Caldicott as Inspector Snow came out of the flat. They watched, mildly entertained, as he fiddled at the doorlock with his handkerchief.

'If you'd like to step back in now, gentlemen,' said Snow, catching Caldicott's eye.

'According to Mr Grimes,' said Snow, nodding towards the shamefaced porter, 'the lady said she wanted access to your flat to regain possession of some highly personal letters. Any comment you'd care to make on that, Mr Caldicott?'

Caldicott glared at Grimes. 'Yes, there is, Inspector, but it would scorch the pages of your notebook.'

'There are no such letters?'

'Search the flat, Inspector. Go on – you have my permission.'

'Sergeant Tipper *has* had a good look round, sir. I'm glad to have it confirmed that that was in order.' Ignoring Charters' and Caldicott's indignant glances, he went on, 'So either Miss Beevers wasn't telling Mr Grimes the truth, or Mr Grimes isn't telling me the truth.'

'The man's a liar,' said Caldicott. 'Sorry, Grimes, but there you are.'

'Yes, I'm inclined to agree with you. Otherwise what was she doing with this?' Snow unfolded the handkerchief he was holding to reveal a key with an identifying tag attached.

'My spare key!' said Caldicott.

'It's a puzzle, isn't it, sir? We've a good idea how she came by it – it's like a self-service counter down in that lobby. But why, *having* come by it, does she want to spin Mr Grimes a yarn to let her into the flat? Or so he tells us.'

'I *did* let her in, sir. I've no *idea* what she was doing with that key and that *is* the truth,' Grimes insisted.

'Well now, Mr Grimes, I think we'd better sort out what's the truth and what isn't. How do you feel about coming back to the station with me? It's not far.'

The body of the dead girl was carried out of Viceroy

23

Mansions on a blanket-covered stretcher and put into a waiting police van. As the door closed, a young woman in a smart grey suit withdrew from the knot of watching bystanders and hurried to the nearest phone box.

With the flat to themselves again, Charters and Caldicott had rejected as unseemly both the cinema and the Club and were recovering from the distressing events of the afternoon in the traditional way. When the level of liquid in the decanter had dropped considerably, Charters, mellowed, stood up. 'You still keep a thoroughly decent dry sherry, Caldicott,' he said, retrieving his umbrella and beginning to put on his raincoat. 'You must invite me to your place more often.'

'Delighted. And of course it makes an excellent base camp for the Odeon, Kensington High Street.' Caldicott paused in the act of returning the 1979 Wisden to the shelves. 'You found that batting average?'

'Yes – and I owe you and the shade of Jock Beevers an apology. Do you think I should send a correction to *The Times*?'

Caldicott was considering the matter when the telephone rang. 'If this is the gutter press after a juicy interview they'll get short shrift,' he said, lifting the receiver.

The call box bleeps stopped and a young woman's voice said, 'Mr Caldicott? It's about the murder in your flat – something you ought to know.'

Caldicott put his hand over the receiver and reported to Charters, 'Unspecified female. Says she knows something about the murder.'

Charters buttoned up his raincoat. 'Crackpot, most likely.'

Caldicott listened. 'Craves a meeting at Cuddles Restaurant in the Earl's Court Road,' he informed Charters, covering the mouthpiece again.

'Never heard of it. Anyway, I have my Green Line bus to catch,' said Charters, rolling up his umbrella in a decisive manner.

'Don't you think we ought to find out what she has to say?'

'Publicity seeker. Waste of time.'

Peeved by Charters' lack of co-operation, Caldicott said to his caller, 'I'm sure I shall find the place. Perhaps you'll allow me to buy you a cup of tea? . . . In about ten minutes then.' He was about to replace the receiver when a thought occurred to him. 'By the way, I don't know your name.'

'Yes, you do, Mr Caldicott. You found my body. This is Jenny Beevers.' She hung up.

Caldicott replaced his own receiver slowly and stared at it pensively for a moment before turning to Charters. 'Could I persuade you to take a later Green Line bus, old chap?'

CHAPTER 3

Cuddles turned out to be a glorified hamburger joint, furnished with ledges instead of tables and the sort of high, narrow stools designed to discourage customers from lingering. The lighting was harsh, the colours blinding and the walls and floors chipped and peeling. Charters and Caldicott, had passed happily through the colourful, noisy, polyglot crowds of the Earl's Court Road, reminded, perhaps, of some Far Eastern bazaar long ago, but in the doorway of Cuddles they came to an abrupt halt, stunned by the plastic squalor that lay before them.

'Good God!' Caldicott gasped at Charters, appalled.

Charters, determinedly up-to-date in the face of Caldicott's helplessness, said caustically, 'What did you expect in Earl's Court? Ann Hathaway's Tea Rooms?' and looked round for Jenny Beevers. A young woman, sitting with a Coke and the evening paper at one of the ledges, glanced up and smiled at them. They hesitated, not recognising her immediately, then went over and introduced themselves with their usual punctiliousness. Regardless alike of the tawdriness of their surroundings and the smirks of the mainly punkish clientele, they raised their hats, shook hands and exchanged greetings, creating a small oasis of civilisation where none had existed before. These formalities completed, Caldicott perched himself on an absurdly high stool beside Jenny while Charters approached the service hatch.

'A pot of tea for two, please,' Charters ordered, ruthlessly cutting into the two assistants' private conversation. When he rejoined the others he was carrying, with immense distaste, a small plastic tray upon which reposed two Styrofoam beakers of tea, two paper sacks of sugar, two mini-cartons of cream and two plastic spatula devices for stirring.

'That's very noble of Charters,' said Caldicott. 'He could have got a waitress to do that. Jenny, you're sure you wouldn't like something before Charters sits down? A muffin, perhaps?'

Charters, now wise in the ways of Cuddles, snorted. 'Don't be absurd old fellow. This isn't Gunter's, you know. And he accuses *me* of being out of touch with the world,' he said to Jenny, putting the tray down on the ledge and taking the stool on the other side of her.

26

'I shouldn't have dragged you into such a dump but I couldn't think of anywhere else,' said Jenny. 'I'm afraid I don't know London very well.'

'You live where these days?' Caldicott asked.

'New York. And I didn't go back to Hong Kong as often as a good daughter should have done. The last time, of course, was for the funeral.'

'We were both so sorry to hear about Jock's death.'

'Yes. I wrote a little appreciation in *The Times*, you know. Perhaps you'd like to read it?' Charters fumbled once more in his wallet but was again thwarted.

'A friend of my father showed it to me. I was very touched.'

'Thank you.'

Jenny turned to Caldicott who was having trouble opening his customer-proof mini-carton of cream. 'Let me do that.'

'Thanks awfully. Never been able to get the hang of these things.'

'Oh, it's just a knack,' said Charters airily, thrusting his thumb through the foil lid of his own carton and spurting cream all over the place. While he fumed and mopped himself up, Jenny calmly poured cream into Caldicott's tea.

'You know, looking at you now, Jenny, I don't see how we could possibly have mistaken anyone else for you, even after all these years,' said Caldicott. 'I'm mightily relieved, I must say.'

'Amen to that,' said Charters.

'There was no resemblance, then? You see, I hardly saw her face. I just saw her lying there and . . .'

Charters patted her hand awkwardly. 'Don't upset yourself, my dear.'

'I'm sorry, but I think I've got plenty to be upset about.'

'Of course you have, after an ordeal like that,' said Caldicott. 'No I don't think there was any resemblance at all, Jenny. The thing was, we both knew we'd seen her before but couldn't place her. When the poor girl was identified as you, of course, the penny dropped – or we thought it had.'

'The question that arises now – this tea is disgusting. It tastes like detergent – is who the unfortunate woman was, and what she was doing with our papers,' said Charters.

'She was called Helen Appleyard. Or, at least, that's the name on *her* papers.' Jenny produced a driving licence and a couple of letters. 'I switched handbags,' she explained, seeing that Charters and Caldicott were baffled.

Caldicott struck his forehead. 'I see. Simple when you know how, isn't it.'

Charters didn't pretend to understand. 'What do you mean, you switched handbags?'

'Oh, really, old man, you're a bit slow on the uptake today,' said Caldicott. 'Jenny let herself in with the spare key from the lobby – we'll inquire into the whys and wherefores of that in a minute . . .'

'I did have a reason,' Jenny put in.

'I'm sure you did, my dear.' Caldicott turned back to Charters, elaborately patient, delighted to get his own back for the mathematics lecture. 'You savvy? Lets herself into flat, finds body, swaps handbags.'

'Why?'

'Come along, Charters, wakey, wakey. Oh dear, oh doctor,' he gloated as Charters continued to look blank. 'You may be hot on the price of lamb cutlets, old man, but logic seems to defeat you. Look – watch closely.' Caldicott, having a whale of a time, doubled his fists and crossed them one over the other, demonstrating what he believed to have happened. 'This is Jenny. This is the body. Jenny swaps places – as you were, handbags – with dead girl. Whereupon what's-her-name, Helen Appleyard, becomes Jenny Beevers and Jenny becomes Helen Appleyard. Switch of personalities. Savvy?'

Charters, who had watched this elaborate pantomime with grim patience, said, 'Yes, I've understood that all along.'

'Well then.'

'But why?'

'Why what?'

'Why switch personalities?'

'Well because,' Caldicott began, then stopped, frowning. 'Yes, dash it, why?' he demanded, turning to Jenny.

'Can I tell you first what I was doing in your flat? I knew Dad had sent you a trunk brimful of diaries and notebooks and stuff.'

'Yes, it's in my custody as it happens,' said Charters.

'I wanted to read them.'

'My dear girl, they're your property now,' said Caldicott. 'You only had to ask.'

'Yes, I know – and that's what I meant to do when I first called round to Viceroy Mansions and you were out. But then I got to thinking that you mightn't let me see what you mightn't wish me to see.'

'What a bizarre idea!'

'Why on earth should we prevent you reading your own father's diaries? See them whenever you like,' said Charters.

'Now?' Jenny asked.

'Well, I *am* in the country, you know.'

'Of course. I remember seeing a snap of you and your wife in the garden.'

'Ruth died, you know.'

'I'm sorry – I never heard.'

'No, I didn't want a song and dance made of it. They were happy years, the few we had.'

Jenny took a deep breath. 'Mr Charters, Mr Caldicott, can I ask you something? What did you actually do before you retired?'

'Do?' Charters asked.

'We were with HMG,' said Caldicott. 'I thought you knew that.'

'Yes, I know, but which branch?'

'The, ah, sort of general branch,' said Charters.

'Were you spies?'

'Ha! The idea,' said Caldicott, pleased as Punch at the suggestion.

'No, no, no, nothing of that kind at all,' said Charters, delighted.

'Flattering though the suggestion is.'

'What did my father do?' Charters and Caldicott looked even more puzzled. 'Oh, I know what he put in Who's Who: first the Army then the Trade Commission. But he didn't know anything *about* trade, did he?'

'What's that got to do with it?' Charters asked, genuinely baffled.

'I think that was a cover and he was an agent of some kind.'

'Old Jock?' Caldicott chuckled. 'A secret agent? Nonsense. With all due respect.'

'How do you think he died?'

'Heart, according to what one heard,' said Charters.

'Your "general" branch of HMG really didn't tell you?' Jenny asked ironically.

'No reason why anyone should tell us anything. We really were very unimportant cogs in a very big wheel,' said Caldicott.

'No need for false modesty, old chap,' said Charters.

'He was murdered.'

'Good God!' and 'How terrible for you!' Charters and Caldicott exclaimed.

'Why, or by whom, I've yet to find out.'

'So you were hoping to find a clue in your father's papers?' Caldicott asked.

'Instead I found the body of this Helen Appleyard, who, for whatever reason, was looking for the same thing. And that's why she died – I'm sure of it.' Jenny paused while a Cuddles assistant cleared the ledge by the simple method of sweeping the debris with his sleeve into a plastic bin. Momentarily silenced, Caldicott and Charters watched this operation with acute distaste.

'I wonder if they mistook her for me?' Jenny went on as the assistant moved away.

'Is that possible?' Caldicott asked.

'You two did. You see, ever since I arrived in London a few days ago, someone – a man – has been trying to find me. He rang the Hong Kong trade people here, posing as my cousin. They gave him the address of the flat I'm renting.'

'Very remiss of them,' said Caldicott.

'Since then I've felt very strongly that I was being followed.'

'If you were, then he could well have taken up a lurking position outside Viceroy Mansions,' said Caldicott.

'All of which explains Jenny's handbag-switching ruse,' said Charters triumphantly.

Caldicott had completely lost track of this strand of the story. 'Quite,' he said unconvincingly.

Charters explained, 'If the police think the dead girl is Jenny, so will the criminal when he reads his *Times* or *Daily Telegraph* tomorrow.'

Caldicott got the point at last. 'Smart girl. So whoever the murderous swine is, you've now got him off your back.'

'Unless that porter of yours spills the beans, Caldicott.' Charters turned to Jenny. 'He's seen the body and he's met you as Miss Beevers, so he must know you're not one and the same.'

'Yet he didn't let on to Inspector Snow,' Caldicott pointed out. 'Knowing Grimes, he has his own reasons for keeping mum. I shall have a word with that lad later.'

Charters turned irritably to address a sulky young couple with loaded trays who had taken up positions immediately behind him. 'Would you mind? We are engaged in a private conversation.'

The couple stayed mutinously put. Caldicott murmured to Charters, 'I believe it's the custom in these establishments to leave the moment one's finished, old chap.'

Jenny stood up. 'I think we've outstayed our welcome.' Pursued by snickers from the young couple, they made as dignified a departure as they could. Outside, it had started to rain and the three paused in the doorway to button up their raincoats.

'Where to now?' Caldicott asked.

'That's the problem,' said Jenny. 'I don't live anywhere.'

'I thought you were renting a flat?'

'Jenny Beevers is renting a flat. But she's dead, isn't she?'

'You don't belong to any of the ladies' clubs, overseas membership?' Charters asked.

Caldicott shook his head. 'The same objection applies, old chap. You can't have the world believing you're dead then roll up to the club bar demanding whisky and soda.'

'No. No, I suppose technically one would no longer be a member.'

'It's a quandary,' said Caldicott frowning. Then he snapped his fingers. 'Got it! Margaret Mottram. An old friend,' he explained to Jenny.

'An old flame,' Charters amended roguishly.

'A respectable divorcée of the very best sort. Runs a temps agency now. She can be trusted implicitly. I knew her in Kenya.'

Jenny smiled at the non sequitur. 'I'm sure that's an impeccable reference.'

The question of Jenny's billet for the night having been settled, Charters was anxious to get home. 'If you're taking a cab, you can drop me at the Green Line bus stop.'

'We'd better confer very soon,' said Caldicott.

'Is that necessary? I've a very full diary next week.'

'We did find a corpse in my flat today, Charters,' Caldicott reminded him acidly. 'I think that takes precedence over your parish council meetings and chrysanthemum shows.'

'Perhaps I could come up for a turkish bath on Monday,' said Charters, ruffled.

'Do.'

Margaret Mottram welcomed Caldicott, strange girl in tow,

31

to her South Kensington mews house without much surprise. An easygoing woman with a clear sense of priorities, she got busy with the gin bottle while she listened to the bare bones of Jenny's story.

'He's improving,' Margaret said to her unexpected house guest at the end of the recital. 'The last time he called he only brought me a goldfish.'

'The old clothes man gave it to me in exchange for a redundant pair of riding boots,' Caldicott explained. 'I thought it needed a better home than I could offer.'

'Now he brings me a beautiful young thing who's left herself for dead on his bedroom floor. Ice and lemon?'

'Please,' said Jenny. 'Am I a nuisance? I could always change my name and find a hotel.'

'You'll do no such thing. If Caldicott hadn't brought you to Chateau Mottram I'd have been livid. If there's anything I can't resist it's a mystery novel – see, I've got them by the yard – and you've stepped right out of chapter one. Put this down you, love, and then we'll get you into a nice hot bath.' Jenny accepted a generous gin and tonic.

'But not until we've rummaged through that swapped handbag of yours, I hope,' said Caldicott. 'There must be *some* clue as to who this Helen Appleyard is – or was.'

'I've been through it once. There's very little to go on,' said Jenny, tired and depressed at the end of a long, upsetting day.

Margaret sympathised. She leaned forward and snapped the bag shut. 'Now that can wait till morning. The owner of that handbag's dead so she's not going to run away.'

'I thought you were gasping to get your teeth into the mystery,' Caldicott protested.

'So I am, when Jenny's had at least ten hours' sleep. That girl's pooped. She ought to be in bed.'

'I'm all right – really,' Jenny said unconvincingly, sipping her drink.

'There you see – tough eggs these Beevers,' said Caldicott.

'All the same, she's had an exhausting and trying day. How would *you* feel if you walked into someone's flat and found a body on the floor?' said Margaret.

Caldicott began to nod sympathetically, then his head jerked upright. 'But I did! And nobody tells *me* I ought to be in bed.'

'Story of your life, dear, isn't it?' Margaret said with a

wink. 'Come along, my girl. Say goodnight to your Uncle Caldicott and he can come and see you again for breakfast.'

Jenny smiled and allowed herself to be led away. 'Do you always call him by his surname?'

'My dear, even his mother called him by his surname.'

Caldicott sipped his drink contentedly, sank deeper into his armchair and tried to look indignant.

Dusk was falling by the time Charters reached home. As he put his key in the lock he heard a banging noise coming from somewhere. Stepping back to investigate he spotted a side window open and swinging gently to and fro. Charters hesitated apprehensively, then opened his front door and went in.

Caldicott had a few words he wished to say to Grimes before he went up to his flat. The porter's desk was deserted but Caldicott pressed the bell in a determined manner and paced up and down the lobby until Grimes emerged from the basement.

'I thought it might be you, Mr Caldicott. Only I've just got back from the police station. The questions I've been asked today, sir!'

'Not to mention the questions you're about to be asked. Come on, man, why did you let that woman into my flat?'

'For £250, sir. She only offered £100 at first but I turned her down flat,' said Grimes virtuously.

'Very commendable, I'm sure. And who was she?'

'I thought that was established, sir. Miss Beevers. Though the name she preferred to give me was Miss Smith.'

'Yes, well her name wasn't Smith and you know damn well she wasn't Miss Beevers.'

'All I know, sir, is that another young woman's been round *calling* herself Miss Beevers. When I heard you say *this* one was Miss Beevers, who was I to argue? I didn't want to get you into trouble, see, Mr Caldicott.'

'You're the one who's in trouble, laddie. Now, what do you know about this woman?'

'Nothing, sir.'

'Nothing? And you let her into my flat? I expect you thought I was giving up the lease and she'd been sent round by the estate agents with an order to view.'

'It's the same as what I told the police and what I've

33

kept on telling them, Mr Caldicott – she said you had some
correspondence of hers that she'd be happier getting back,
on account of she was getting married.'

'And you believed her!'

'Not for me to say, is it, sir?' Grimes smirked.

'No, it's merely for you to pocket 250 smackers, isn't it?
Where did she come from – she didn't just walk in out of
the street?'

'That's just what she did do, sir. Came in yesterday –
looking very upset and could she have a word. Spun me a
tale and then asked was there any particular day I could be
sure of Mr Caldicott being out, and when he *did* go out,
could I ring her right away at this number.'

Caldicott grabbed the crumpled piece of paper Grimes
produced. 'Did you give the inspector this number?'

'Not me, sir. I told him what he asked me about and no
more. So if you should want to keep this phone number quiet
– he thinks she came back by appointment, style of thing.'

'Did you just wink at me, Grimes?' Caldicott demanded,
outraged.

'Twitch in the eye, Mr Caldicott.'

'Yes, well look here. You and I are not in collusion over
this business. Do I make myself clear?'

'Oh yes, Mr Caldicott.'

Caldicott made as if to go, then stopped and asked in what
he hoped was an off-hand manner, 'That duplicate key, by
the way. What did Inspector Snow make of it in the end?'

'Same as I made of it. She must have snitched it while my
back was turned – in case I had second thoughts and wouldn't
let her in. Only explanation there *can* be – isn't it?'

'Yes, I expect you're right.'

'I suppose it's got to go to the landlords, sir – about me
letting her in?'

'It certainly ought to, Grimes. You've betrayed a trust.'

'I know I have, sir, and I'm ever so sorry. If there was
anything I could do . . .'

'There's one thing you *can* do, laddie, and that's keep your
trap shut.'

'I understand, Mr Caldicott.'

'You don't understand anything, Grimes, and you don't
have to. Except this. Someone wanted to kill the real Miss
Beevers. Thanks to a series of fortuitous misunderstandings
they now think they have. Until the murderer is brought to

book, that's how we need it to remain. And that's all you need to know. Now you're on probation, Grimes. If any of this gets out, you're for the high jump.'

'Yes, sir. Thank you, sir.'

'Very well.' Caldicott strode off to the lift, reaching it just as the doors opened to let out a woman holding a collecting tin. 'Ah, another victim,' she beamed, pouncing on Caldicott.

'Good evening,' said Caldicott coolly.

'Would you like to give something to the Children's Fund?'

'Of course.' While Caldicott fumbled for change, the lady gushed, 'It's not really our flag day until tomorrow, but I find people are much more generous if I beard them in their dens.'

'Flag Day!' Caldicott gasped, giving a decent imitation of Paul on the road to Damascus.

'I hope you don't mind. It's in a very good cause.'

'Indeed it is, dear lady, indeed it is.' To the woman's utter astonishment, Caldicott whipped out his wallet and stuffed a fiver into her tin. Brushing aside her thanks, he stepped into the lift. 'Oh, and by the way,' he said, pressing the floor button. 'The porter there is also good for a fiver.'

Highly excited, Caldicott hurried into his flat, threw down his hat and umbrella and headed straight for the phone.

'Tudor Cottage. Charters speaking,' Caldicott heard. 'Oh, it's you, Caldicott.'

'Charters, are you busy at the moment?'

'Well, it is rather an inconvenient time, since you ask.'

'This won't take a sec, old man, and it is rather important. It's just come to me where we've seen Helen Appleyard before. Do you know who she was, Charters? She was the flag seller outside the Club. You remember – selling petunias although it wasn't Petunia Day.'

'Yes, I remember.'

'Clearly she was double-checking that we were where Grimes had told her we'd be, before nipping smartly round to the flat. I say, Charters, you don't seem very surprised.'

'No, I'd already worked it out for myself.'

'Oh,' said Caldicott, peeved. 'Then here's something I bet you haven't worked out. Do you remember that chauffeur standing next to her, lolling against the Jag?'

'Vividly.'

'There was only a handful of chaps in the Club before lunch. We knew all of them and none of them runs to a

35

chauffeur-driven Jag. Do you know what I think, Charters? I think that chauffeur was Helen Appleyard's accomplice.'

'I'm inclined to agree with you. Is that all you have to say, Caldicott?'

'Is that all *you* have to say, Charters?' said Caldicott indignantly.

'As I've already said, you've caught me at an inconvenient time. Goodbye, Caldicott.'

'Goodbye, Charters,' said Caldicott, hurt as well as angered by Charters' inexplicable attitude. He put the phone down.

At the other end of the line, in his cosy cottage, Charters also replaced his receiver. He sighed, then spun round in his swivel chair to face, once again, the chauffeur Caldicott had correctly identified as Helen Appleyard's accomplice. He was holding a revolver aimed straight at Charters' heart.

CHAPTER 4

In spite of his uniform and a fittingly obsequious manner, the chauffeur managed to exude a kind of seedy menace more suited to a small-time crook. 'Very good,' he said as Charters put the phone down.

'That's as may be,' said Charters.

'You were sensible.'

'I was prudent.'

'Prudent, then. Now you prudently unlock that trunk.' Jock Beevers' battered and rope-bound trunk had been dragged down as far as the half-landing of the open staircase. Charters had evidently disturbed the chauffeur before his job was finished.

'You clearly have something to learn about the English language, Mr . . .? You are English, aren't you?' Getting no reply, Charters went on, 'Prudence is the virtue of caution. As a cautious man, I'm unlikely to turn over the contents of Colonel Beevers' trunk to an armed intruder without credentials.'

The chauffeur was unimpressed. 'I've already scratched your nice parquet landing getting it so far. If I have to drag it out to the car it's going to cause a lot more damage.'

'French polishing is no problem in these parts,' Charters said airily. 'We're blessed with some very fine craftsmen. Moreover, dragging that trunk out will take time – a commodity you don't possess.'

'I've all the time in the world – time to tie you to that chair and persuade you – no, that's not the right word either – to hand over those keys.'

'I think not. That telephone call just now was from my friend Mr Caldicott.'

'Clairvoyant, is he?'

'We've been in many tight spots together, he and I. We've therefore evolved a system of speaking in code.'

'So when you say he's ringing at an inconvenient time, that's a signal for him to dial 999,' the chauffeur sneered, not believing a word of it.

'Something of the sort.'

'Pull the other one, it's got bells on.'

Right on cue, they heard the siren of an approaching police car. The chauffeur, startled, dashed to the window as the

37

car, its roof light flashing, drew up outside the cottage. Charters, who couldn't have been more surprised if Concorde had landed on his front lawn, pulled himself together with difficulty. 'You see,' he said smugly. Yet even with help at hand, Charters, no coward, made no attempt to stop the chauffeur as he fled through the back door. Nor did he mention his intruder to the two policemen standing on his doorstep.

'Good evening, Mr Charters, sir,' said the sergeant. 'Sorry to make such a racket but it's the only way we could get through them sheep. That lane's jam-packed with the beggars.'

'They roll over the cattle grid, you know – sheep have more nous than is generally appreciated. Come in, Sergeant Bellows. Constable – what can I do for you?'

'We're on an errand for Scotland Yard, sir,' said Bellows, preceding his constable into the cottage. 'An Inspector Snow. Says he's already had discussions with you and he'd like us to take possession of a trunk.'

'Oh, yes. A moment, Sergeant Bellows. Let me shut the back door,' said Charters, missing another opportunity to unburden himself to the Law.

'By the way, I don't suppose that's your Jag parked on the verge back there, Mr Charters?'

'Hardly my style, Sergeant,' said Charters. A truthful man, he hesitated before going on, 'I don't know whose it is.'

'Sheep rustler, could be. We'll have a look at it on the way back, Jim,' Bellows said to his constable.

'We'll have to be quick, Sarge,' said the constable, looking out of the window as the Jag went past at high speed. 'He's making some time up. He'll have stopped for a leak, most like.'

'It wouldn't be the first time my hedge has been used as an ablutions. Now about this trunk, Sergeant, I'm not at all sure I can help you,' said Charters, reluctant to part with the trunk, even to the police, before Jenny had had a chance to search through it.

'The inspector said you did know the circumstances, sir.'

'Indeed I do.'

'He said the contents of the trunk might throw light on the matter under investigation.'

'I appreciate that, but there is a procedure for this sort of thing, you know, Sergeant Bellows.'

'Yes, sir. He did suggest if there was any, well, difficulty, we could always apply for a warrant.'

'From the local magistrate.'

'That's it, sir.'

'But *I'm* the local magistrate.'

'Yes, sir.'

'This is absurd.'

'Well – awkward.' The sergeant noticed the trunk on the half-landing for the first time. 'Is that it, Mr Charters?'

'Yes.'

'Is it on its way somewhere, sir?'

'No, no – I anticipated your visit,' Charters stammered. Trapped, he gave in. 'Very well, Sergeant, take the thing. I shall want a receipt, mind.'

Charters watched the police officers load the trunk into the boot of their car and drive away, then went indoors to telephone the latest news to Caldicott. Caldicott, however, was enjoying a whisky and soda and a pipe while listening to *Any Questions?* on the wireless and was in no hurry to answer. Only when his pipe was going to his satisfaction did he pick up the receiver.

'There you are,' said Charters. 'I'm at liberty to speak now.'

'Who's that?' Caldicott asked unnecessarily.

'Charters. Who do you think?'

Caldicott, still smarting from Charters' off-hand treatment of his own phone call earlier that evening, was in an unforgiving mood.

'Oh, very well,' Charters snapped, after listening to Caldicott's excuses. 'What time does your wretched *Any Questions?* programme finish? I'll ring you then.'

Caldicott, smirking, turned up the volume on his radio. Charters, fuming, tuned in to *Any Questions?* himself and before long began to relax.

The following morning, Caldicott stepped briskly out of Viceroy Mansions and headed for the nearby flower stall. After careful examination of its wares, he bought a bunch of flowers and continued on his way, ignoring the battery of newspaper placards bearing news of the murder in the Mansions. A young, effeminate-looking man of foreign appearance watched this transaction from a discreet distance. A compulsive eater, Cecil St Clair, as he styled himself, was

39

working his way through a bar of chocolate he'd broken into
pieces in his gloved hand. Upon Caldicott's departure, he
popped the last square into his mouth and strolled into
Viceroy Mansions.

'Good morning. And I see from the board that one of the
flats is for sale,' said St Clair, in a Slavic accent, to Grimes.

Grimes scented a tip. 'Number ninety-one, sir. Snip. You
at all interested, sir?'

'I should like to see it. Who has the keys? The agents?'

'*I* have the keys, sir. Tell the truth, you don't want to
bother with the agents. You'll get a better price if you deal
with the individual owner. I could give you her number.'

'And you get commission?'

'Oo, nothing like that, sir,' said Grimes, shocked. 'No, it's
just a labour of love style of thing. 'Course, if anyone *did*
want to show their appreciation . . .'

St Clair, with Grimes at his elbow, gave the flat a perfunctory inspection, then produced a fat wallet. 'No, no, it is too
. . .'

'Empty, sir?' Grimes suggested, eyeing the wallet. 'Perhaps
you were looking for more your furnished style of thing?'

'Yes. For instance number thirty-six.'

'Mr Caldicott's flat? Very nice indeed. Only I don't think
he's contemplating a move.'

St Clair handed over some notes which Grimes accepted
as of right. 'That's for your trouble. You see, Mr Grimes, I
am a writer of mystery stories.'

'Oh yes, sir,' said Grimes, keeping a straight face.

'Atmosphere is everything to a writer. I am always interested to see the actual place where a crime has been
committed.'

'Must come very expensive, sir. Still, I suppose you can
claim it off tax.'

St Clair's survey of Caldicott's flat was considerably more
protracted. 'And by the way, the body was facing this way
or that way?' Grimes indicated the position on the bedroom
floor. 'I see. This is all most fascinating to a writer.'

St Clair continued to look around in a leisurely manner.
Grimes, already nervous of discovery, became increasingly
agitated as the minutes passed. 'Was there any piece of
atmosphere you were looking for in particular, sir, or are
you just soaking it up in general,' he asked, in a desperate
attempt to hurry St Clair along.

Grimes' anxiety would have been even more acute had he happened to glance out into the street just then and seen Caldicott retracing his steps towards Viceroy Mansions. But instead of entering the flats he went back to the flower stall where he bought a second, identical bunch of flowers and once more went purposefully on his way.

Grimes at last succeeded in easing St Clair out of Caldicott's flat and back down to the lobby where he hung up Caldicott's spare key and accepted a handsome tip. 'Thank *you*, sir. And if you do need to do any more of your researches – like if you get writer's block style of thing – I'll see what I can do.'

'Thank you, Mr Grimes.'

'There's nothing you want me to look out for? No particular detail?' Grimes probed, mystified by St Clair's interest.

'No, thank you. And by the way, this interview did not take place.'

'Trust me, sir. I never remember a face. Noted for it.' Grimes watched St Clair leave with puzzled speculation.

'They're lovely. You shouldn't have,' said Jenny, arranging one of Caldicott's bunches of flowers in a vase.

'Given that he did, though, it was diplomatic of him to bring us a bunch each,' said Margaret, arranging her own flowers and smiling to herself, pleased with the gift. Caldicott sipped his coffee complacently, wallowing in their gratitude and satisfied that he'd done the right thing.

'The wisdom of Solomon,' said Jenny in answer to Margaret.

'Don't tell him that, Jenny, or he'll want a baby to saw in half.' Margaret gave a final twitch to an errant carnation. 'Now – to work.' The murdered girl's handbag was lying on a glass-topped occasional table in front of Caldicott. Margaret picked it up and tipped out the contents.

'What's this? Kim's game?' Caldicott asked.

'Or Cluedo,' said Margaret, picking up a lipstick. 'The deadly deed was committed in the library by Colonel Mustard and the murder weapon was a lipstick.' She stopped abruptly and cast a sidelong glance at Jenny. 'Sorry, ducks, I was forgetting you actually *did* find the body in the library.' Jenny gave a feeble smile.

Caldicott selected a key with a plastic tag attached from

41

the paraphernalia in front of him. 'I'm not entirely clear what a clue looks like but this must surely be one. "Thamesview",' he read off the tag. 'That nineteen-thirties block of service flats at World's End. And a telephone number – my goodness, the old Flaxman exchange that was.' He took a scrap of paper out of his pocket and compared it. 'Yes, the number Helen Appleyard gave Grimes. I rang it last night. No reply.'

'There wouldn't be, seeing as she was unavoidably detained at the mortuary,' said Margaret witheringly.

'Her accomplice might have been there, smarty-boots.'

'I haven't told Jenny about him yet,' said Margaret, glancing apprehensively at the younger woman.

'Evidently he was after your father's trunk,' said Caldicott. 'He broke into Charters' cottage and threatened him with a gun.'

Jenny was frightened. 'The man who's been trying to find me?'

'Yes, well don't take on, love. The police have got hold of him now,' said Margaret.

'They haven't, actually,' Caldicott confessed. 'Charters let him go.'

'Let him go! You didn't tell me that bit! Why did the idiot let him go?' Margaret demanded.

'Ah, well, you see, he was anxious not to blow Jenny's cover.'

' "Blow her cover!" You've been reading spy stories again,' said Margaret, amused.

'You know what I mean, Mottram! Once they'd got him in for questioning they'd twig that the late Helen Appleyard wasn't our Jenny.'

'And?'

'Well – it'd get into the papers and whoever's after Jenny would then know she's alive and kicking.'

'But whoever's after Jenny could well be Helen Appleyard's accomplice.'

'Yes! . . . Not necessarily.'

'Who, if Charters had turned him in, would be behind bars,' Margaret went on relentlessly.

'No!' said Caldicott, thoroughly confused now. 'Well, very probably.'

Margaret interpreted for Jenny. 'What Caldicott means is that we don't really know who's after you, or why they're after you – except that it's something to do with your father's

42

trunk – or how many of them there are, or what they might do next. So you'd better lie low. Correct, Caldicott?'

'Exactly what I said – she mustn't blow her cover. Meanwhile Jenny, that trunk is as safe as if it were in Fort Knox.'

Jenny was not consoled. 'You mean the police have it.'

'Fret not – Charters got a receipt. We'll have it back the moment they've finished with it.'

'But why do they want it? What are they doing with it?'

Margaret had been sifting through various papers from the handbag. She held up a letter she'd been scanning. 'The same as we're doing – looking for clues. And this looks like a real one. "From the desk of Josh Darrell",' she read.

'Never heard of him,' said Caldicott.

'Yes, you have – I've talked about him. London president of the Zazz Corporation of California.'

'Soft drinks,' said Jenny.

Caldicott shuddered, 'Never touch them.'

'Regretting he had to break their lunch engagement,' Margaret went on. 'Been trying to reach her, blah, blah, interested in her proposition – *that* sounds intriguing – would she call his office to make another date.' Margaret gave the letter to Caldicott. 'You *have* heard of Josh Darrell, Caldicott. The one who's always asking me for dirty weekends at his flash country house in darkest Bucks. Or I assume they're dirty – I'm giving him the disbenefit of the doubt.'

'How do you come to know him, Margaret?' Jenny asked.

'My temps agency. I've supplied him with so many office girls he should really be getting a trade discount. I suppose one of these days I ought to find out what he does with them all – I might be the next best thing to a madam.'

'Do . . .' Caldicott and Jenny began in unison.

'Go ahead,' said Caldicott.

'I was going to ask – do you think you could fix *me* up as a temp with the Zazz Corporation?'

'Not as Helen Appleyard, ducky. As you see from the letter, he evidently knows her.'

'That's the whole point, Margaret. If I went as Miss Brown or somebody, I might find something in the files about her.' Jenny smiled wrily. 'Besides, being homeless, stateless and nameless, and possessing only what I stand up in, I need the money.'

'Miss Brown it is, then. It's worth a try.' Margaret turned to Caldicott. 'And what's on *your* tiny little mind?'

'Those dirty weekends he invites you to . . .'

'Yes?' Margaret prompted. Then, 'No!' she said emphatically, suddenly seeing the way his mind was working.

'But if he has the who, what and wherefore about Helen Appleyard, what better opportunity to . . .'

'. . . get myself chased round the summerhouse by Josh Darrell,' Margaret finished for him. 'N – O.'

'I don't mean you to go alone, Margaret. Charters and I could go with you.'

'Oh, I see. Dear Josh, arriving as per standing invite re orgy, and is it all right if I bring my own spares,' said Margaret scornfully.

'Ha, ha.'

'Well, I suppose I *could* pass you off as a couple of English toffs – he likes a bit of tone.'

'That's my girl. Let me try Helen Appleyard's number again.' Caldicott picked up the phone and began to dial. 'If there's still no answer I might chance popping over and having a quick look-see through her belongings.' He listened for quite a while, then quietly replaced the receiver.

'Still no one there?' Jenny asked.

'Oh, there's someone there all right,' said Caldicott grimly. 'Somebody who picked up the phone but didn't speak. Somebody who's worked out what must have happened to Helen Appleyard. Somebody who's just waiting. As if a blessed spider had answered the phone.'

Jenny shuddered and Margaret put a protective arm round her shoulders.

CHAPTER 5

Charters and Caldicott, lobster-pink and sweating it out in
the steam room of the Club's turkish bath, still managed to
cling onto a shred of towel-clad dignity: each had equipped
himself with a now-soggy copy of *The Times*, carefully folded
at the crossword.

'Reading lights should help its elucidation,' said Charters.

'Doubt it, old chap. It's the steam.'

'No, no, no – that's the clue. One down.'

'Oh, I see. Reading lights should help its elucidation. Beats
me.'

'Nine letters. Something something O, something S, something something something something.'

'Where do you get the O from?'

'Five across. Overt.'

'You didn't pass that on to me.'

'Didn't think I'd need to,' said Charters, smugly. 'It's
obvious.'

'It is, now you mention it.' Caldicott wrote in the word
before asking, 'Why overt?'

'Obvious. "Unconcealed – six balls to a T." '

'Yes?'

'Six balls to an over.'

'I'm aware of that, Charters.'

'Add an over to a T and you've got overt. Unconcealed.'

'Obvious,' said Caldicott, disgusted with himself.

Charters returned to puzzling over one down. 'Reading
lights should help its elucidation.'

The figure of Venables, the clubman, also towel-clad but
still looking distinguished, materialised out of the steam.
'Crossword,' he stated.

'Yes, difficult one today,' said Caldicott.

'That's the answer. Reading lights should help its elucidation. Nine letters. Crossword.'

'How do you make that out?'

'Reading *lights*. Crossword lights – in other words, clues.'

'Yes, thank you, Venables,' said Charters, irritated.

'Not at all, Caldicott.'

'Charters!'

'Sorry.' Venables drifted away and was swallowed up by
the steam.

'He did that to annoy us,' said Charters.

'Mixed our names up? Doesn't annoy me.'

'Told us the answer to one down. Just when I was on the verge of solving it.'

'Never mind, old man. Now we know that nineteen across begins with a D. Four letters.'

Charters brightened. Then hearing a cough behind him, he clutched his newspaper to his damp chest, fearing another intrusion into his crossword. 'Now look here, Venables . . .' he began before recognising the Club porter through the steam. 'Oh, it's you, Barstow. What is it?'

'There's a gentleman to see you both, sir,' said Barstow.

'Gentleman? What gentleman?'

'A Mr Snow, sir.' Barstow lowered his voice. 'Well – Inspector Snow, to be more exact.'

'In the Club? I shall write to the Committee!'

'I should think the Committee will be writing to *us* when they get wind of the police tramping up and down the grand staircase,' said Caldicott. 'Where have you put him, Barstow?'

'In the smoking room, sir.'

'Then take him *out* of the smoking room and put him in the library where no one'll find him,' said Caldicott, much agitated by this breach of Club etiquette.

'Fifth floor,' said Margaret, studying the directory board in the main entrance of the prestige office-block in Mayfair that housed the Zass Corporation. 'Don't steal anything I wouldn't steal.'

'Wish me luck,' said Jenny, Josh Darrell's new temp. She turned to go in and almost collided with the mysterious Cecil St Clair, who also seemed to have business in the building. He stepped back and clicked his heels.

'See you for lunch,' Jenny called over her shoulder to Margaret.

Margaret cast an amused glance at St Clair. 'Unless you get a better offer – Miss Brown.'

While Inspector Snow waited for Charters and Caldicott, he entertained himself by straightening all the pictures that covered one wall of the Club's library. Eventually he reached a very large portrait of Sir Robert Peel, hanging high above the mantelpiece. Here he had to admit defeat. Undeniably askew though it was, Snow couldn't reach it without a ladder.

Charters and Caldicott, who had dressed with utmost speed, paused on the threshold of the library and glanced over their shoulders to reassure themselves that no one was following them in. Peering round the library anxiously, they registered not one but two distressing sights: Inspector Snow, wiping dust from his hands as he stared regretfully up at Sir Robert, and another member already in occupation and reading a newspaper.

Charters and Caldicott approached the Inspector on tiptoe. 'Inspector Snow,' Caldicott whispered.

'Sorry to barge in on your Club, gentlemen,' said Snow in normal tones, to the anguish of the pair.

Charters raised a warning finger to his lips, pointed to a prominent Silence sign, and hissed, 'Yes it *is* rather unusual.'

'Grimes said you'd be here, Mr Caldicott, and I did want to get you both together,' Snow went on more quietly. 'Saves a special journey up to town, look at it that way, Mr Charters.' Charters grunted. Snow nodded towards the portrait and said, 'Sir Robert Peel. My governor as was.'

The clubman in Caldicott overcame his hostility to the Inspector's intrusion. Beckoning Snow to lean closer, he whispered, 'Yes, and how he comes to be up there since he was never a member is rather a curious story. It seems that the first chairman of our wine committee was something of a gambler, who in his cups one evening . . .'

'Can we get on,' Charters interrupted. 'Is this about the murder, Inspector?'

'Related matters.'

'It comes to the same thing. You see, there's no reason why you should be acquainted with our Club rules, Inspector, but under them we're not permitted, while *in* the Club, to do business.'

'A murder inquiry isn't what I'd call business, Mr Charters.'

'Ah, but it's business to *you*, Inspector,' said Caldicott, keeping an anxious eye on the other occupant of the library. 'Pursuit of your profession, don't you see? For example, supposing I brought you in here for a quiet Scotch as my guest and you started trying to flog me life insurance.'

'We could always go down to the Yard,' said Snow, his

voice rising. 'Or there's the Club steps outside, if you'd find that more convenient.'

The other member coughed pointedly. Charters flapped an agitated hand towards the Silence sign and murmured, 'Shall we sit down?'

They selected a table as far as possible from the other member, pulled chairs up close and put their heads together – literally. 'That's another thing,' Charters hissed as Snow set his briefcase down on the table. 'Our guests usually leave their briefcases in the cloakroom.' The inspector gave him a long, withering look. 'Not allowed to, eh? Well, I suppose you have your rules as we have ours.'

Inspector Snow, pointedly putting an end to further discussion of Club ethics, snapped back the lock catches of his briefcase. 'I've spent most of the weekend sifting through all Colonel Beevers' documents and papers. Grubby job, I can tell you. There was the dust of ages in that trunk.'

'I can well believe it. Something of a squirrel, our Jock,' Caldicott whispered.

'You'd say that, would you?'

'One-man lumber room. Old diaries, letters, reunion dinner menus, photographs . . .'

'Score cards,' Charters supplied.

'We all keep scorecards, Charters.'

'Not bridge scorecards, Caldicott.'

'True.'

The other occupant of the library, tired of rustling his newspaper in a critical manner, got up and departed with an angry glare.

'Yes, quite a bundle of those,' Snow agreed, abandoning his hunched position over the table with relief. 'So you'll have had a good look through the trunk yourselves, gentlemen?'

'Certainly not!' said Caldicott, successfully distracted from the shame his fellow member had inspired in him. 'Colonel Beevers' hoarding tendencies were well known to all and sundry. Why, he even saved our old school mags.'

'Yes, I know. They were in the trunk,' said Snow, opening his briefcase.

'Have you brought them with you?' Charters leaned forward eagerly but all the inspector took out was a passport. 'That name ring bells?'

Caldicott glanced at it. 'Buckton.'

'D. W. Buckton?' Charters asked.

'Ducky Buckton! Bowling average eight point something, batting average nil. Literally.'

'Our house captain. Superb bowler – couldn't bat for toffee.' Charters waved an arm at the Wisdens on the shelves. 'It's all there if you're interested.'

'The missing volume turned up, by the way, Inspector,' said Caldicott. 'You'll recall it was because we couldn't find the 1979 Wisden that we went back to my flat and discovered the body.'

'Yes, it hadn't been taken away – simply carelessly replaced in the wrong order,' said Charters.

'Quite a weight off my mind,' said Snow.

'Ducky Buckton,' said Caldicott, drifting back on a wave of nostalgia. 'Bought it in North Africa, poor chap. But why did Jock Beevers have his passport?'

'Did he?' Snow asked.

'Didn't he?'

'You tell me.'

'Need we play cat and mouse, Inspector?' said Charters, exasperated. He picked up the passport. 'Either it was in Colonel Beevers' possession or it . . .' He stopped abruptly, staring goggle-eyed at the photograph in the passport. 'But this *is* Colonel Beevers!' He thrust the passport in front of Caldicott.

'To the life!' said Caldicott excitedly. 'I'm out of my depth here. What is Jock Beevers doing on Ducky Buckton's passport?'

'Interesting isn't it?' said Snow. 'Like the false-bottomed Bible it was tucked inside.'

'What are you suggesting?' Charters demanded. 'That this is a forged passport using the name of a schoolmate who died for his country?'

'What are you suggesting, Mr Charters? That it isn't?'

'Give it here, Charters.' Caldicott snatched the passport and opened it. 'Russian visas,' he said, stunned.

'Quite a regular visitor, wasn't he,' said Snow.

'Good God,' said Charters, lost for a decent excuse.

Caldicott, totally bewildered, asked, 'But why?'

'To be briefed and debriefed, I suppose. About what isn't my pigeon, thank goodness.' Snow went on casually, after scarcely a pause, 'What's Moscow's interest in Hong Kong, would you say?'

'Oh, enormous,' said Caldicott. 'British presence, Chinese

49

presence, lease running out, secret negotiations, no doubt. There's a hell of a lot going on in that little melting-pot that the Russkies would give their . . .' He stopped, belatedly realising what Snow was getting at. 'I don't believe it!'

'That he was a spy? What was he then – a travel courier?'

'It'll take more than this to convince me, Inspector,' said Charters loyally, giving the passport back to Snow. 'You see, I *knew* Colonel Beevers.'

Inspector Snow replaced the passport in his briefcase in precisely the correct position and took out two photocopies of a short letter. 'I know you did, Mr Charters. That's why I'm here. He left you both a letter, by the way. I'm surprised you didn't stumble across it.'

'We didn't stumble across it because we hadn't looked in the trunk,' said Caldicott heatedly.

'Don't rise to the bait, old man,' said Charters. 'What letter?'

'Well, more of a note, really,' said Snow. 'In fact, he does seem to have assumed that in the event of his death you *would* open the trunk.'

'Do you mean to say you've read it?' Charters demanded.

'I've made you a photocopy each. You can keep it.'

Charters seized his sheet. 'Thank you! Thank you very much!'

Caldicott read his copy. ' "Dear old chaps, just in case my plane nosedives or the old ticker packs up before I get there – Mix Well and Serve. Yours aye, Jock." End message.' Caldicott looked up. 'Never much of a correspondent, old Jock.'

' "Mix Well and Serve",' said Charters, mystified.

'Yes, I was wondering about that,' said Snow.

'Quotation, is it?' Caldicott asked.

'Conundrum?' Charters suggested.

'Code?' Snow asked, at which Caldicott suddenly looked wary and said unconvincingly, 'Catchphrase. I've remembered. Does it come back to you, Charters?'

'What? Oh, indeed,' said Charters, loyally if equally unconvincingly responding to this verbal kick on the ankle.

'Not a message, then?' Snow asked.

'Well, farewell message after a fashion,' said Caldicott.

'No, I meant a message asking you two to do whatever he would have done himself if he'd made it back to the UK.'

'Contact the Soviet Embassy, I suppose,' said Charters

derisively. 'I'm sorry to disappoint you, Inspector. As Mr Caldicott says, it's no more than a catchphrase.'

'What does it mean?'

'It means . . . Mr Caldicott remembers better than I,' said Charters, cravenly passing the buck.

'Doesn't mean anything, really,' said Caldicott. 'It was just what he used to say when he had his dry martini, wasn't it, Charters?'

'That's it. Mix Well and Serve.'

'Sort of like "Cheers"?' Snow asked.

'Or "Chin chin",' said Caldicott.

'Or "Bottoms up",' said Charters.

'Or "First today",' the inspector offered. Charters and Caldicott frowned. Their kind of catchphrase belonged to the officers' mess, whereas this one was distinctly public bar. 'Mix Well – I thought dry martinis were supposed to be shaken not stirred.'

'Colonel Beevers, Inspector, had no affinity with James Bond,' said Caldicott firmly.

Inspector Snow locked his briefcase and stood up. 'No, rather the reverse.'

Charters and Caldicott hurried their unwanted and embarrassing guest out of the library and down the grand staircase. 'Still, as I say, the espionage end of all this isn't really my baby,' said Snow, pausing to straighten a portrait on the wall. 'There'll be someone in touch with you about that end. And I warn you, gentlemen, when those lads get cracking they make the Murder Squad look like a game of Twenty Questions.'

Charters and Caldicott exchanged anxious glances. They could almost hear the cell door clanging shut behind them. They propelled Inspector Snow across the lobby, past the ever-watchful eye of Venables who was pretending to read a newspaper and out onto the steps. But just as they hoped to be rid of him, Snow stopped. 'You'll be going to the funeral?'

'Shall we?' Charters looked at Caldicott.

'I hadn't thought. What's the form?'

'The form of what?' Snow asked.

'When peripherally involved with murder. Is it usual to pay one's respects to the unfortunate victim?'

Snow gave him an odd look. 'It is if you're friends of the family.'

Embarrassment, plus the fear that a fellow member,

descending the Club steps, may have overheard some of this, threw Charters and Caldicott into confusion. Worse still, another member, about to enter the Club, stopped to talk to the departing member only a few feet from where Charters, Caldicott and Snow were standing.

Caldicott gave the pair a hideous, glassy smile. 'Quite,' he said desperately.

'I'll send you the details,' said Snow.

'Do. Most grateful.' To allay the imagined suspicions of his fellow Club members, Caldicott went on more loudly, 'Well, goodbye, Snow, old chap.'

'Cheerio, Snow,' said Charters, backing him up.

To their immense relief, Snow nodded and seemed about to take his leave at last. Then he turned back again with yet another final thought. 'Tell me, had Colonel Beevers quarrelled with his daughter, do you happen to know?'

'Not to my knowledge,' said Charters. 'It's some years since we actually met, of course.'

'I'll tell you why I ask. As you were saying, Mr Caldicott, he was a great hoarder. There must be enough snapshots in that trunk to fill a dozen family albums.'

'I don't doubt it.'

'And yet there isn't one single, solitary photograph of the murdered girl, his daughter. Odd, that, isn't it?'

Charters and Caldicott exchanged worried glances. 'Very,' Caldicott gulped, finally.

Josh Darrell buzzed through to his secretary on the intercom and summoned her, plus notebook, to his office. 'And ask Mr St Clair if he can give me three more minutes.'

Cecil St Clair, who had followed Jenny into Darrell's outer office and had since been patiently reading *The Financial Times*, half rose. 'That's quite all right. I have all the time in the world.'

The secretary picked up her notebook and departed. Jenny watched the door close behind her, then glanced over to St Clair. She caught his eye and they both smiled. With assumed nonchalance, Jenny walked over to the filing cabinet, opened one of the drawers and searched through the files. Finding the one she was looking for she took it out, cast a wary look at Darrell's office door and a disarming smile at St Clair, and began to go through its contents. Unnoticed by Jenny, St Clair watched with great interest.

Charters and Caldicott repaired to the Club bar for a much-needed restorative aperitif. ' "Mix Well and Serve," ' said Charters thoughtfully as the barman poured them two dry sherries.

The barman looked up in surprise. 'Not the sherry, Eric,' said Caldicott. 'Mr Charters was just thinking aloud.'

Charters signed the chit and when the barman had moved out of earshot, said, 'What was the idea of claiming it was a catchphrase?'

'Because *he* thought it was a coded message between the three of us. He was just on the verge of accusing us of taking Moscow gold.'

Charters snorted. 'Easier to make *that* kind of accusation against the dead! I still can't credit that yarn, Caldicott.'

'I wish *I* couldn't, Charters – but thinking about it, you know, Jock Beevers *did* move in mysterious ways. And how do we account for the forged passport? There can only be one explanation.'

'There could be two. That he was an agent for *them*, as Inspector Snow professes to believe, or, as *I* prefer to believe, an agent for us.'

'That's what Jenny thinks, if you recall. Whichever way round it is, it could certainly explain why he was bumped off and why all the world and his wife were hell-bent on getting hold of that trunk.'

'It could even explain why that wretched Helen Appleyard was murdered in mistake for poor Jenny.'

'Why "poor" Jenny?'

'Well – if she hears about this Russian spy nonsense.'

'Need she?'

'You're right, Caldicott. Not a word.'

Caldicott mused in his turn upon Jock Beevers' odd message. ' "Mix Well and Serve." He was trying to tell us something, you know Charters.'

'Yes, I realise that, Caldicott. I'm not a complete dunderhead, you know.'

'Or, more specifically, asking us to do something, in the event of his not getting here. "Just in case my plane nosedives or the old ticker packs up before I get there – Mix Well and Serve." '

Charters produced his own photocopy and studied it. 'Do you know what, Caldicott? I'm pretty sure this is one of Jock's little games.'

'I've gathered that, Charters. Nor am *I* a complete dunderhead.'

'We were neither of us a match for Jock Beevers, with his conundrums and teasers and riddles, were we?'

'What was that thing he always used to catch me with? Brothers and sisters have I none but my wife's mother is my uncle's son – no, that's not it. Now how does it go?'

Charters had been scribbling on the back of his copy of the letter. 'Rex ends Mall view,' he said.

'Come again?'

'Anagram of Mix Well and Serve. Rex ends Mall view.'

'That's brilliant!'

'Just a knack,' said Charters modestly.

'Rex ends Mall view. What does it mean?'

'How the devil should I know?'

'Then we're back where we started.'

'Not quite, Caldicott. I shall make a close study of this. I have a hunch that in setting this puzzle Jock Beevers was relying on my expertise with *The Times* crossword.'

'We *both* do *The Times* crossword, Charters,' said Caldicott, hurt.

'Of course we do, old fellow. Of course we do. Let's have another sherry. Eric!'

'I say, Charters, you don't suppose Inspector Snow suspects, do you? I mean, that his body isn't really Jenny Beevers? Or that we're holding something back?'

'No, no, no – hasn't got the imagination. Policeman Plod, that's his mark.'

'Yes, he does carry an aura of size eleven boots, doesn't he?' Caldicott agreed, comforted.

The purpose of St Clair's visit has been puzzling Grimes. In Caldicott's absence, he decided to do a little snooping on his own account to see if he could find out what was so interesting about the flat. Moving gingerly from room to room, looking for he knew not what, he was startled to find himself suddenly face to face with Inspector Snow.

'Left the door open, didn't we?' said Snow.

'No reason why it should be locked,' said Grimes, making a quick recovery.

'Every reason why it shouldn't be. Anyone comes back unexpectedly, it's just a case of having popped in to see if everything is all right, isn't it? Heard a strange noise, taps running, breaking glass, smell of burning. Which was it?'

'I *am* the resident caretaker, Inspector Snow,' said Grimes with attempted dignity.

'Yes, I know. I'm asking which was it. What are you doing in Mr Caldicott's flat?'

'Just checking, sir.'

Inspector Snow went over to an antique table. 'Checked this, have you?' He made as if to wrench open the drawer.

'Careful, sir! There's a knack of opening that.'

'How do you know?'

'I've seen Mr Caldicott do it.'

'Oh yes? Has you round, does he? Social occasion? Glass of sherry?'

Grimes licked his lips nervously. Snow, in no hurry, looked round the room. 'So what are you looking for, Grimes?'

'Nothing – swear to God.'

'Now that's a silly reply, that is, isn't it. What are you looking for?'

'I don't know, sir.'

'That's better. I can believe that.'

'There *has* been a murder, Inspector. Just call it natural curiosity.'

'No, I won't call it that. I'll call it something that'll look good on a charge sheet. If I have to, that is. Shall we have another chat, Mr Grimes?' Inspector Snow, with all the time in the world, produced his notebook and two pens and laid them neatly on a side table, then he plumped up the cushions in an armchair until they suited him.

Grimes watched aghast. 'We can't talk here, Inspector. What if Mr Caldicott comes back?'

'Caught me red-handed, you could try him on,' said Snow, his attention distracted by two matching vases on the mantelpiece. One of them was a fraction out of place. Snow adjusted it, stepped back to confirm that the arrangement was now exact, then turned again to Grimes. 'Let's go back to the day of the murder, shall we, Mr Grimes? Mr Caldicott paying you to keep your mouth shut, is he, or do you have reasons of your own?'

CHAPTER 6

The funeral of 'Jenny Beevers' took place in a large, forlorn-looking, deserted cemetery. Inspector Snow waited alone outside the chapel, watching the unaccompanied hearse approach down the long avenue that led from the gates through rows of neglected graves. Only when the undertakers' men were preparing to carry the coffin into the chapel did he move inside. Charters and Caldicott, soberly dressed in dark suits, their bowler hats at their feet, were the only other mourners. Snow took a seat across the aisle from them in the front row. When the simple coffin had been placed on trestles before the altar and the pallbearers had retreated to the back of the chapel, there was an unexpected addition to the congregation. Venables, approaching on tiptoe, took the pew next to Charters and bent his head in prayer. Charters stared at him and nudged Caldicott. Seething with indignation and curiosity, the pair were forced to keep quiet and wait until Venables completed his devotions.

Charters allowed a decent interval to elapse after Venables had straightened up, then hissed, 'Venables?'

'Caldicott,' Venables whispered back.

'Charters!'

'My mistake.'

'I wasn't aware you knew Jock Beevers.'

'I didn't.'

'Much less his daughter.'

'No.'

Charters felt that an explanation was called for. While he waited for one, Caldicott, to his exasperation, leaned across and said, 'In that case, Venables, decent of you to swell our numbers.'

'Not at all. It was my duty.'

Charters bristled. 'What do you mean?' But before Venables could answer, the verger called upon those present to rise, the duty clergyman bustled in and, without any preliminaries, began to read the funeral service from the Alternative Service book. Poor 'Jenny' was just one more on the day's production line to him.

The Lord is my shepherd, therefore can I lack nothing,
He will make me lie down in green pastures, and lead
  me beside still waters,
He will refresh my soul, and guide me in right pathways
  for his name's sake . . .

As the words rolled on, Charters and Caldicott became increasingly restless. This was not the way they liked their funeral services to be conducted. 'Modernistic claptrap,' Charters muttered, finally irritated beyond endurance. 'I don't approve of this at all, Caldicott.'

'Nor I. From religious trendies may the Good Lord preserve us.'

'Ssh! Respect for the dead, chaps,' said Venables mischievously. Caldicott looked contrite, Charters seethed and the clergyman read on.

Though I walk through the valley of the shadow of death,
I will fear no evil,
For you are with me,
Your rod and your staff comfort me,
You spread a table before me
In the face of those who trouble me . . .

The service ended and the clergyman led the small procession out of the chapel and along one of the straight paths that cut through the cemetery. He glanced surreptitiously at his watch, then stepped up the pace a little to remain on schedule. Charters and Caldicott dropped back and took up a position one on either side of Venables.

'Venables,' said Charters, 'This is neither the time nor the place but we have a question to ask. And before you answer, I'd like you to be clear that my name is not Caldicott.'

'No, your name is Charters,' said Venables obligingly.

'*My* name is Caldicott,' said Caldicott, anxious that there should be no room for misunderstanding.

'Agreed.'

'Then that's established. Now let's establish something else. What's your game?' asked Charters bluntly.

'Game, Caldicott? Charters, I should say.'

'What are you up to?'

'Why are you here, if that's not a leading question?' said the more conciliatory Caldicott.

'Ah. For my sins I happen to be the Official Mourner.'

Charters glared at him. 'Official Mourner? What's that?'

'Appointed by the Home Office. Unpaid, of course, though one receives a small honorarium against expenses – black tie allowance and so on.'

'So you're with the Home Office, Venables,' said Caldicott. 'We've often wondered what you did.'

'I wouldn't say *with* the Home Office. One's merely called in from time to time. When some unfortunate leaves this mortal coil with no kith or kin to pay their last respects, it falls to the Official Mourner to act in *loco bereavis*.'

'*Bereavis*! There's no such word, man!' Charters snorted.

'Latin was never my strong point.'

'Furthermore, Venables, I happen to be well versed in public life and this is the first time I've ever heard of such an appointment as Public Mourner.'

'One doesn't court publicity,' said Venables, drifting forward to walk beside Inspector Snow.

'Official Mourner, my foot!' said Charters angrily as they drew near the graveside.

'Woman born of woman has but a short time to live,' the clergyman began. 'Like a flower she blossoms and then withers; like a flower she flees and never stays. In the midst of life we are in death; to whom can we turn for help, but to you, Lord, who are justly angered by our sins?'

For a while, Charters and Caldicott were too distracted by their irritation at these words to notice that first Inspector Snow, then Venables, were staring intently away from the graveside. Caldicott spotted them at last, turned to see what had attracted their attention, then nudged Charters. A man stood on the other side of the boundary railings. It was the chauffeur, respectfully holding his uniform cap under his arm as he followed the last rites. Charters and Caldicott looked at each other, worried, but when they turned back to the railings, the man had gone.

At the graveside, the clergyman had reached the final words of the service. 'We have entrusted our sister Jennifer to God's merciful keeping, and we now commit her body to the ground, earth to earth, ashes to ashes, dust to dust, in sure and certain hope of the resurrection of eternal life . . .'

Venables, in his capacity as Official Mourner, stepped forward and scattered earth over the coffin.

'If this is Venables' idea of a practical joke, it's in very questionable taste indeed,' said Charters.

'Well, was I buried in style?' Jenny asked.

'Like a duchess,' said Caldicott, opening champagne for Jenny, Margaret and himself. 'The Official Mourner was there.'

'Who?' Margaret asked incredulously.

'Just a small courtesy HMG extends on these occasions. Charters wasn't impressed. I was. There we are, my dear,' said Caldicott, handing a glass of champagne to Jenny. 'Mix well and serve, eh?'

'What's he muttering about?' said Margaret. 'If you want a swizzle stick you only have to ask.'

'No, it wasn't that. It's just a phrase that's been puzzling me. Doesn't mean anything to you?' Jenny shook her head. 'It was in a note your father left. See what you make of it.' Caldicott produced his copy of Jock's letter and Jenny and Margaret pored over it together.

'No, I give up,' said Margaret finally.

'Me too,' said Caldicott. 'Charters thinks it's one of Jock's teasers, Jenny. You remember how he liked his crossword clues served – the more cryptic the better.'

'Yes – it's as if he's giving you directions of some kind. You know, like in a treasure hunt.'

'Exactly what I said to Charters. Look, we do have another copy even if one didn't know it by heart. Would you like to hang onto this, Jenny, and see if inspiration strikes?'

Jenny took the copy but said doubtfully, 'I'm not very good at this sort of thing. Big flightless bird in three letters is about my level.'

'Big flightless bird in . . .' said Caldicott blankly, almost ruining what little reputation he had as a solver of crossword puzzles. 'Oh, the ubiquitous emu!'

Jenny put down her father's letter and produced some papers of her own. 'Swap?'

'What's that?'

'The Zazz Corporation file on Helen Appleyard, such as it is. I photocopied it.'

Correspondence concerning Helen Appleyard ran to only three pages. There was a letter from her saying that she'd be at Thamesview for a few days and would Darrell be interested in some valuable information about a company in Oldham called Norton and West; a copy of Darrell's reply, the original of which she'd had in her handbag, saying that he would be; and a memo from Zazz's northern manager reporting that he couldn't find a link between Helen Appleyard and Norton and West.

Caldicott scanned the pages then asked. 'Who Norton and West?'

'We looked them up,' said Margaret. 'Old-established family firm bottling lemonade.'

'Sounds as foul a temperance brew as Zazz.' Caldicott raised his glass. 'I'll stick to the devil I know. Chin chin.'

'Cheers. I must say this is better than a ham tea, Caldicott. You must go to more funerals.'

'Cheers.' Jenny sipped her drink and shivered. 'Someone walking over my grave.'

'Helen Appleyard's chauffeur chum, I shouldn't wonder,' said Caldicott. 'That's someone else who turned up today.'

'At the actual funeral?' Jenny asked.

'Hovered on the touch-line. Which indicates that he's put two and two together and savvied that it's not our Jenny Beevers who's dead but his Helen Appleyard.'

'He was bound to work that out, unless he has an IQ of zero,' said Margaret robustly, adding reassuringly to Jenny, 'It's all right. He can't possibly know you're here.'

'All the same, I'm not altogether happy about leaving her alone for the weekend,' said Caldicott.

'She's got a fridge full of food, a bottle of gin and orders to keep the chain on the door and watch telly till we get back.'

'See that you do, my girl,' said Caldicott sternly. He looked again at the photocopies she'd brought. 'What do you suppose can be the connection between Zazz, Helen Appleyard and this Norton and West outfit?'

'If we knew that, ducky, we wouldn't be letting ourselves in for a weekend with Josh Darrell,' said Margaret.

'Here we are, Charters,' Caldicott called, spotting him at last, half-hidden behind a trolley stacked high with enough suitcases to last a world cruise. He waved to attract his attention.

Charters completed the long trek down the station platform and drew up beside the open door of the first-class carriage. 'I hardly imagined you'd be in the guard's van,' he snapped, out of breath and uncomfortably hot in his country tweeds and ancient fishing hat. 'Give me a hand with these, would you, Caldicott? The profession of railway porter seems to be a thing of the past.'

Huffing and puffing, they chain-ganged the suitcases into the modern, open-plan carriage. Charters and Caldicott, unfamiliar with the lay-out, spent some time locating the luggage spaces, cunningly hidden between seats and in separate compartments at each end. Margaret Mottram, sitting coolly and cosily with a copy of *Country Life*, watched their exertions with amusement. 'What, no cabin trunk?'

'My dear Mrs Mottram, when you've knocked about as much as I have, you'll realise the benefits of travelling light,' said Charters. 'Is that *The Times*, Caldicott? I left mine behind. Pass it over, there's a good chap.'

Caldicott had been about to settle down with it but he handed it over, though with ill grace, just as the guard came down the platform slamming doors. As the whistle went, Cecil St Clair, wearing a Chelsea boutique's version of country clothes, complete with leather patches, pleated pockets and mysterious flaps, and carrying an expensive weekend case, hurried through the barrier and ran for the train. He leaped aboard the last carriage and passed through the train until he came to the crowded first-class section where Charters was doing the crossword in Caldicott's *Times*, Margaret was engrossed in her magazine and Caldicott was twiddling his thumbs – literally. St Clair paused in the aisle beside them.

'By all means,' said Caldicott in answer to St Clair's smile and inquiring glance at the empty seat beside him. St Clair tucked his case under the seat, sat down and unfolded his *Financial Times*. Charters, who didn't care for strangers, looked grumpy.

The train travelled some distance without a word from anyone, then Charters broke the silence. 'Five down. Could low joint be ankle?'

'I've really no idea, old man,' Caldicott said huffily. 'I haven't had an opportunity to look at the crossword this morning.' Charters grunted. Caldicott, after sulking for a bit, relented and asked, 'What progress has that razor-sharp mind made on "Mix Well and Serve"?'

Charters didn't look up from his crossword. 'Very little so far, I'm afraid. It'll come, Caldicott, never fear.'

'Hm. Are you going to be all day with that *Country Life*, Margaret?'

'I've only just started it!'

Charters rustled Caldicott's *Times* impatiently. 'Do you mean to say you haven't brought anything to read?'

'Really!' Caldicott exploded but before he had time to lodge a strong protest, St Clair leaned over and offered him his *Financial Times*. 'Oh, if you've finished with it, very kind of you. Very kind of you indeed.' Caldicott was not familiar with the *Financial Times*. He opened it with every expectation of pleasure but his expression soon changed to one of strained concentration and then to total bafflement. He might as well have been reading *Micro-Chip Monthly* for all the sense it made to him. Finally he admitted defeat, lowered the newspaper and began to play a little game of blowing up his nostrils.

'Margaret,' said Caldicott when the amusement palled.

'*Yes*, Caldicott,' said Margaret, irritated.

'What was the name of that lemonade factory up in Oldham again? Old-fashioned sounding place – puts me in mind of those matchstick-men paintings by what's-he-called.'

'Lowry,' said Charters.

'No, that wasn't it.'

'Norton and West,' said Margaret.

'Got it. They make some concoction known as Birdade. Ever heard of them, Charters?'

Charters had noticed that St Clair seemed to be taking an interest in their conversation. 'Pas devant la domestique,' he warned in schoolboy French.

'Oh, quite,' said Caldicott hastily.

'No, *not* quite, my dear sir. Do I look like a female domestic servant?' St Clair asked. 'By the way, you need have no fear of my blabbing your confidences. Your conversation is double Dutch to me.'

'I beg your pardon,' said Charters.

'Please do not mention it.'

Deeply embarrassed, Charters and Caldicott buried themselves in their newspapers. Margaret winked at Caldicott from behind her magazine.

St Clair carefully broke a bar of chocolate into pieces and offered some to Margaret who declined with a smile. Charters, glancing up from his crossword, shook his head politely. St Clair gave up and popped a square into his own

62

mouth before he noticed that Caldicott was gazing at him longingly, like a spaniel under the dinner table. Caldicott gratefully accepted St Clair's belated offer.

'And, by the way, I was so anxious not to miss my train – it does stop at Percival St Mary?' St Clair asked, taking advantage of the slight thaw in the atmosphere.

'I sincerely hope so, otherwise we're all in trouble,' said Caldicott.

'You're going there also?'

'The whole pack of us,' said Caldicott, ignoring Charters' disapproval of his getting into conversation with strange foreigners.

'Incidentally, it is a most pleasant spot.'

'So I believe.'

'Worth a detour, as Michelin would say.' St Clair translated, for the benefit of Charters, the French expert of the company, 'Mérite un detour.'

'Very probably,' said Charters, burying himself deeper in *The Times*.

Margaret decided to be polite. 'Do you live there?'

'On the contrary, this is my première visit.' St Clair offered some more chocolate to Caldicott who took another piece and said, 'Ah, misunderstood.'

'I'm sorry. My English is not very good.'

'Your English is perfect, old lad. I meant we got hold of the wrong end of the stick in thinking you were well-acquainted with the place.'

'As to that, I've heard all about it from my host.'

'Then you're staying there' Margaret asked.

'Now you have the right end of the stick. Yes, at the Old Priory. Do you know it possibly?'

'Good Lord! Talk about small worlds!' said Caldicott.

'You are going there also?'

'We certainly are,' said Margaret. 'To stay with Josh Darrell.'

'The smallest of worlds, as you say.'

'Well, well, well. Well, on that note, I think we'd better introduce ourselves,' said Caldicott heartily. 'Mrs Mottram.' St Clair half rose and clicked his heels. 'Charters.' St Clair repeated the performance and Charters, not to be outdone in civility, also half rose, but naturally omitted the heel-clicking. 'And I'm Caldicott.'

'Saint Clair,' their fellow guest announced with a final clicking of heels.

'Sinclair,' said Charters, not quite catching it.

'If you'll permit me – *Saint* Clair. It is an unusual form of the name, by the way.'

'Most unusual,' said Charters drily. 'Well, if we're all house guests together that puts us on a quite different footing. I'll accept some of that chocolate, if I may.' To Caldicott's great annoyance, Charters reached over and took St Clair's last piece.

The atmosphere became almost genial and as the train sped through open countryside, the four engaged in desultory conversation. St Clair, apparently a compulsive eater, carefully peeled an apple with a Swiss Army knife and said, 'As a matter of fact, our host is a most entertaining fellow.'

'So Mrs Mottram tells us,' said Caldicott. 'Charters and I have not yet had the pleasure.'

St Clair turned to Margaret. 'Do you know him well, by the way?'

'Business acquaintances. Do *you* – by the way?' Margaret asked, deadpan but mocking.

'Not frightfully well. You know, we spent some little time together in Hong Kong, just a few months ago. Mr Darrell made himself most agreeable.'

'Really!' said Caldicott, suddenly alert.

'Really. Charming fellow.'

'Yes, I'm not so much interested in his charms as in the fact that he was in Hong Kong recently. Precisely what is Josh Darrell's connection with . . .' Caldicott broke off with a gasp of pain and glared at Charters.

'Sorry, old chap. I'm afraid my foot caught your ankle. Pleasant spot, Hong Kong,' said Charters in what he thought to be an offhand manner.

'You know the place?'

'Oh, yes. Bustle, that was my chief impression. Do you have business interests there?'

'I have business interests wherever I chance to be, you know.'

'A cosmopolitan,' said Charters, with a faint sneer.

'As you say, a cosmopolitan.'

Having, as he imagined, approached the subject in a roundabout way and allayed suspicions, Charters, to Caldicott's disgust, leaped in with both feet. 'And what precisely is Josh Darrell's connection with Hong Kong?'

St Clair turned to Margaret. 'By the way, you must know he began his career with the Zazz Corporation in the Far East?' Margaret hadn't known it but she nodded. 'One imagines he likes to keep a toe in the water, you know.'

'If you were doing business in Hong Kong you must have come across a friend of ours. Colonel Beevers,' said Caldicott.

St Clair started nervously at the name but made a quick recovery. 'I believe not.'

'Of the British Trade Commission,' said Charters.

'No.'

'One would have thought your paths might have crossed,' Charters persisted. 'Beevers. Ruddy-faced, shock of white hair, Colonel James, otherwise Jock, Beevers.'

'I didn't know him,' said St Clair woodenly.

'Hm,' Charters grunted.

'Hm,' Caldicott echoed, equally dissatisfied.

Margaret decided to take a hand. 'But you knew he was dead?'

'Excuse me?'

'You spoke in the past tense. Not I *don't* know him, but I *didn't* know him.'

'My colloquialisms leave much to be desired. I didn't know your Colonel Beevers when I was in Hong Kong. That is not correct?'

'It's correct.'

'I don't know that he is dead. Am I still on the straight and narrow?'

'More or less.'

'Then we have no problem.'

'No problem.'

'By the way, I am sorry your friend is dead,' said St Clair to Charters and Caldicott. 'And now who will have a piece of apple?' He held out a slice speared on his knife blade.

Charters and Caldicott shook their heads at the apple but Caldicott exclaimed, 'I say, St Clair, *that's* a knife and a half.'

'The Swiss Army knife, Caldicott. You know it has a blade for every purpose.'

'*Every* purpose?'

'Except scrimshaw,' said Margaret gravely. 'For that you need a Swiss Navy knife.'

Caldicott guffawed but St Clair said seriously, 'You know, I am afraid someone has been pulling your leg, Mrs Mottram. Switzerland is landlocked and thus has no navy.'

Margaret exchanged a long-suffering look with Caldicott and tried to exchange one with Charters. 'He's right, you know,' said Charters.

Percival St Mary, a small country station, actually ran to a porter. Obligingly, he piled all the luggage onto his trolley and pushed it towards the ticket barrier.

'If Darrell's sent his car, as you say, where's his driver?' Charters asked, peering past the ticket collector to the road outside.

'Probably took one look at your luggage and zoomed off,' said Margaret. 'Never mind, we'll borrow that station parcels van.'

At the barrier, Charters and Caldicott hesitated, eyeing each other, while Margaret waited resignedly.

Caldicott opened the batting. 'Tickets, Charters.'

'*You* have the tickets, Caldicott.'

'If you will excuse me, I will look for the car,' said St Clair, handing in his own ticket and making his escape.

'*You* have the tickets, Charters.'

'No, *you* have the tickets, Caldicott,' said Margaret.

'There, you see!' said Charters triumphantly.

'That is, you have your ticket and my ticket,' Margaret went on, adding to the smug Charters, 'You have your own ticket.'

'Do I?' Charters began a panic search through his waistcoat pockets.

While Charters and Caldicott were arguing and dithering, the porter, helped by the uniformed chauffeur, had been loading the luggage into the waiting Jaguar. When the other three finally emerged from the station, they found St Clair hovering by the open front passenger door. 'Shall I take the seat by the driver?' he said to Margaret. 'I think you will be more comfortable in the back, you know.'

'Fine,' said Margaret, climbing in and taking a seat in the middle.

'Take care of the porter, old man, would you?' Caldicott said to Charters, patting his own pockets ineffectually.

'Oh, very well!'

'After all, you've had the most use out of him.' Caldicott followed Margaret into the car and closed the door.

The chauffeur banged shut the boot lid on the last of the luggage and went round to open the other passenger door. Charters tipped the porter and, as he climbed into the Jaguar, caught sight of the chauffeur's face for the first time. It was Helen Appleyard's accomplice. Caldicott noticed Charters' uneasy expression, looked past him and also recognised the chauffeur. The pair exchanged anxious looks across Margaret who, never having seen the man, was quite unperturbed. The chauffeur slammed the passenger door, climbed into the driver's seat and drove off, his face impassive throughout.

CHAPTER 7

No one spoke as the Jaguar cruised up the long drive and stopped outside Josh Darrell's country retreat, an impressive pile with enough towers, turrets and battlements to do credit to a fair-sized castle. Two servants emerged and began to unload the luggage, a butler hovered by the main entrance in a supporting role and the chauffeur, inscrutable as ever, opened the door for Charters to get out.

Charters thanked him coldly. 'I still don't have your name.'

'Gregory, sir.'

'We seem to be seeing a lot of one another, Gregory.'

'Don't we just? I expect we'll be seeing a lot more,' he said, suddenly menacing, and went to help the servants with the cases.

A shot rang out as Caldicott, Margaret and St Clair strolled round the car to join Charters. They started nervously and looked about them. 'The butler did it,' Margaret joked. Then she froze, staring at two large, well-muscled men who appeared round the corner of the house and took up positions, sentry-style, on either side of the path. Their host, carrying a gun and followed by dogs, strode between his bodyguards and came towards them. Margaret, reassured, called, 'Don't shoot. We're on your side.'

Josh Darrell was American, youngish for his powerful position, and very attractive, a man who carried his responsibilities with an easy confidence. He embraced Margaret and shook hands with St Clair. 'Glad you could make it,' St Clair clicked his heels. Margaret began to make introductions but Darrell brushed formalities aside. 'And you're Messrs Caldicott and Charters.'

'Charters and Caldicott, we're usually known as,' said Charters, apologetically.

'Like Morecambe and Wise,' said Margaret.

'It's just something that's become established,' said Charters.

'How've you been?' said Darrell.

'Quite well, thank you,' said Caldicott. 'What do you shoot here?'

'Anything that moves. Come along in. If you like guns, I have a whole museum of them.'

Gregory watched thoughtfully as the party moved into the house.

It was the custom, *chez* Darrell, to dress for dinner. Caldicott had donned an old-fashioned boiled shirt and red braces and was knotting his bow-tie when Charters came into his room. Charters had taken up the sartorial option of a cummerbund and was having trouble with his own neckwear.

'You might tie my tie, Caldicott. I'm a little out of practice.'

'Oh, it's like. riding a bicycle. Once learned, never forgotten.' Caldicott took hold of the ends of Charters' tie. 'Now let me see. Right over left.'

'No, no. Left over right.'

'*Your* left over right, but my right over left.'

'Nonsense,' said Charters impatiently. 'My right over left, your left over right.'

Caldicott made a few practice passes. 'Which are you calling left?'

'Look here, Caldicott, get behind me and do it in the mirror. Then tie it as you would your own.'

'Easier said than done, old boy.' Caldicott moved behind Charters. 'Ah, got it. Right over left.'

'Precisely what I said.'

'No. What I said. *You* said left over right.'

'Just get on with it, Caldicott. Has Gregory been in touch with you at all?'

'Who Gregory?'

'The chauffeur.'

'Oh, *your* friend. I'm surprised he hasn't been in touch with you. You're the one he holds up with Smith and Wesson .38s. Gives one a certain rapport, I would have thought.' Caldicott gave the tie a twist. 'Is that too tight old boy?'

'Not if your object is strangulation.'

'Sorry, old chap. I suppose he *will* make contact as soon as he gets the chance. I only hope he doesn't do it with a blunt instrument.'

'I'm quite sure friend Gregory is as anxious to talk to us as we are to talk to him. Odd that he turns out to be working here, wouldn't you say?'

'Not if he and Josh Darrell turn out to be pieces in the same jigsaw.' Caldicott made a final adjustment to the tie. 'How's that?'

'It'll have to do, I suppose. What do you make of Darrell?'

'Too early to say. Seems open and above board so far.'

'You think that, do you?'

'I think so,' said Caldicott, uncertainly. 'What do you make of him?'

'I'll tell you what I make of him, Caldicott. I took a walk outside before dressing. Now I use my eyes, as you know.'

'Well?'

'Everything is not what it seems in this house, Caldicott.'

'In what way?'

'Polystyrene gargoyles.'

Margaret, elegant in silver and black, paused in the doorway and glanced around at those of her fellow guests who were already assembled in the great hall. Spotting Cecil St Clair seated at the grand piano, playing light, cocktail-hour music, she strolled over to do a little sleuthing of her own.

She listened to a few bars, then said, 'Ever since we met on the train, I've had this feeling I've seen you somewhere before.'

St Clair stiffened but continued to play. 'Is that possible?'

'you didn't used to work in the music department at Harrods, did you?'

'I regret no.' St Clair scowled down at the piano keys.

Josh Darrell, smart in a restrained tartan jacket and cravat, joined them. 'All right, break it up, you two. I want Margaret and a champagne cocktail to myself before this place starts to look like the Concorde departure lounge.' He took a drink for Margaret from one of the waiters and led her towards the terrace. 'You're looking great, do you know that?'

St Clair's eyes, as well as his music, followed them. He too wondered where he and Margaret had met before.

'So we got you at last,' said Josh. 'Where did I go right?'

'I haven't been playing hard to get, Josh. I've *wanted* to come down for ages.'

'But your chaperons were busy. Do those two guys take good care of you?'

'When I want them to.' Margaret nodded to where Josh's bodyguards were hovering in the shadows. 'Do yours?'

'Rocky and Rocky II. They come with the job.'

'You mean you get them off tax.'

'Kidnap, hijack, they're as much executive risks as a coronary these days. Now, tell me about your two. What do they do?'

'Not a lot,' said Margaret laconically.

'What did they used to do when they did it?'

'Oh, they were sort of abroad a great deal. *You* know.'

'Foreign Service?'

'Not quite.'

'Colonial types, what?'

'You're getting warmer. I don't know quite what the department was called. It was a sort of overseas branch of the Civil Service where they posted well-meaning chumps to stop them making even bigger chumps of themselves at home.'

Darrell laughed. 'Oh, we have that. We call it the Diplomatic Service.'

Charters and Caldicott, veterans of many a country-house weekend, had provided themselves with a hip-flask of whisky with which to launch the evening. Caldicott topped up their toothglasses and asked, 'Well now, what's our plan of action?'

'Keep our eyes and ears open, do some discreet pumping and evaluate Darrell's taste in friends – for example, that fellow Sinclair, or Saint Clair, as he chooses to style himself.'

'Yes, rum customer. Mark you, he *is* foreign.'

'A foreigner of the worst sort, I'd say – all that heel-clicking. But there's more to him than mere foreignness, Caldicott. Look how he wriggled and shuffled when I asked him if he'd known Jock Beevers. It was as plain as the nose on your face he knew who we were talking about, yet he pretended he didn't. Why?'

'Natural shiftiness, probably. Still, he did tell us one thing we didn't know – that Josh Darrell had strong connections with Hong Kong.'

'I wonder if *Darrell* knew Jock Beevers?'

'Doubt it, or Jenny would have mentioned it. Still, we can always drop the name into the conversation and see how he reacts.'

'Casually, mind.'

'That goes without saying, Charters,' said Caldicott with quiet dignity. 'Shall we go down?'

Charters picked up the empty glasses. 'I'll just rinse these out. It's a poor guest who leaves his toothglass reeking of whisky.'

Caldicott called him back. 'Just tie my tie, would you, old chap?'

The subdued roar that greeted the pair as they reached the top of the grand staircase indicated that the party was already in full swing. The great marble hall, hung with tapestries and surrounded by arched galleries, made a spectacular setting. Charters and Caldicott paused and looked down on the scene. Hell would have made a more inviting prospect. Below them swirled representatives of every world they despised as cheap and shoddy. Darrell had chosen to fill his home with rich trendies and photographers, advertising executives and models, pop singers and show business personalities, chat show habitués and hairdressers. Leopardskin leotards vied with silk dungarees, punk zips and pink hair bayed at glittering ballgowns, scarlet legwarmers shrieked to purple satin shorts, technicolour jockey outfits gossiped with split leather, near-topless little black frocks crowed at camouflage-grey suits.

At this bizarre fancy dress party, Darrell's tartan jacket seemed on the conservative side. Charters and Caldicott, impeccable in old-fashioned dinner-jackets, might have emerged from the Ark. At the sight of them, standing rigid and goggle-eyed at the head of the stairs, the party babble died. Suddenly aware that they were being stared at, they remembered their manners as guests and began to descend, self-consciously tugging at their collars. St Clair struck up 'Hello Dolly' on the piano. Charters and Caldicott continued to walk down the stairs, sublimely unaware that they were doing so in time to the music.

Darrell watched, amused. Margaret put her hands to her face to hide her giggles and fled out onto the terrace to pull herself together. At the sight of Gregory, standing in a pool of light below, smoking and staring up at her, her laughter died and she went back indoors.

Darrell took a couple of glasses of champagne over to Charters and Caldicott. 'Hi. Now who don't you know?'

'Pretty well everyone, I'm afraid,' said Caldicott.

'We don't get about much these days, you know,' Charters apologised.

Darrell, a courteous host, led them on a tour of introduction. 'Here we go. This is Milo Dashwood, the artist. Alex Meyrick, the photographer, Sarah Meyrick. Ed Jollard, who produced "Evil Out of the Deep" – great movie, Ed; thanks for the tape. Jane Leslie, who *is* the evil out of the deep. Helen Hyman – you know the name' – they didn't – 'that's the face. Peter Price, the agent. Richard Shadd you *must* have heard of' – they hadn't – 'Carla Woodman . . .'

The introductions to names and faces Charters and Caldicott had never heard of or seen before and hoped earnestly never to meet again seemed interminable. They endured stoically, greeting everyone with a punctilious 'How d'you do' and a handshake. The assorted personalities responded with a wave of a cigarette holder, a kiss, a smile, a nod. 'Cecil St Clair you've met. And that, I guess, must be the lady you came in with,' said Darrell as Margaret, a recognisable member of the human race, joined them. 'Henry Grice, the writer, and a cast of thousands.' The host to these abominable hordes raised his voice and clapped his hands. 'OK, gang, let's eat. Carla, you can't cut me dead in my own home . . .'

Margaret, Charters and Caldicott were forced to mingle with the garish throng drifting towards the dining-room. 'I'm going to get you for this, Mottram,' Caldicott hissed.

'I did warn you. What did you expect? The Cliveden Set?'

'No, but really! I wonder what frightful oiks we're going to be sitting with at dinner . . .' Caldicott's indignant mumblings faltered and stopped as he and Charters took in Darrell's feeding arrangements for the evening. Instead of the formal dining-table they'd been expecting, the room was laid out like an after-theatre buffet at a five-star, American-owned hotel. Guests were expected to queue for food at a long table, then carry their plates to small, lamp-lit tables that were spread around the room. Margaret surveyed the scene with amusement, Charters and Caldicott with deep disgust.

'Good God! It's like the tourist-class dining-room on a cruise-liner,' Charters snorted.

'Do you suppose there'll be tombola with the coffee and liqueurs?' Caldicott sniggered.

'Don't be such a couple of snobs,' said Margaret. 'And don't sit with me. I'm going to see if I can get anything more out of my new little friend Mr St Clair.' She looked round and saw that he was in earnest conversation with Darrell.

Charters and Caldicott, when their turn came, each accepted a plate of pigeon pie and another of salad from waiters at the buffet. Faced with the problem of equipping themselves with bread, Caldicott asked Charters to hold his salad plate.

'How the devil can I?' Charters demanded, himself similarly encumbered.

'Oh, very well, give one of your plates to me.'

Seeing them juggling ineffectually with their plates, Darrell came to their assistance. 'Let me do that. Come on, I have influence with the maître d' here.' He provided them with bread and guided them over to a vacant table which was equipped, like the others, with an open bottle of wine and another of Zazz. 'Chateau Latour or chateau-bottled Zazz?'

Charters, desperate but unfailingly courteous, said, 'With pigeon pie? Which would you suggest?'

'I'm only kidding.' Josh poured them some wine. 'Though millions drink Zazz with every meal they eat.'

'Good God!' Caldicott gasped. 'That is – Good Lord!'

'On every conceivable occasion. Would you believe, in Hong Kong Zazz is the speciality drink at funerals?'

'Really?' said Charters.

'It's true. But you're most likely familiar with that custom, right?'

'No, I wasn't.'

'But you are familiar with Hong Kong?'

'I wouldn't say familiar,' Charters hedged. 'We've passed through once or twice.'

'I guess you knew Jock Beevers at your Trade Commission?'

'Did we not,' said Caldicott heartily. 'So you *did* – or should I say, *did* you know Jock?' Charters gave Caldicott a filthy look for falling into Darrell's trap.

'No,' said Darrell. 'Not really. We bumped into one another at parties. I guess we were on "How are you?" terms, that's all.' Charters and Caldicott were smoked out and silenced. Darrell was enjoying himself. 'OK, so who else don't we number among our mutual acquaintances?'

Caldicott decided he might as well be hung for a sheep as a lamb. 'Helen Appleyard?' Darrell shook his head. 'She was mentioned to us as a possible contact with Norton and West.'

'Birdade?'

'Ah, so Norton and West you *do* know?' said Charters.

'It's my business to know them. They make a rival product. They can't sell it but they make it! So?'

'Well, we thought . . . Margaret thought,' Caldicott stumbled, tugging nervously at his collar, 'You might know someone there we could talk to.'

'About a little proposition of ours,' said Charters, trying to be helpful.

Darrell was curious. 'A proposition for Norton and West? Would it interest Zazz?'

'I hardly think so,' said Charters quickly. 'No, no, no, far too modest.'

'No problem.' Darrell stood up. 'If you'd like an introduction, just say the word.'

'You're very kind,' said Caldicott.

'Any time. Excuse me while I circulate.'

Charters and Caldicott reached for their glasses with heartfelt sighs of relief. 'I must say *that* conversation took an unexpected turn,' said Caldicott.

'Yes. He was trying to draw our fire.'

'That was my impression. I say, Charters, do you suppose he's guessed we have an ulterior motive in being here?' Charters' long-suffering look answered him. 'Oh. Then we'd better hope Margaret's playing her cards closer to her . . .' He paused, then made a delicate amendment to his words. 'Closer to *her*.'

Margaret had succeeded in capturing St Clair as her supper partner and had seated them at a little table apart from their fellow guests.

'This is a most agreeable pigeon pie,' said St Clair.

'Delicious.'

'He shoots them himself, you know.'

'I don't think I want to know that.'

'And by the way, now I recollect when we saw each other once before. You were escorting a young lady to Mr Darrell's office. Rather, I should say a lady even younger than yourself,' he corrected himself with ponderous gallantry.

'Thank you. That would be one of my temps, Miss Brown. It was her first day. I thought I'd better hold her hand.'

'And what is this "temps"?'

'Temporary. It covers a whole range of jobs.'

'Industrial spy?'

'Not according to her references. More your audio typist,' said Margaret, coolly concealing her shock.

'The reason I ask is that I saw your Miss Brown prying into our host's confidential files. Very unusual behaviour for a so-called "temp" on her first day, wouldn't you say?'

'Oh, that's our Miss Brown all over, I'm afraid. A compulsive Nosy Parker.'

'A common failure, Mrs Mottram.'

'Isn't it just, Mr St Clair? Would you excuse me? I'm not sure the pigeon pie was as agreeable as we thought.' St Clair rose and bowed as Margaret made her escape with as much dignity as she could muster.

Emerging a short while later from an upstairs bathroom where she'd been restoring her equilibrium as much as her make-up, Margaret happened to pass the open door of Darrell's study and heard him talking on the phone. 'You don't sound surprised? You *knew* they were staying here? How did you know? I didn't know myself until two days ago.' Margaret dawdled outside, pretending an interest in a nearby picture. 'Then did your little bird tell you who the hell they are and why they're asking questions about your operation? . . . That's right! . . . Don't give me that – we all have something to hide in this business – Norton and West more than most operations, am I right?' Darrell suddenly noticed that his door was open and kicked it shut. Margaret, seeing that one of Darrell's weirder guests was heading towards her, was forced to abandon her listening post and make for the stairs.

Coffee and liqueurs were being served in the great hall. Margaret ran Charters and Caldicott to earth there and helped herself to half Caldicott's brandy before saying grimly, 'Those pigeons we ate for dinner. I think between us we've set the cat among them.'

CHAPTER 8

After such an unpromising start to their weekend's investigations, Charters and Caldicott decided to cut their losses and concentrate on the more traditional country pursuits. The following morning, clad and equipped for fishing, they strode through the deserted great hall and out into the fresh air. As they paused to assess the weather, a car sped down the drive and drew up beside them. A smart, young accountant-type got out, retrieved his slim-line, black executive case and weekend grip from the back seat and nodded coolly to them. They nodded back and were about to continue on their way when Josh Darrell called down to them from his balcony, 'Meet Gordon Wrigley.'

Charters and Caldicott turned back civilly to greet a fellow guest.

'Of Norton and West,' said the newcomer, making no move to shake their outstretched hands.

'Ah,' said Caldicott.

'You wanted to see me?' said Wrigley.

There was a pause. 'Yes,' said Caldicott.

'A proposition?'

'Yes. Well, you see, the thing is,' Caldicott stammered after an even longer pause, 'Charters and I are inordinately fond of Birdade, aren't we Charters?'

'Inordinately.'

'Glad to hear it,' said Wrigley.

'Drink it all the time, don't we, Charters?'

'Perpetually.'

'Good. And what's your proposition?'

'Well not so much a proposition, just an idea, really,' said Caldicott, cornered. 'We thought, Charters and I, that what Birdade could do with is a slogan.'

'A slogan?'

'Yes.'

'What slogan?'

'Tell him your slogan, Charters.'

'Very well,' said Charters, rising loyally to the challenge. 'For what it's worth – "Birdade – gives you back your fizz".'

'Of course, that's only a rough draft,' said Caldicott hurriedly.

' "Birdade – gives you back your fizz",' Wrigley repeated.

77

'Something along those lines,' said Caldicott.

'I'll think about it.'

'Do. Well, we have an appointment with some trout,' said Caldicott, beginning to shuffle away.

'Don't let me keep you. See you at lunch.'

'Look forward to it,' said Charters, joining Caldicott in undignified retreat.

'We'll have another chat,' said Caldicott. Their tactical withdrawal turned into a disorderly rout.

Wrigley, totally bemused, looked up at the balcony from which Darrell, amused and intrigued, had watched Charters' and Caldicott's discomfiture. Darrell shrugged elaborately.

Charters and Caldicott reached the sanctuary of the riverbank and fished for some time in silence. 'I've just made a discovery,' said Caldicott finally. 'There are some moments in life so hairy that even fishing can't blot them out.'

'Yes, it *was* rather embarrassing. But of course it was meant to be. Shock tactics, Caldicott. Trying to find out what our game is.'

'I'll tell you one thing. I couldn't possibly face that Norton and West chap at lunch.'

'Nor I. I think we should run for it.'

'The old telegram trick?'

'They don't have telegrams now, more's the pity. I'll say we've had an urgent telephone call. Your sister ill – that should sound convincing.'

'I haven't got a sister.'

'Very well, then, *my* sister.'

'Better.'

With escape in sight, they both cheered up. Charters consulted his watch. 'If we left at once, we could be back for the start of play.'

'Good-oh. Which is it to be? Lord's or the Oval?'

'Difficult question. Middlesex are in good form but on the other hand I wouldn't mind seeing Surrey thrashed.'

'We could do Lord's this morning and the Oval after lunch,' Caldicott suggested.

'No, no, no – far too unsettling. We'll decide this in the traditional way.'

Caldicott nodded and produced a coin. 'Heads Middlesex v Warwicks, tails Surrey v Essex. Agreed?' He threw the coin up but the result went unheeded. Gregory was standing motionless on the opposite bank, staring across at them.

'Who killed Helen Appleyard?' Gregory called.

'That's what a good many people would like to know,' said Caldicott.

'Perhaps *you* did it, Gregory,' said Charters. 'Accomplices do fall out.'

'She wasn't my accomplice. She was my wife.'

'Sorry about that. I didn't know,' Charters mumbled.

One of Darrell's dogs ambled into sight along the river-bank. Judging his master to be not far behind, Caldicott called urgently, 'Look here, Gregory, we can't go on bawling at one another across the river like this. Isn't there somewhere we can talk?'

'The gun museum. At eleven.' Gregory turned and walked away.

'Eleven? That's cutting it a bit fine,' said Charters.

'I say!' Caldicott shouted after Gregory. 'You couldn't make it a bit earlier, could you? We have some rather urgent business in Town.' But Gregory was out of earshot.

Charters and Caldicott communicated the change of plan to Margaret and delegated her to tell their host, with appropriate excuses, while they changed into their cricket-watching clothes and packed their cases.

'Josh has gone shooting. I've left him a note,' said Margaret when they joined her in front of the house where she was supervising the loading of the luggage into the Jaguar.

'That's the ticket. Saves embarrassment all round,' said Charters.

'The clock on the belfry strikes eleven. Should I come with you?'

'Better not,' said Caldicott. 'You might inhibit him. You can be looking up trains.'

'yes, sir.'

Charters and Caldicott came across St Clair on their way to the gun room. He greeted them from the stone bench where he was sitting peeling yet another apple with his Swiss Army knife. 'Forever eating, that fellow,' Charters muttered. 'Case of tapeworm there, I shouldn't wonder.'

The walls of the museum were lined with guns of all kinds, ages and sizes. Revolvers, duelling pistols, muskets nestled next to military and sporting rifles. Yet more exhibits were laid out in glass display cases.

'Bloodthirsty hobby, collecting all this stuff together,' said

Charters as they wandered round the room. 'Give me triangular stamps any day.'

'Everything clean, bright and lightly oiled, you'll notice. There must be enough hardware here to slaughter a regiment.'

Charters consulted his watch. 'It's gone eleven. Where's Gregory?'

Caldicott, exploring further afield, spotted one exhibit they had overlooked. He called to Charters and together they hurried across to where Gregory lay, half-hidden by one of the display cases, blood oozing onto the floor from a wound in his chest.

'Shot?' Caldicott asked.

'Knifed, I'd say.'

'A knife! In this place!' Caldicott stared round in disbelief at the arsenal of guns surrounding them. 'Now there's a case of coals to Newcastle, if ever I saw one.'

Once again, Inspector Snow followed the Club porter up the stairs and into the library. The solitary occupant put down his newspaper and rose from his armchair to greet him.

'Inspector Snow, good of you to spare me your valuable time,' said Venables, the clubman.

The likelihood of finding bodies in the Club billiards room being, on the face of it, remote, Charters and Caldicott met there for a game of restorative snooker and a breather from the relentless attentions of the police. The game was not going Caldicott's way. When a hiss of sharply indrawn breath distracted him as he was about to pot yellow, he turned to Charters in irritation.

'Do you mind, old boy?'

'I didn't utter a sound. It's the radiators.'

'Sorry.' Caldicott re-applied himself to the shot and again was stopped by a gasp. Turning, he discovered that Inspector Snow had joined them and was taking a critical interest in his game.

'Go for the pink, Mr Caldicott. Then you'll be in line to pot that red there, which should bring you up to the black.'

'I'm aware of that, Inspector. I was just considering my options.'

'Inspector, I don't wish to appear rude, but have you been

elected a member of this Club?' said Charters, bristling with annoyance.

'Come along, Mr Charters, you know why I'm here.'

'That poor devil Gregory, I suppose. We've already been closely questioned by the Buckinghamshire constabulary, you know.'

'Yes, I do know. They tell me that what seemed to concern you most was missing a cricket match at the Oval.'

'Lord's, actually,' said Caldicott.

'Don't let me interrupt your game of snooker, Mr Caldicott.'

'I concede, Charters,' said Caldicott, laying down his cue. 'Look here, Inspector, I hope we're not creating an impression of callousness, but after all we didn't know the man from Adam and it was only our bad luck that we chanced to be the ones to find him.'

Snow began absent-mindedly to retrieve the snooker balls and replace them in their positions. 'Oh, chance, was it? So you hadn't gone to the gun museum to meet him?'

'Why should you think that?' Charters asked, bluffing boldly.

'Well, you see, Mr Charters, you have your luggage loaded in the car in ample time to catch the 11.18 to Marylebone – you're anxious to get to the Oval, or Lord's, it doesn't matter which – yet you then go wandering off to the gun museum when there isn't another train until 2.40.'

'Yes, and the next one after that isn't until five, as we have good reason to know,' said Charters bitterly.

'All the more reason for catching the earlier train. That yellow please.' Caldicott obligingly rolled the yellow ball down the table to Snow.

'Look here, Inspector, this murder, if murder it was, took place far outside the province of the Metropolitan Police. Now, unless you've been brought into the case . . .'

'Black, Mr Charters,' Snow interrupted. Charters shoved the ball viciously towards him. 'Let's say I brought myself into it. As soon as I'd heard you'd found another body.'

'You're not suggesting *we* had anything to do with these deaths?' Charters demanded.

'You're one of my common denominators. I'll put it that way.'

'One of them? Are there others?' Charters asked.

'Oh, yes. You know Gregory came from Hong Kong?'

81

'Did he, by Jove,' said Caldicott.

'Interpol have a file on him. Petty drug-runner, porn merchant, part-time pimp. I imagine that's why Mr Josh Darrell gave him a roof over his head when he turned up there. He'd have plenty of use for Gregory's type of services – you know the company he keeps.'

'Do we not!' said Caldicott feelingly, the memory of his fellow guests still nightmarishly vivid.

'Hardly your style, I would have thought.'

'Yes, well, we were taken there by a friend,' said Charters. 'I can tell you, it's the last time I spend a weekend with an unknown quantity.'

'You won't be spending any more weekends away in the near future, gentlemen, will you? No holidays abroad, for instance?'

'We don't take holidays abroad, Inspector, we've been abroad.'

'That red,' said Snow. When Caldicott had rolled it to him he completed the frame, moved it into its exact position and crouched down to check it at eye level. Satisfied, he removed the frame from the balls and wiped the chalk off his hands with his handkerchief. 'Just let me know if you *do* decide to take off anywhere, won't you? Washroom's down the stairs, isn't it?'

Snow's departure was more than welcome but Charters hastily redirected him. 'There's a nearer one this way, Inspector. Down the back staircase and through the kitchens.'

'Thanks,' said Snow drily, moving towards the green baize door. 'Sorry to be an embarrassment, gentlemen, but if you *will* get mixed up in all these murders.'

'Let him know if we go away?' said Charters, as Snow followed his directions into the nether regions of the Club. 'That's tantamount to warning us that anything we say may be taken down and used in evidence! I don't like this, Caldicott. He quite clearly suspects that we know far more about Gregory than we've admitted.'

'Probably. I'll tell you something he *doesn't* suspect, though, Charters – the existence of the flat at Thamesview.'

'How do you make that out?'

'He spoke of Gregory having been given a roof over his head at Darrell's place. Evidently he and Helen Appleyard – Mrs Gregory – kept their little hideaway to themselves.'

'What's that to us?'

'Well, don't you see, Charters? With Gregory out of the way, and the police still in blissful ignorance of the place, there's no reason why we shouldn't go round to Thamesview now and have a thorough nose round.'

'What? Before lunch?'

'Well, after lunch.'

They took up their cues again. 'My break, I believe,' said Charters.

'You won't let me interrupt you at all, Mr Grimes,' said Snow, his shadow falling across the newspaper Grimes was using to help him fill in his football pools.

''Scuse me, Inspector, slack period.'

'Good. We can have one of our little chats. Anyone been up to thirty-six of late?'

'Only Mr Caldicott himself.'

'And?'

'And Mr Charters.'

'And?'

Grimes smirked. 'Well, *you* know, Inspector.'

'No, I don't know.'

'That Mrs Mottram once or twice. And that's all, to my knowledge. Of course, if you'd like me to keep a special look-out style of thing.'

'I don't pay for information, you know, Mr Grimes. You're supposed to give it to me for nothing. If you don't, it's called withholding evidence and you get arrested for it.'

'I've got nothing else to tell you, Inspector. Honest to God, I kid you not.'

'Good. I prefer to be kidded not.' Snow produced a batch of photographs from his briefcase and showed Grimes a wedding picture of Helen Appleyard. 'Now, we all know who this is, don't we?'

'The dead girl, Jenny Beevers as she was known.'

'What do you mean "as she was known"?'

'Well, it's who everybody *said* she was style of thing, isn't it?'

'You have reason to believe it wasn't Jenny Beevers?'

'Not for me to say, Inspector Snow. I know nothing about her in any shape or form whatsoever.'

'You've never heard Mr Caldicott casting doubt on it being Jenny Beevers?'

'Oh, he wouldn't, sir. Not to me. Not to staff. He's not what you'd call a big confider, see?'

'All right, Mr Grimes, what about this fellow?' Snow showed Grimes a wedding snap of Helen Appleyard and Gregory arm-in-arm. 'Ever seen him before?'

'Never.'

'Yes you have. He's on page one of that newspaper you've got there.'

'I only read the sports pages, sir. Never look at the front page – I mean to say, it's only bad news, isn't it?'

'It is for him. Has he ever been here?'

'Not to my knowledge.'

'Never asked to see Mr Caldicott?'

'No.'

'And you didn't slip him the spare key to Mr Caldicott's flat? Or leave this grille unlocked so he could help himself?'

'More that my job's worth, Inspector Snow.'

'Your job isn't worth fivepence at the present moment in time, Mr Grimes. You're a liar, aren't you?'

'I don't have to stand here and take that from you, Inspector.'

'Yes, you do. You work here.'

'I swear to God I've never set eyes on that man in that picture.'

'I didn't say you had. I said you were a liar. As to what you're lying about, we'll find out sooner or later.' Snow put the photographs away and looked at his hands. 'Just chuck me one of those tissues, will you?'

'Do you want me to mention to Mr Caldicott you called round,' Grimes asked as Snow carefully wiped his hands.

'You'll do whatever suits you best, won't you?' said Snow, throwing down the dirty tissue and leaving. Grimes scowled, picked it up and put it in his waste-paper basket.

The sign opposite the lift said, 'Thamesview South Block Nos. 100–200' and an arrow pointed down a long, featureless corridor. 'Soulless establishment, isn't it,' said Charters as they followed the arrow. 'Like a Swedish clinic.'

'You pays your money and you gets your privacy. Very much a port of call for ships that pass in the night, I believe. Here we are.'

They went into a tiny service flat, just a bed-sitter with doors leading off to a kitchenette and bathroom. It obviously hadn't been tidied since Helen Appleyard went out for the last time. The bed was unmade, clothes were strewn carelessly about and an open suitcase stood on top of the wardrobe. Looking around, Caldicott found underwear hanging on the shower rail in the bathroom and unwashed crockery in the kitchenette. 'Exactly as she must have left it,' said Charters, wrinkling his nose. 'You'd have thought someone would have been in with a vacuum cleaner.'

'Only if she'd opted to shell out for maid service. As evidently she hadn't. Which suggests, Charters, there's something in this room that Helen Appleyard and Gregory wouldn't have wanted anyone else to see.'

Charters tried the door of the wardrobe. 'Locked. What do you suppose we're looking for, exactly?'

'Hard to say until we find it. The Hong Kong connection, as the thriller writers would have it.'

'She might at least have emptied her ashtrays.' Charters picked up a full one with disgust. About to empty it into the waste-paper basket, he stopped short and stared. 'There's your Hong Kong connection, Caldicott,' he said, pointing into the basket. A long spiral of fresh apple peel lay in the bottom.

'St Clair?'

'And his Swiss Army knife.'

A loud creak came from behind them. They turned as the wardrobe door swung open gently to reveal St Clair, half-eaten apple in one hand and knife in the other, standing inside it. Gravely, St Clair clicked his heels.

'Yes, we should have known it wasn't locked, Charters,' said Caldicott. 'There was no wardrobe key in her handbag.'

'So you have Helen Appleyard's handbag? And did it contain anything of interest?' St Clair asked, stepping out of his hiding place.

'What's Helen Appleyard to you, St Clair?' said Charters.

'I may as well ask what is she to you? Not to mention your friend Mrs Mottram and – I suppose one would say her sidekick, Miss Brown. Is that her name?'

'We'll keep that young lady out of this, St Clair,' said Caldicott.

'As you wish. And now since you have nothing you wish to tell me and I have nothing I wish to tell you, I suggest you leave.'

'I'll be hanged if we will!' Charters exploded.

'Then with regret I must call the management and put the problem to them. Oh, and by the way, my spare key if you please.'

'*Your* key? Do you mean to say this is your flat?' Caldicott asked.

'Since today. I explained to the management that I was a friend of Miss Appleyard, whom she had asked to look after her flat while she is away.'

Charters snorted. 'Most accommodating of them.'

'They are accommodating types. Especially when a month's rent is due. The key.'

Caldicott dropped it into his hand. 'And *were* you a friend of Helen Appleyard?'

'As to that, she had many friends – as you may have gathered.' St Clair opened the front door. 'And by the way, I will set your minds at rest, gentlemen. There is nothing here for either of us. We are all looking for the same crock of gold – but so to speak this is not the end of the rainbow.' He clicked his heels. Charters and Caldicott, completely mystified, took their leave.

CHAPTER 9

'So there we are, Jenny, your story so far,' said Caldicott, delving into his steak pie in search of some elusive kidney.

'But no happy ending in sight,' said Jenny ruefully. At the end of a successful morning's shopping, she and Margaret were taking Caldicott to lunch so that he could bring Jenny up to date with the weekend's events.

Margaret frowned at a dish of vegetables lying untouched. 'Are you going to eat that spinach, Caldicott?'

'No, I've got enough here, thanks.'

'Then why did you order it?'

'I'm sorry. I thought it was table d'hôte, like at the Club.'

'Yes, well it isn't. Just for that you'll get no pudding.' Margaret transferred the spinach onto her own plate. 'Jenny, assuming you won't be settling in London – and that is not a roundabout invitation to leave my house, don't think it – will you be going back to New York or have you things to tie up in Hong Kong?'

'Margaret, without wishing to sound stubborn or melo-dramatic or like a potential squatter – I don't mean to go anywhere until I've found out who killed my father and why.'

'Yes, I must confess I've rather been losing sight of our real objective, Jenny,' said Caldicott. 'I've been exercising myself as to who killed Helen Appleyard and why and who killed Gregory and why.'

'They all link up, though, don't they?' asked Margaret.

Jenny nodded. 'The Hong Kong connection.'

'I wonder why everyone who has been connected with Hong Kong denies having known your father?' said Caldicott.

'Perhaps they didn't. It's not a tiny village, you know.'

'But he was in the British Trade Commission and they were in trade. You would imagine paths would cross.'

'Everybody in Hong Kong is in trade of one kind or another. And besides, I can't prove it but I'm still sure of it. His job in the Trade Commission was only a front for some-thing else.'

'So you say,' said Caldicott, his attention distracted by the sight of Venables, the clubman, standing by the restaurant's reception desk, reading a newspaper while he waited for a table.

'I suppose you and Charters couldn't go out to Hong Kong

yourselves and see what you can ferret out there,' said Margaret, unaware that she'd lost her audience.

Caldicott turned to her. 'Impossible.'

'The cost,' said Jenny.

'It's not so much that as the fact that we're coming up to the Test season. Besides, Inspector Snow has more or less in so many words confined us to barracks.'

'Are you still speaking to Inspector Snow?' Jenny asked.

'All too often. Why do you ask?' Venables, Caldicott noticed unhappily, was being led by the receptionist in their direction.

'Would you see if you can persuade him to give my father's belongings back, so that we can thoroughly examine them?'

'I'll certainly try to jolly him along, my dear,' said Caldicott evasively. 'But you know what the rheumatic arm of the law is like.'

'Charters, my dear chap!' said Venables, stopping beside their table.

'Caldicott,' said Caldicott automatically.

'Of course.' Venables turned to Margaret. 'Good morning,' he said, hovering pointedly.

Caldicott reluctantly introduced her. 'And Miss . . .'

'Brown,' said Margaret.

'How do you do, Mrs Mottram. We met at Sandra and Jeremy Willoughby-Fox's wedding five and a half years ago. Remember?'

'So we did,' said Margaret who didn't.

'Miss Brown, and how are you enjoying your visit to London?'

Jenny exchanged an anxious glance with Caldicott. 'And what makes you think I *am* a visitor?'

Jenny's jacket lay across an empty chair, its label clearly visible. Venables nodded at it. 'Michaelo of Fifth Avenue. A Londoner would go to Michaelo of Bond Street.'

'Miss Brown is staying with her family,' said Caldicott.

'The Pont Square Browns?'

'No,' said Jenny, baldly.

'My mistake. I thought I glimpsed you in the vicinity the other day. Strong Far Eastern connections – imports and exports.'

'No,' Jenny repeated.

The receptionist, having discovered she'd mislaid her client, had returned crossly to reclaim him. 'I believe your table's ready, Venables,' said Caldicott with relief. 'We don't want to lose you but we think you ought to go.'

'Ah. A great pleasure, Miss Brown – enjoy your stay. How very well you're looking, Mrs Mottram. Charters.' Venables drifted away leaving the three of them thoroughly rattled.

'Nosy devil, isn't he? Sharp-eyed with it,' said Margaret.

'Yes, who *is* that man?' Jenny asked.

'Oh, I don't think we need worry about Venables, Jenny,' said Caldicott uneasily. 'We belong to the same Club.' He picked up the menu. 'Margaret, am I *really* not allowed pudding?'

'Did Inspector Snow get hold of you?' Grimes called out as Caldicott crossed the lobby of Viceroy Mansions.

'Get hold of me when?'

'Not half an hour ago, sir. I told him to try the Club.'

'Yes, well I wish you'd stop telling him to try the Club, Grimes. It's beginning to look like Savile Row police station.'

'Sorry, Mr Caldicott, only he did say it was fairly urgent style of thing. He said would you give him a ring as soon as you came in.'

'Right. Will do.' Caldicott turned towards the lift, then paused. 'Did Inspector Snow have anything else to say, Grimes?'

'About like what, sir?'

'You know very well "about like what". Has he been here asking questions, snooping about the flat?'

'Not while I've been here, Mr Caldicott. I mean to say, he'd need a search warrant to get past me, Mr Caldicott.'

'Yes?'

'You know me, sir!'

'Yes,' said Caldicott acidly.

When he'd spoken to Snow, Caldicott tried to contact Charters and Margaret but neither was at home. Mr Charters, Caldicott learned from his cleaning-lady, was in court playing at magistrates. After a moment's hesitation, Caldicott picked up his hat and hurried out. The news from the Inspector was too serious to wait.

Happily unaware that Caldicott was, at that moment, entering the court building, Charters, the chairman of the bench, listened attentively to a point being made by the defending solicitor. 'Yes, we're in some difficulty here, Mr

Wellbeloved. Mr Neaps admits driving his motor cycle along the pavement.'

'Yes, your Worship.'

. 'Yet he pleads not guilty to driving without due care and attention.'

'That is true, your Worship.'

'But surely, driving along the public pavement is as blatant a case of driving without due care and attention as one is ever likely to come across in a month of Sundays.'

'With respect, sir, the offence with which Mr Neaps is charged refers specifically to his allegedly scraping his handlebars, or allegedly allowing his handlebars to scrape, against the fruit and vegetable stall on the corner of Butter Cross Lane. He . . .'

Charters, impatient with waffle, cut in, 'Yes, yes, we know all about that, Mr Wellbeloved. But you see, he couldn't have scraped against the fruit and vegetable stall if he hadn't been driving on the pavement in the first place. Yes, Mr Charles?' The clerk to the court had risen. He whispered into Charters' ear and sat down again. 'Mr Wellbeloved, was your client driving on the pavement carefully?'

'He will say that he was, your Worship.'

'Then that may very well put a different complexion on the matter. Now you say you wish to call an expert witness on a particular aspect of this case?'

'If your Worship pleases. That is, if he has arrived from London.'

'He's either arrived or he hasn't. We can't be kept hanging about, Mr Wellbeloved.'

'Of course not, your Worship.' Mr Wellbeloved murmured to a police sergeant who nodded and left the court, boots squeaking.

'Now, what is this particular aspect in which your witness is an expert, Mr Wellbeloved?' Charters asked.

'Sir, the witness is a trained beekeeper . . .'

Caldicott, who had been staring blankly at the noticeboard in the lobby for some time, greeted the sergeant with relief. 'Ah, officer! Is that Mr Charters' court?'

'It is that. Been sitting two hours or more, so he has.'

'Thank you,' said Caldicott, heading for the door.

'Oy, where do you think you're going?'

'In there. You said the court was sitting.'

'So it is, but you can't just go barging in when you think fit.'

Caldicott stopped, surprised. 'Can't I?'

'You just park yourself on that bench and wait till I calls you.'

'Oh, that's the form, is it?' Caldicott did as he was told while the sergeant tiptoed back into court.

'You see, Mr Wellbeloved,' Charters was saying, 'this swarm of bees should have been brought up earlier.'

'I agree entirely, your Worship. I apologise that my client didn't mention it under examination.'

'If he was driving carefully along the pavement, then the swarm of bees could well be a mitigating factor.'

'That is what I aim to establish with the help of my expert witness, your Worship.' Mr Wellbeloved bent his head to listen to the sergeant. 'I've just learned that he has in fact arrived.'

'Then for goodness sake have him called and let's get on with the case. I have a flower and produce show to judge in half an hour.'

The sergeant went outside and beckoned to Caldicott. 'Right. Let's be having you.' Caldicott followed him into court.

'Now it may very well be in law, Mr Wellbeloved, if Mr Neaps was attacked by a swarm of bees at the point where he was approaching the fruit and vegetable stall, then he was no longer in control of the machine and technically not driving at all.'

'I believe that could be the case, your Worship.'

'If you can establish to the court's satisfaction that bees, if sufficiently angry, would . . .'

Caldicott's circuit of the court in the squeaking steps of the sergeant had been invisible from the bench. Seeing his old friend popping up in the witness-box out of nowhere, Charters' eloquence deserted him.

'What are you doing in my witness-box, Caldicott?' he demanded, suspecting a practical joke.

'I was put here, Charters,' said Caldicott, thoroughly bemused.

'Sir!' said the sergeant.

'Yes, officer?'

'You call his Worship "sir"! Or "your Worship".'

Caldicott was happy to oblige. 'Oh sorry. Sorry Charters, sir – your Worship. Didn't know the drill.'

Charters knew that it was up to him to bring the giggling courtroom back to a state of magisterial dignity. He did his best. 'Now look here, Mr Wellbeloved, I doubt whether I can continue this case. I have to declare an interest in this – that is to say, this gentleman is known to me. Besides, I thought you were calling an expert witness?'

'Indeed, your Worship, but . . .'

'He's not an expert on anything.'

'Thank you very much!' said Caldicott from the witness-box.

'You're not a trained beekeeper, are you, Caldicott? *Mr* Caldicott, I should say.'

'You know very well I'm not – Mr Charters. Sir. Your Worship.'

'There's evidently some mistake here. Step down, Mr Caldicott.'

Charters exchanged a few murmured words with his colleagues on the bench. 'In the absence of your witness, Mr Wellbeloved, I shall have to take precedents into account in the matter of these bees. Case adjourned until Wednesday.'

The magistrates began to shuffle out. 'All rise,' the sergeant called.

Caldicott, who had stepped down, as instructed, popped back into sight in the witness-box like a jack-in-the-box.

Charters was putting his papers in order when a policeman showed Caldicott into his anteroom. 'Now, what's the meaning of this, Caldicott? You've just interrupted a most involved and intricate case.'

'You don't have to tell me that, old chap. I couldn't make head nor tail of it.'

'Yes, well, the layman can't be expected to understand the complexities of case law,' said Charters, mollified. 'Now I hope this is important, Caldicott.'

'I haven't come all this way to discuss the cricket score, Charters.'

'No, I don't suppose you have. What *is* the score, by the way?'

'Fifty-two for three at lunch, I'm afraid. And now I'll give you something to look even more glum about. Inspector

Snow has found out that Helen Appleyard wasn't Jenny Beevers.'

'Well he was bound to in the end, wasn't he? He knows she was Gregory's wife, presumably?'

'It's what she was before she was Gregory's wife that's more to the point. He's got it all from the Hong Kong police.'

'Yes?'

'She was Jock Beevers' mistress.'

'Good grief!'

'That was, shall we say, her unofficial role. More formally she was Jock's secretary.'

'Par for the course, I'm afraid. The old rascal always did have a weakness for . . .' The full implications of this piece of news suddenly sunk in. 'Hold on a minute! Jenny Beevers didn't know who she was.'

'Exactly,' said Caldicott, who'd had a tiresome bus journey in which to examine the information from all angles.

'Didn't know her from Adam! Had never seen her before! Didn't know her name or anything about her!'

'Precisely.'

'How could Jock Beevers' daughter never have heard of her own father's secretary?'

'There's only one explanation, Charters, isn't there?'

'Jenny Beevers isn't Jenny Beevers.'

'And come to think of it, we've only ever had her word for it that she *was* Jenny Beevers. We didn't recognise her after all these years – neither of us did.'

Charters was still busy trying to sort out the loose ends. 'But the handbag she switched with Helen Appleyard was chock-full of Jenny Beevers' papers. Passport and everything. We saw them!'

'Forgeries? Unless the real Jenny is dead and the bogus one has literally stepped into her shoes.'

'Who the devil is she and what's her game?'

'She's certainly well-informed enough about poor old Jock, that's plain enough. And in common with several others, she's after something in poor old Jock's trunk, that's equally plain. But who she really is, old lad, or where she's turned up from, I can't even begin to guess.'

Charters abandoned speculation as a new aspect of the situation occurred to him. 'You've considered *our* position, I suppose?'

'I most certainly have,' said Caldicott forcefully. 'We've been taken for the most monumental ride!'

'More than that, Caldicott. We've been harbouring an imposter – very likely a murderer – why else should she pretend to be what she's not? You know what this makes us, don't you? Accessories after the fact.'

'I say! That's serious, isn't it, Charters?'

'More so for me than for you. I'm a magistrate! I'm supposed to have knowledge of these things – I can't even plead ignorance!'

'You think it'll come to that, do you Charters? Pleading?'

'I sincerely hope not, Caldicott.'

'You don't think we should make a clean breast, then?'

'I'll tell you what I think we should do, Caldicott. Get the bogus Jenny Beevers out of Mrs Mottram's house and into a hotel, then tip off the police anonymously and hope she doesn't implicate us.'

'Rather a caddish thing to do, turning copper's nark, isn't it?'

'Murder is a caddish business, Caldicott. Does Mrs Mottram know about this?'

'Not yet. I've kept ringing her but she's out.'

'She must be informed as soon as possible. It's not very nice, you know, having an imposter eating one's bread and using one's towel and linen.'

'I know – I haven't been able to get hold of her yet.'

Charters nodded towards the phone. 'Try her again. And if you do get through, bear in mind the call has to be paid for. It wouldn't do to impose the burden on our borough treasurer.' Caldicott picked up the phone and dialled. 'Come,' Charters called in answer to a knock on the door and the sergeant brought in a copy of the evening paper.

'I thought you'd like your cricket results as usual, sir.'

Charters thanked him. 'Nice day for the show.'

'It is that, sir.'

'Are you exhibiting this year, Sergeant?'

'Just in the orchid class, sir.'

'Good man. I mustn't play favourites as one of the judges, but I wish you luck.'

The sergeant departed. While Caldicott waited for someone to answer the phone, Charters turned to the cricket scores. 'A hundred and twelve for four. That's better.'

'Not much. See if there's a later score in the Stop Press.'

94

Charters turned to the back page. 'No . . . Hello!'

'Still no reply.' Caldicott hung up and took the paper from Charters. '"Viceroy Mansions murder mystery deepened today when dead girl believed to be colonel's daughter Jenny Beevers . . ."' he read, appalled. 'Why the blazes did he have to give it to the papers? I wonder if Margaret's seen this?'

'Has the so-called Jenny Beevers she's harbouring under her roof? That's more to the point. Who knows what that girl might do in her panic?'

Caldicott looked worried. 'You know, it's odd, there being no answer from Margaret's phone. When she goes out, she usually puts her answering machine on.'

'How do we know she *is* out, Caldicott?'

They stared at each other. 'How quickly can we get to London, Charters?'

Charters looked at his watch. 'Have you ever judged a lily, Caldicott?'

'No more than I've trained bees, Charters.'

'No matter – I'll mark your card. First prize to our worthy Sergeant, second to Miss Elphinstone, third to the school caretaker, Mr Nebbs. If I go through the marrow class like a dose of salts we should just catch the express coach to Town.'

Charters and Caldicott, each wearing an orchid buttonhole presented by a grateful prizewinner, completed their journey to Margaret's house by taxi and hurried up to the front door. Getting no answer to his determined ringing, Caldicott groped along the ledge over the door and found the key.

'Idiotic place to leave one's latch key, if I may say so,' said Charters.

Caldicott unlocked the door. 'Not so idiotic that it hasn't saved us from shinning up the drainpipe.'

The door to the guest bedroom stood open and the room bore clear signs of a hurried departure. Drawers had been left open, tights and a glove dropped and abandoned on the floor and a copy of the evening paper read and discarded.

'Our bird's flown, Charters, that's for sure.'

'I'm afraid there's been a struggle, Caldicott,' said Charters, glancing towards an overturned chair.

Caldicott threw open the living-room door in some trepidation. Here were more signs of a fight. Rugs had been scuffed up, small tables knocked over, lamps overturned. In the middle of this chaos sat Margaret, bound to a chair and gagged. While Charters hurried over to unfasten her gag and begin work on the knots, Caldicott, with a fine sense of priorities, went for the decanter.

'I think we'll omit your usual dash of soda under the circumstances,' he said, pouring out a stiff brandy.

Margaret stretched her arms and winced. 'None of your small ones, Caldicott. And if that little bitch has taken my best pigskin suitcase, I'll kill her.'

CHAPTER 10

Golf was not Charters' and Caldicott's favourite game but their club lay outside the jurisdiction of the Metropolitan Police, none of the few women members called herself Jenny Beevers and there was no cricket at Lord's or the Oval.

'Do you know what I regret, Caldicott?' said Charters as they pushed their golf-trolleys gloomily towards the first green.

'The demise of the old-fashioned caddy.'

'Now how the deuce did you know I was going to say that?'

'You always do, old boy – every time we approach the first tee.' Caldicott waved disparagingly at his own trolley. 'I do see what you mean, though. You know what these things always remind me of?'

'Shopping at Niceprice supermarket.' Charters had also heard it all before.

'Actually, I've transferred my allegiance to More Store, but let it pass,' said Caldicott, nettled. 'Your usual five, Charters?'

'What do you mean, my usual five?'

'I traditionally allow you five strokes over and above your handicap.'

'There's nothing traditional about that concession, Caldicott. You were kind enough to allow me five strokes when I sprained my wrist'.

'Better now, is it?'

'It still plays me up from time to time,' Charters halted his trolley and turned to his companion. 'Caldicott, before we tee off, shall we make a pact?'

'Omit the lake hole? Now just because you always lose your ball, Charters.'

'I'm quite prepared to take my chance at the lake hole, Caldicott, I didn't mean that. I was about to suggest that, as you seem a little on edge today . . .'

'*I'm* not on edge, Charters,' Caldicott barked.

'Caldicott, after the sum of our recent experiences we are *both* on edge. Now I'm about to propose that we put those wretched murders and all associated with them out of our minds for one day, and concentrate on a relaxing round of golf.'

'I'll drink to that, Charters.'

'Good. I'll accept my usual five strokes if that's all right with you.'

They played the first two holes amicably enough. By the time he reached the green on the third hole, Caldicott, at least, was restored to good humour. Amused and patient, he waited to make his own, easy putt while clods of earth and sand from the adjoining bunker showered round him. Charters' ball finally trickled up onto the green followed by its perspiring owner.

Caldicott tapped his ball into the hole. 'Seven. That's only two over, Charters. I'm somewhat on form today. Good God!'

Charters, about to tee off, looked up and stared ahead in amazement. A club-carrying figure had emerged from a distant bunker and was ambling towards them straight down the middle of the fairway. 'What the blue blazes! Fore! Fore, I say!'

'You there! Wrong way!' Caldicott called.

'The secretary shall hear of this, Caldicott. The man's a complete ignoramus.'

'This is what we get when we tout for business memberships, Charters. Commercial travellers whose natural habitat is a seaside putting-green. Fore!'

The errant golfer, deaf to their shouts, disappeared into a dip in the ground. As he came up the other side he proved to be the ubiquitous Venables. Charters and Caldicott leaned on their clubs in exasperation as he strolled towards them.

'Good morning to you,' said Venables, genially.

'What's the meaning of this, Venables?' Charters demanded.

'My anti-clockwise approach? Awfully remiss of me, I know, Caldicott.'

'No, I'm Caldicott,' said Caldicott.

'He knows that perfectly well,' Charters snapped. 'I could have done you a serious injury, man, do you know that?'

'I had my eye on you, never fear. By the way, I'd advise a three iron from this tee.'

'Thank you, Venables, but I've always driven off from the third with my trusty number two wood.'

'Then that's all right. Even if you had hit the ball, you'd have sliced well clear of me.'

'Is this a social visit, Venables? You're interrupting a match, you know.'

'Ah, then you've started. Not just limbering up, then?'

'I should jolly well say not,' said Caldicott. 'I'll have you know I took the first in six as against Charters' nine, and the second in seven as against his fourteen. And that's not counting the five I gave him over and above his . . .'

'Venables doesn't require a blow-by-blow account of our game, Caldicott,' Charters interrupted. 'I haven't played for some while on account of a sprained wrist – I'm just finding form.'

'Then you won't mind starting again?' said Venables.

'Starting again,' said Caldicott, puzzled.

'In a threesome. You see, my partner hasn't turned up and I've no one to play with.'

'But as a threesome, the rules say we must start from the tenth.'

'I've no objection to starting at the tenth,' said Charters, cheering up and at once moving off with Venables.

'Of course you haven't, because then you miss the lake hole,' said Caldicott, trailing after them. 'Besides, I always do better on the first nine.'

'I'm sure you'll run rings round us, Charters,' said Venables.

'No, I'm Charters,' said Charters, cheerfully.

Charters' good humour turned out to be justified. At the tenth hole he drove off after Caldicott and watched the progress of his ball with satisfaction. 'Not far short of the green, I fancy.'

'Well done,' said Venables.

'Shame your landing in the rough like that, Caldicott. I'd advise discouraging your right shoulder from rolling with your drive.' Charters demonstrated what he imagined to be Caldicott's fault. Caldicott fumed and ignored his advice.

'Your friend Jock Beevers, by the way,' said Venables, teeing up last.

'Yes?' said Charters.

'I thought we'd agreed to give the topic a rest,' said Caldicott crossly.

'If Venables has something to say, let him say it.'

'Thank you. You'll be relieved to hear he wasn't a Soviet spy after all. Not that he's been given an entirely clean bill of health. No, it transpires he was a considerable smuggler of Russian icons.'

Charters and Caldicott forgot their differences and stared

at each other in astonishment. 'The old rascal!' said Caldicott as Venables swung his club back.

Venables lowered his club. 'Would you mind, Charters?'

'Sorry, Venables. I'm Caldicott, actually,' said Caldicott as Venables swung his club again. Venables glared at him.

'Do let's not chitter-chatter on the green, Caldicott,' said Charters. 'Sorry, Venables.'

Venables played off at last. 'More luck than judgement there, I'm afraid,' he said, pleased with his shot. 'Yes, one gathers he was in league with a certain Colonel Pokrovski in Moscow, if that name means anything to you.'

'It does as a matter of fact,' said Caldicott as they made their way down the fairway. 'Jock often used to yarn about him.'

'His Russian opposite number when he was with the Control Commission in Berlin after the war? Best days of his life, he used to say,' said Charters.

'They probably were. That must have been when they hatched this highly profitable scheme out,' said Venables. 'One doesn't know what Pokrovski made out of it but I hear your friend Beevers finished up with not far off a cool million.'

Caldicott whistled. 'But not a spy,' said Charters.

'Not a spy.'

'That's very good news, Venables,' said Charters. 'Very good news indeed. I always knew in my bones that Jock Beevers was incapable of treachery.'

'Yet you don't seem surprised that he was capable of icon-running.'

'Oh, indeed not. He always had a weakness for that type of exploit, didn't he, Charters?' said Caldicott.

'A distinct Boy's Own Paper streak, I'd say.'

Venables, about to stroke his ball to the green, considered that last remark. 'I was never a big reader of the Boy's Own Paper –' he broke off to hit the ball, 'Left, you brute, left! – but I don't think their heroes usually made a practice of defrauding Customs and Excise while in the service of HMG, what?'

'Quite,' Charters grunted, shamefaced.

Charters and Caldicott digested this new information about Jock while they completed the tenth hole and teed off at the eleventh. As the golfers followed their balls, Caldicott said,

'So that accounts for his forged passport, false-bottomed Bible and all the rest of it.'

'Yes, I expect it does,' said Venables.

'You haven't come across Jock Beevers' daughter Jenny during your inquiries, have you Venables?'

'Inquiries, my dear fellow? What inquiries?'

'You know very well, Venables!' said Charters, firmly. 'The inquiries that led you to the conclusion that Jock was not a spy but a smuggler.'

'Oh, that. Shall we say that it came to my notice.'

Venables putted to within a couple of inches of the eleventh hole and held up the pin for Caldicott. 'If one *is* allowed what you term an "inquiry", however, I suppose you chaps know nothing about your friend's extramural activities over the years – that goes without saying?'

Charters, who had reverted to his usual form, emerged from a bunker in the wake of a shower of sand. 'Then why say it?'

'What was that curious phrase in that note to you both from Beevers? "Mix Well and Serve", was it?'

'How did you know about that?' Charters demanded.

'Oh, it came . . .'

'To your notice, yes,' Charters finished. 'Look here, Venables, let me ask you a question. Just who the devil are you?'

Venables straightened his tie and said reproachfully, 'You know me, Caldicott. We belong to the same Club.'

'I'm aware of that and my name's Charters.'

'Well, then! Venables – chairman of the Wine Committee.' And with that he sunk his ball smoothly.

'M15, I'd say, or M16 – whatever cloak and dagger name they give themselves these days,' said Caldicott, stirring his tea thoughtfully. He and Charters had omitted their customary visit to the nineteenth hole and had hurried straight to Margaret Mottram's to give her the latest news.

'I don't think so, Caldicott,' said Charters. 'Otherwise he'd have lost interest once it was established that Jock Beevers was never involved in spying activities. No, he's still got the bit between his teeth. Police Special Branch, that's my guess.'

'Is that a promotion or demotion from Official Mourner at funerals?' asked Margaret, amused.

'Official Mourner, my Aunt Fanny,' Charters snorted. 'Excuse me, Mrs Mottram.'

101

'If he's heard of your Mix Well and Serve conundrum, he can only have got that from your chum Inspector Snow, can't he? So perhaps he *is* some kind of policeman.'

'Could be,' said Caldicott. 'Although he didn't rise to the bait when I mentioned Jenny Beevers, did he, Charters?'

'Venables isn't given to rising to bait, Caldicott. There's much of the basking shark in that man's make-up. I know one thing. If we allow him to ply his seedy trade on the golf course, they'll be letting in double-glazing touts next. I shall write to the secretary.'

'In the strongest terms,' said Caldicott. 'And now I suggest, Margaret, that we mark our formal detachment from all these recent unpleasantnesses with a modest celebration.'

'Oh, goody – are you going to get me drunk?'

'No, we are not going to get you drunk, my girl – we are taking you to the pictures.'

'We thought the local Classic,' said Charters. 'It *is* in English.'

'Oh, yippee,' said Margret drily.

'Come on, Mottram, put your bonnet on,' said Caldicott. 'Or would you rather spend the next couple of hours sipping cold tea and endlessly chewing over a case that no longer concerns us?'

'I wouldn't mind if it was cold gin, but you're right. Unless that fake Jenny Beevers turns up on my doorstep to return my best pigskin suitcase I never want to hear of that little cuckoo in the nest again. I'll just go and powder my . . .'

As if on cue, the doorbell rang. The three of them jumped, and stared at each other in consternation. 'Milkman wanting his money,' said Margaret, relaxing, and going to answer the door.

Charters consulted the evening paper. 'You realise we've seen this film before?'

'Oh yes, when it first came out. 1962, wasn't it?'

'Even earlier than that. It was the year School thrashed Harrow.'

'No, that was 1959. It was the year Winchester thrashed School 1962.'

The pair squabbled over the date, using their usual cricketing terms of reference, while Margaret chatted on the doorstep. She seemed to be taking a surprisingly long time to pay for a few bottles of milk.

'We'll soon settle the matter,' said Charters. 'If Mrs

Mottram would oblige us by hurrying herself. 'They always print the date on the credit titles.'

'Yes, Charters, but only in roman numerals. Can't make head nor tail of them.'

'Ah, now there's a particular reason for that practice, Caldicott,' said Charters knowledgeably. 'You see, when the film is reissued as this one is now, it may not be in the distributors' interests to let their audiences know just how ancient the . . .' He broke off, thunderstruck, as Margaret came back into the room accompanied by Inspector Snow.

'Well, I'll be blowed,' Caldicott exploded. 'Did Grimes tell you you'd probably find us here? I'll skin that little weasel alive!'

'There's such a thing as unwarranted intrusion, Inspector,' said Charters. 'First you hound us in our Club, now you gatecrash this lady's private tea party. Mrs Mottram, you don't have to receive him in your drawing-room, you know. He can just as well conduct this interview in the kitchen.'

'Wouldn't be the first time,' said Snow. 'Don't worry, Mrs Mottram, it won't take a minute.'

'Yes, but we don't happen to have a minute at our disposal,' Caldicott objected. 'We're just off to the pictures.'

'Nobody's stopping you, Mr Caldicott.'

'Good,' said Caldicott. Then the words sunk in. 'Eh?'

'It's Mrs Mottram I've come to see. Just an informal word, Mrs Mottram.'

'With me? Why?' asked Margaret nervously.

'Mrs Mottram knows nothing whatever about this business, Inspector,' said Caldicott.

'Except what you've told her, eh?'

'We're old friends. We have discussed the case, naturally.'

'Including the fact that the dead girl originally believed to be Jenny Beevers turned out to be Helen Appleyard from Hong Kong?'

'That much was in the papers,' said Margaret, recovering her composure.

'Married to Josh Darrell's chauffeur, likewise found dead on the one weekend all three of you happened to be staying at Mr Darrell's place in the country.'

'That's right.'

'Why?'

'Why was he killed? I don't know, Inspector, I'm not a detective.'

'No, I don't mean why was he killed. I mean, why were you there?'

'Like the other twenty or thirty guests, I was invited. I do a lot of business with Mr Darrell.'

'Yes, but these two don't. They didn't even know him.' Snow began absent-mindedly to pile the used tea things onto the tray.

'If you really want to know, Josh Darrell is an incurable lecher. I couldn't turn down his invitation because I needed his business. But I asked Mr Caldicott and Mr Charters along as my – well – minders, I suppose.' Charters and Caldicott straightened their shoulders and puffed out their chests in a doomed attempt to look like minders.

'Mm. No question of the three of you going to Mr Darrell's to see what you could find out?'

'About what, Inspector?' Charters asked.

'About why the murdered wife of his chauffeur was being passed off as the daughter of your old friend Colonel Beevers.'

'But until you told us otherwise we didn't know she *wasn't* Jenny Beevers,' Caldicott lied.

'Didn't you, Mr Caldicott? No, I'll tell you why I ask. You see, it transpires that when she slipped Grimes £100 to let her into your flat . . .'

'A measly £100! He told me £250.'

'Yes, well he would tell you that – it puts him in a better light. But you see she never claimed to be Jenny Beevers at all. Whereas a different young lady who called at Viceroy Mansions asking for you *did* claim to be Jenny Beevers.'

'Really?' said Caldicott faintly.

'Really. As you know.'

'*How* do I know?'

'Grimes told you. As he told me – eventually. And you advised him to keep his trap shut.'

Caldicott made a recovery. 'I advised Grimes to keep his trap shut because he changes his story from one minute to the next. He'll say anything to get himself off the hook.'

'A notoriously unreliable witness, friend Grimes, Inspector,' said Charters.

'Yes, there's a lot of it about, Mr Charters. Now, I won't keep you, Mrs Mottram. I'm just wondering about this girl you've had staying with you.'

Margaret, shaken, seized on the fact that Snow was holding

the teapot. 'Shall I get you a clean cup, Inspector?' she asked in an unnaturally high voice.

'Not for me, thanks.'

'Oh, then thank you for clearing up my tea things.'

'I do it automatically. Drives my wife barmy, I don't know why. You know which girl I'm talking about, Mrs Mottram? Usually in a grey suit. Until Friday when she left with a pigskin suitcase.'

Margaret winced at the mention of her case but said easily, 'There are girls coming and going all the time, Inspector. I run a temps bureau – I prefer to interview new recruits here where it's quiet rather than in my office with the phones ringing like Bow Bells.'

'And do they all have pigskin suitcases?'

'If it was Friday, that's not so very unusual. The kind of girls I employ usually go away for the weekends.'

'And they usually wear grey suits?'

'Practically their uniform this season. Sloane Rangers, you know – they're like peas in a pod.'

'And if it came to it, I suppose you could produce the very girl who was seen leaving here with a suitcase at three-fifteen on Friday?'

'I don't have my diary here but I expect I could – if it came to it. But you're chasing a red herring, Inspector.'

'I am that, Mrs Mottram,' said Snow, preparing to take his leave. 'And when I catch it I shall have it kippered for breakfast.'

CHAPTER 11

'Now you guarantee this hasn't got an eagle-eyed detective in it?' said Margaret, settling herself into her seat in the sparsely filled cinema.

'Firm promise,' said Caldicott. 'Boggle-eyed butler, yes, eagle-eyed detective, no.'

'He's on to us, you know.'

'Evidently, as Grimes appears to have blown the gaff. But he isn't on to the murderer. And so long as we keep from under Inspector Snow's feet, that will remain his main preoccupation. Ah, good show, Charters.'

Charters pushed his way along the row carrying ice-cream tubs. 'One chocolate chip, one raspberry ripple,' he said, handing them out.

'How very kind,' said Margaret, fumbling in her handbag.

'No, no, no.'

'Thank you.'

'We'll settle up later.'

Margaret allowed her grateful expression to fade and turned back to Caldicott. 'I know you're the eternal optimist but you can't seriously imagine the inspector isn't going to bother us again?'

'I'm quite sure he is. All the more reason why *we* shouldn't bother *him*. Keep out of his hair and don't concern ourselves with other people's murders.' Caldicott stopped abruptly, staring into his ice-cream tub as if it contained worms. 'This is raspberry ripple!'

'I couldn't agree with you more,' said Charters. 'On both points. A. I've said all along we should leave it to the police and B. I just said it was raspberry ripple.'

'I must say I haven't quite the appetite I had,' said Margaret.

Caldicott turned to her eagerly. 'You don't want your chocolate chip? Why not swop it for my raspberry ripple?'

'My appetite for playing Sherlock Holmes, fool! But I do wish we'd cracked that Mix Well and Serve conundrum.'

'I shall one day, given peace of mind to concentrate,' said Charters. 'I'm convinced Jock Beevers wanted to tell us something or lead us somewhere. Is there anything wrong with that raspberry ripple, old chap?'

Caldicott glared at him. 'I'm sure it's an excellent raspberry ripple, old chap, but I asked for a strawberry ripple.'

'You asked for a raspberry ripple.'

'I hate raspberries. I've always hated raspberries, as you know.' The lights dimmed and the music began but Charters ignored these signs that the film was about to start. 'I *do* know. That's why I was quite surprised when you asked for a raspberry ripple.'

'Strawberry ripple.'

'Raspberry ripple.'

A voice from a couple of rows away urged them to shut up. 'You must have misheard, old boy,' said Caldicott, ignoring this interruption.

'My hearing's perfect! You asked for a raspberry ripple!'

Other people began to glare and mutter. 'The natives are getting restless,' said Margaret. The pair piped down. Charters fumed and scooped up his ice-cream, Caldicott sulkily dabbed at his ripple with the spoon and Margaret smiled to herself.

The credit titles for the old black and white movie appeared on the screen. When the copyright date in roman numerals came up Charters remembered another grievance. 'That's something else I'm not mistaken about, Caldicott. This film was made in 1959.'

'How do you claim to know that?'

'It was there in black and white, man. "Copyright 1959."'

A young couple further along their row invited them to keep their voices down. '*You* say it was 1959, old man. To me it was just MX something or other – like myxomatosis,' said Caldicott.

The young man hissed even more angrily at them. Charters gave him an apologetic grimace, lowered his voice slightly and went on, 'No, no no. M – that's a thousand. CM – nine hundred. L – fifty. Then IX – *Good God*! I've licked it, Caldicott!' The entire audience turned to glare at him.

'Your raspberry ripple?' said Caldicott acidly. 'I told you it was foul.'

'M-I-X, Caldicott! Mix Well and Serve! Come along! You too, Mrs Mottram.' He stood up and pushed his way excitedly along the row, followed by a bewildered Margaret and Caldicott. Caldicott murmured 'Excuse me,' to the furious couple as he climbed over them, then a kind thought struck him.

He turned back and gave the young woman his raspberry ripple.

The urgency and excitement of the situation seemed to warrant a taxi to Viceroy Mansions. They paid it off, hurried into the block and across the lobby. About to enter the lift, Caldicott glanced back thoughtfully to Grimes's desk, his recent talk with Snow coming back to him. 'You two go up. I shan't be a tick,' he said, handing Charters his keys. He went back and peered over the counter, then banged the bell for attention. Grimes, who had been crouching out of sight since he'd seen the taxi unexpectedly unload Caldicott and his friends, rose obsequiously.

'Oh, it's you, Mr Caldicott. Only I was just straightening out my shelves style of thing.'

'I thought you couldn't bend, Grimes. On account of the slipped disc that compels you to take three afternoons a week off at your osteopath's.'

'Been told to exercise it, sir. Only it seizes up otherwise. See, your spinal cord, Mr Caldicott, it's like kind of a set of interlocking . . .'

'Never mind my spinal cord, Grimes. You've been blabbing to Inspector Snow, haven't you?'

'Got interviewed again, was I not! He's a crafty devil, though, isn't he, Mr Caldicott? I mean, the way he wriggles things out of you – you don't know what you've said till you've said it style of thing. He's clever, he is!'

'I hope at least you've now told the sordid truth about why you let the late Helen Appleyard into my flat.'

'Oh, I have, sir.'

'That it was nothing to do with incriminating letters and all to do with a dirty great fistful of fivers.'

'I was tempted and I fell, I freely admit it.'

'What did you do with that money, Grimes?'

'Put it to a good use, sir. That's why I wanted it, why I was tempted. It's gone to pay for a week in Lourdes.'

Caldicott could hardly believe his ears. 'Lourdes?'

'Like a pilgrimage.'

'For a slipped disc?'

'Worth a try, Mr Caldicott. Faith can move mountains, so they say. So you never know, sir – that grubby £250 might do some good in the world after all.'

They had reached the nub of the matter. 'Yes, but it *wasn't*

£250, was it Grimes? You let that woman into my flat for a piddling £100!'

'Is that what the inspector told you, sir?'

'That's what the inspector told me, Grimes. So as your 250 quid trip to Lourdes turns out to be total fiction, I'll ask you again. What did you do with the money?'

Grimes thought fast. 'Put it down as a deposit, sir. On a pilgrimage to Lourdes.'

'Then it's in a good cause after all,' said Caldicott, heavily sarcastic.

'Trouble is, though, if I don't come up with the other hundred and fifty before the end of the . . .'

'Grimes!'

'Yes, sir.'

'Are you about to ask me for £150?'

'Only as a loan style of thing, Mr Caldicott. I mean to say, there's a lot has to be done round Viceroy Mansions, and I can't give complete satisfaction if I'm a martyr to a slipped disc, now can I?'

'No, indeed, Grimes. What *would* give complete satisfaction is if you were a martyr to rigor mortis!' Caldicott stormed off to the lift, leaving Grimes looking deeply wounded.

Caldicott found Charters already examining the Mix Well and Serve letter through a magnifying glass while Margaret was fixing herself a drink. 'Do you know what that cheeky blighter Grimes just had the nerve to . . .' Caldicott burst out as soon as he was inside the flat.

'Never mind that, Caldicott,' said Charters. 'Come over here. I've taken the liberty of unearthing your magnifying glass.'

'And I've taken the liberty of unearthing your gin,' said Margaret.

'Now then, look at that.'

'Jock's letter? I know it by heart, old boy,' said Caldicott.

'But do you? Look at it again.' Caldicott did as he was told. 'Concentrate on the cryptic message, Mix Well and Serve. Now we've established what Mix indicates.'

Caldicott looked up, surprised. 'Have we? When?'

'In the cinema, Caldicott! Why do you suppose we came rushing out?'

Caldicott still looked baffled. 'Think of a number,' said Margaret helpfully.

'A number? Ah, myxomatosis. Those roman numerals.'

'Exactly,' said Charters. 'M-I-X. One thousand and nine.'

'I say, that's clever. One thousand and nine! That's damned ingenious,' said Caldicott, profoundly impressed by this display of learning. 'One thousand and nine what?'

'That's what we're trying to work out, ducky,' said Margaret. 'We've cracked the first word, now what about the second?'

Caldicott resumed his study of Jock's letter. '"Well". Now, what's that in roman numerals?'

'It isn't anything in Roman numerals, Caldicott, but it isn't "Well" either. See?' Charters stabbed his finger at the word.

Caldicott peered more closely at it through the glass. 'I'm with you, Charters. There's a sort of curly bit at the end of the word.'

'What we call an S,' said Margaret.

'Wells. One thousand and nine wells. Which wells? Oil wells?'

'Or perhaps Wells the place. As in Bath and. He didn't come from that part of the world, did he?' Margaret asked.

Charters shook his head. 'No, no, he was a Kentishman.'

'Man of Kent, actually,' said Caldicott. 'Little place called Yabble, after the river of that name.'

'Yes, he meant to retire there. Be that as it may – Wells. What other kind of wells are there.'

'Water wells,' Margaret offered.

Caldicott snapped his fingers. 'H.G.'

'Smart thinking, Caldicott,' said Charters.

'His fellow Man of Kent!'

'Or Kentishman. H. G. Wells,' said Charters, turning excitedly to Margaret. 'Jock's favourite author. *The Time Machine*, *War of the Worlds*, *Tono-Bungay* – never tired of reading them. H. G. Wells, that *must* be it. Some reference, an allusion, something he'd expect us both to pick up on.'

'A page number, perhaps,' said Margaret.

'Page 1009? It'd have to be a pretty thick volume.'

'He wrote some pretty thick volumes. *The History of the World*, to name but one.'

'No, I'm not familiar with the history of the world.'

'Oh, it's riveting. Lots of kings and queens.'

While Margaret teased Charters, Caldicott had been running his eyes along his bookshelves. Finally, he took out a thick, cloth-bound volume stamped with a crest and blew dust off it. 'Here we are. House prize for the best-kept study

– The Collected Comic Novels of H. G. Wells. I bagged it in my last year – the only prize I ever did get.'

'And Jock Beevers the year before! Give that here, Caldicott.'

'I'm quite capable of looking up page 1009, Charters,' said Caldicott, holding the volume out of Charters' reach while he leafed through the pages. 'Kipps – Mr Polly – Oh.'

Margaret looked over his shoulder. '"Bealby"?'

'What?' asked Charters.

'One of the less memorable H. G. Wells comic tales. One thousand and nine is the title page. "Bealby". That's all it says.

'Yabble,' said Charters.

'No, Bealby.'

'Yabble,' said Margaret. 'Oh, I see. It's an anagram. But where have I heard that name before?'

'I mentioned it not a moment ago,' said Caldicott.

'Jock's home village. Where he meant to retire,' said Charters.

'The foxy blighter!' Caldicott exclaimed, the penny dropping. 'He must be telling us to go there.'

'Of course he is! Mix Well and Serve – proceed to Yabble.'

'. . . and Serve?' Margaret wondered.

A foursome was in progress on the Yabble village tennis courts. The vicar, Adam Lamb, a dyspeptic-looking man in late middle-age, just failed to reach a high lob which soared over his head and bounced over the perimeter fence. 'Would you mind?' he called to a passer-by walking past the courts.

Obligingly, she picked up the ball as it trickled towards her and tossed it back. A map tucked into her pocket marked her out as a stranger to the village. It was the young woman who had been calling herself Jenny Beevers.

'Thanks awfully,' said Lamb, scooping up the ball. 'I say, that ramblers' map's not very good. Are you heading anywhere in particular?' 'Jenny' smiled and shook her head. 'The point I'm making is that there are a good many trespassing opportunities in these parts. I'd advise you to get our little guidebook from the Post Office Stores. That'll keep you on the straight and narrow.'

'Jenny' thanked him and walked on briskly. Lamb, having made clear his disapproval of *ad hoc* rambling, returned to his game.

Charters and Caldicott, both armed with the sort of sticks town-dwellers regard as indispensable when travelling beyond the suburbs, were loitering outside the Post Office Stores waiting for Margaret. Charters who had been studying a timetable fixed to the wall, said, 'I say, Caldicott! I believe I've found what we're looking for.'

Caldicott stopped pushing small pebbles about. 'Already?'

'Almost definitely. See here.' He pointed to the timetable. 'If I take this four-twelve cross-country bus to Sevenoaks, there's a connecting bus through to Reigate that should drop me practically at my door. It'll save my returning to Town and you and Mrs Mottram having to make a tiresome detour to Victoria coach station.'

Caldicott glared at him. 'I'm glad we've got your travel arrangements sorted out, Charters. Now, perhaps if you're not too pressed for time we can start our inquiries.'

'No need to take that tone, old chap. We do have a clear five hours to find out why we're here. With a break for lunch, of course.'

'What would you say to the village pub?'

'We'll study the menu, certainly. Probably our only option.'

'I meant in which to begin our inquiries! Unless Margaret has culled any better ideas from her book of words,' Caldicott added as Margaret came out of the stores with the village guidebook in her hand.

Margaret shook her head. 'Not much of riveting interest here, unless you're keen on farmhouse cream teas.'

'Alas, I have to catch the four-twelve to Sevenoaks,' said Charters.

'None of the Beevers family extant, apparently, but Mrs Post Office Stores says there are Beeverses without number in the parish churchyard, so I suggest we start with the vicar.'

'Ah. Not the village pub?' Caldicott asked.

'Or the village pub,' Margaret agreed readily. 'But don't let me drink more than two real gins or I shan't be fit to drive back.' She broke off, staring incredulously across the village green.

'What is it, Margaret?' Caldicott asked.

'You mean "Who is it?" That girl coming towards us.'

Charters and Caldicott peered at an approaching figure. 'No, I can't make her out,' said Charters.

'It isn't Jenny Beevers, surely?' Caldicott asked.

'No it isn't, but it's the girl who's been passing herself off as Jenny Beevers. And before you two start putting her through the third degree, I want to know what she's done with my best pigskin suitcase.'

As they watched, the girl faltered, turned and hurried away. 'Blast,' said Caldicott. 'She's seen us. She's turning back, Charters.'

'Yes, I'm not totally blind, Caldicott. What the devil is she doing here?'

'The same as we're doing here,' said Margaret, as 'Jenny' hopped over a stile on the other side of the green. 'When we find out what that is.'

'Little point in giving chase, I suppose?' said Caldicott.

Charters grunted. 'You can rule me out, I'm afraid. My running and jumping days are over.'

'And it's going back a bit since *I* won the girls' hundred-yards sprint, but I'm going after her,' said Margaret determinedly. 'I'll find you around the village.'

'Margaret! Be careful!' Caldicott called.

'Wasn't I always?' she shouted back with a cheeky grin.

Caldicott gazed wistfully after her across the village green. Charters gave him an affectionate glance and said gruffly, 'A penny for them, old chap.'

'Oh, I was just wishing . . .'

'Yes?'

'That we could have seen a spot of village cricket on this splendid green.'

Charters and Caldicott decided to postpone their researches in the village pub until Margaret's return and to investigate instead the churchyard. The Reverend Adam Lamb, passing the church a short while later on his way from tennis to lunch at the vicarage, was puzzled to hear organ music coming from inside. He entered, and discovered Charters, playing "Abide With Me" with more enthusiasm than skill, watched admiringly by Caldicott who was doing the vocal accompaniment in a tuneless drone.

'I do beg your pardon, Vicar,' said Charters, stopping his playing abruptly and in some confusion as he caught sight of Lamb. 'I don't know what you'll think of this unwarranted intrusion . . .'

'He never could resist a church organ. You see, they won't let him play in his own parish,' said Caldicott.

'Really! It's not that they won't let me – they have a

competent enough organist already! I should have asked your permission, Vicar, but I wouldn't like you to think I don't know how to handle the instrument. It will have come to no grief under my hands, I assure you.'

'He did organ studies at school,' Caldicott confided.

Lamb nodded. 'I know. To get out of rugger.'

'Yes, well, you see, I'd always been a soccer man at my prep . . .' Charters broke off and stared at the omniscient clergyman.

'I've been expecting you. My name's Lamb – appropriately enough, I suppose, considering my trade. Follow me.' He led the way up into the belfry. 'I was beginning to wonder when you'd get here.'

'Thanks to Jock's fondness for confounded conundrums, it was only by a fluke that we did,' said Caldicott.

'I wouldn't say that, Caldicott. Applied logic, that's what got us here.'

'A pity you didn't apply it earlier,' said Lamb coldly. 'I'd like to get this business off my hands.'

'Lamb. That name rings a bell,' said Caldicott.

'More than this rope ever will,' said Lamb, untying a bell rope that had been separated from the others and wound round a rail. 'That's Old Tom, pensioned off with a crack a yard long.'

'Weren't you with Jock in postwar Berlin?'

'I was his padre. He got me my living here – so all this tomfoolery is by way of repaying him the favour.' Lamb gave the rope a deft tug and an old deed box came tumbling down from the rafters. Lamb unlocked it and took out an official-looking document which he passed to Caldicott. 'This was his idea, not mine. Left to myself, I should have kept this in the crypt safe.'

'As I've always said, a strong Boy's Own Paper influence,' said Charters.

'His last will and testament,' said Caldicott.

'He didn't like lawyers – probably because he equated them with the law – and he'd got the idea into his head that if he shipped the will directly to you with his other things it would have gone missing,' Lamb explained.

'There's certainly been no shortage of suspicious characters trying to get their fists on Jock's effects,' said Caldicott.

'I happened to be out in Hong Kong for the Christian

Missions convention earlier this year, so he placed it in my hands with endless instructions and admonitions.'

'I can imagine,' said Charters, amused.

'Together with this letter addressed to you both.'

Charters took it and glanced through it. Caldicott, meanwhile, was scanning the will. 'Appoint Reverend Adam Lamb sole executor – cash sum to steeple fund – books to school library – billiard table to Hong Kong Travellers Club – bequests to charity,' he muttered. 'I say, Charters! He's left practically everything to us!'

'How embarrassing.'

'"I give and bequeath to my oldest friends Hugo Lovelace Charters . . ." Charters winced, 'and Giles Caldicott . . .'

'Giles *Evelyn* Caldicott,' said Charters, spitefully.

' ". . . my remaining capital and investments." '

Charters turned to Lamb. 'Amounting to what?'

'The last time I looked in the City pages, something over two million pounds.'

Caldicott whistled. 'I expected nothing more than his signed Kent county cricket bat,' said Charters, stunned. 'We can't possibly accept this bequest, of course.'

'Hold on, Charters, there's more,' said Caldicott. ' "Said investments to be realised at their discretion to finance any expedition on which they may embark, and the proceeds from such expedition to be distributed as they think fit." What expedition?'

'How should I know?' said Charters.

'Doesn't it say in that letter?'

'No no, it's purely personal. Cricket reminiscences and so on.'

'Now there's a thought. Perhaps Jock means us to do what we've always talked about and follow the England Test team around Australia and New Zealand.'

'With over two million pounds? Don't be absurd, old fellow – surely the exchange rate's not as bad as all that. Vicar, I know you're anxious to wash your hands of us, but until we've some idea what it is that Jock desires us to do –'

'If you're asking me to keep the will stuffed up my belfry, the answer is no,' said Lamb firmly. 'I want shot of it.'

'You *are* his executor.'

'But I've no wish to be his accessory.' Lamb relented. 'I shall be in Town tomorrow. If you like, if you're nervous of taking possession of all this stuff, I'll deposit it with your bank.'

'That should do admirably.'

'Good idea,' said Caldicott, without thinking. 'Why?' he added, when he had.

'Why? It's obvious why,' said Charters. 'In case there are any more attempts to steal it.'

'Oh, I see,' said Caldicott, but still he didn't. 'Why should anyone wish to steal it?'

'Why should anyone wish to steal it? This is a very valuable document.'

'Only to us, old man. Nobody else can do anything with it.'

'Yes, well,' Charters began, suddenly as baffled as Caldicott.

'Except dispose of it,' said Lamb.

'There you see!' said Charters triumphantly to Caldicott. Still puzzled, he frowned. 'Why should anyone – oh, I see. A previous will.'

'A copy of it. The original vanished before he could destroy it.' Lamb handed the copy to Caldicott who skimmed through it.

'Aha! Under this you *would* have got the signed cricket bat, Charters.'

'That's more like it.'

'And I his collection of scorecards and other memorabilia.'

'You'd have appreciated that.'

'And the bulk of his estate, had this will not been revoked, would have been divided between – guess who?'

'Do get on with it, Caldicott.'

' "My daughter Jennifer Beevers and my secretary and friend Helen Appleyard." '

116

CHAPTER 12

'What happened between Jock and his daughter, do you know?' Caldicott asked Lamb as they climbed down from the belfry.

'He never mentioned her. From the odd word dropped in the Hong Kong Travellers Club I gather she got into a bad lot – drugs and all that. Playing the heavy father, he settled an allowance on her on condition that she cleared out of Hong Kong and never came back. She went to America, as you probably know, and then vanished.'

'It must have come as a nasty shock to you when you thought she'd been found dead in my flat,' said Caldicott.

'Not entirely. He anticipated someone coming after the will, though he didn't spell out who – hence the elaborate precautions. So I wasn't altogether surprised at the bad penny turning up again – as I thought – no.'

'But then the body in the case proved to be a different bad penny. Did you meet Helen Appleyard at all?'

'Briefly. A great influence on Jenny, so I was told. A great influence on Jock, come to that – you know the idiot nearly married her? Would have done, too, if he hadn't found her in bed with his driver.'

'Yet Jock continued to employ her as his secretary,' said Charters. 'I find that baffling.'

'Gossip, old boy,' said Caldicott. 'You know what it's like in these far-flung English communities. If he'd thrown her out bag and baggage, it'd have been like something out of Somerset Maugham. Isn't that so, padre?'

'And, of course, she knew a great deal about Jenny, and probably about his own affairs, that he wasn't keen to have broadcast. I wonder how she came by Jenny's identity?'

'Planted on her. By an imposter posing as Jenny,' said Caldicott brusquely, the knowledge that they'd been duped still rankling. 'Who, as a matter of interest, is even now roaming this village.'

'Or so we believe – our eyesight isn't what it was.' Caldicott shook his head slightly, disowning this remark. 'If it is her, then of course she, too, is after the will.'

'She among others,' said Caldicott. They walked down the aisle – passing, without a glance, a figure kneeling in one of the pews, apparently in prayer. It was Cecil St Clair.

'Well, Charters, can you fit an expedition into your crowded engagement programme?' Caldicott asked as they came out into the porch.

'It depends entirely on where he intends us to go. It could be Timbuktu or the moon for all I know.'

'No hints to you, padre?'

Lamb shook his head. 'I didn't encourage him to tell me. It's probably something illegal and I'm not of the branch that takes confessions.'

'You didn't like Jock very much did you?' Charters asked.

'Let's say I didn't approve of his activities, his wheeler-dealering.'

Charters dismissed this tolerantly. 'Small beer.'

'Two million pounds?'

'Oh that! Icon smuggling,' said Caldicott laconically.

'Russian icons?'

'In cahoots with that fellow who was his Soviet opposite number in your Berlin days,' said Charters.

'Colonel Pokrovski. As big a rogue as Jock himself. I'm sure he must have told you about the ex-U-boat commander they interrogated over some currency racket or other.'

'Often,' said Caldicott. 'The chap who was supposed to have scuttled a submarine-load of gold bullion. And spilled the beans as to its whereabouts in exchange for their leaving the cell door open.'

Charters chuckled. 'Romantic poppycock, saving Jock's soul. If all the German U-boats containing gold bullion were laid end to end – Caldicott! Do you remember what that fellow St Clair said to us at Thamesview just as we were leaving?'

'Yes I do,' said Caldicott slowly, the same thought dawning on him. ' "We're all chasing the same crock of gold – but this isn't the rainbow." '

'This expedition, Caldicott. You don't suppose he means us to find that gold?'

'Possible, knowing Jock.'

'Probable, I'd say,' said Lamb with disapproval.

'But where are we supposed to look?' Caldicott asked.

'There could be a map or a chart or something of the sort,' said Charters. 'Probably in that confounded trunk.'

'What about the place he bought for his retirement, padre?' Caldicott asked. 'Is there any of his stuff there?'

'The Old Oast-house? Oh yes, it's just as his sister left it when she died last year. Chock-a-block with wartime souvenirs and relics – you'd probably find enough to get him cashiered retrospectively. Key at the Post Office Stores – say I sent you. I shall want your bank details – drop back to the vicarage for a sherry.'

'Will do. Though I think, Charters, we ought to find Margaret first. I'm getting rather worried.'

'Never fear, Caldicott. Mrs Mottram will find *us* – at the first chink of the vicar's decanter.'

Charters and Caldicott collected the key from the village shop but it turned out to be unnecessary. The Old Oast-house was unlocked. 'That's of no particular significance,' said Charters, a rural resident himself. 'Country folk are very lax in these matters.'

In spite of this reassurance, Caldicott pushed open the front door very slowly. His caution was justified. Someone had been there before them and ransacked the place. Papers were scattered everywhere, drawers had been pulled out and emptied, regimental paraphernalia and German souvenirs examined and discarded, furniture overturned and pictures torn from the walls.

'*Very* lax, said Caldicott.

'Yes, well we know who's been here, do we not?'

'Fortunately we also know that she hasn't found what she's looking for,' said Caldicott, wandering round straightening ornaments and picking up papers from the floor. 'Though what use Jock's will would be to her, now that we know she isn't the real Jenny Beevers, I can't readily fathom.'

'But *do* we know it, Caldicott?'

'We've proved it, old boy. Why do you think she fled? Because the real Jenny Beevers must have recognised her own father's ex-mistress-cum-secretary.'

'Who's to say she *didn't* recognise her – and murder her?'

Caldicott turned this possibility over in his mind. 'All right – then why should she go through the charade of swopping places with her, when simply by coming forward as herself, she could have inherited a fortune?'

'Ah, but you see she *doesn't* stand to inherit a fortune, unless the later will is destroyed. I'll tell you why she changed places with Helen Appleyard, Caldicott. She hoped to keep the dead girl's husband, Gregory, in the dark long enough for her to unearth the will unmolested. Easy enough then to resuscitate herself and claim the inheritance.'

'Not so easy if she really did murder Helen Appleyard.'

'Then perhaps she didn't.'

'But you just said she did.'

'Only on the assumption that she is, after all, the real Jenny Beevers.'

'But according to you, old chap, she *is* the real Jenny Beevers.'

Charters glowered. 'I said she could be. If you've any more plausible theory, Caldicott, I should be delighted to hear it.'

'I've no theory, Charters.'

'Very well then.'

'I'm as foxed as you are.'

'I'm not foxed, Caldicott. I've just produced as rational an explanation of this entire case as you're likely to hear. If it seems to you flawed, I apologise.'

Such furniture as remained upright was covered in dustsheets. Huffily Charters plumped himself down in a swathed armchair. Dust swirled upwards and settled gently over him. Caldicott sat in another chair and maintained a brief, sulky silence.

'I say, Charters,' said Caldicott, who had been brooding.

'What is it, Caldicott?'

'Jock's letter. You might let me see it.' Charters handed it over silently and Caldicott glanced through it. 'This is an odd sort of rigmarole, isn't it?'

'I don't think so,' said Charters stiffly.

'But it is odd, Charters. All this stuff about school cricket.'

'Seems perfectly straightforward to me.'

'But what he says about half last year's averages being wrong – he can't be serious.'

'Never more so,' said Charters, relenting slightly. 'The record as set forth in Wisden doesn't reconcile with the analysis in the school year-book. He wishes us to correct the error. What's so extraordinary about that?'

'Wisden wrong? It's unheard of!' said Caldicott, scandalised.

'It's not Wisden that's wrong, Caldicott, it's the school year-book.'

'Oh, I see.'

'They'll have to send out gummed errata slips.'

'It *is* rather a mish-mash, isn't it? "For R. H. L. Johnson as captain, read N. Orton, whose innings figure should be the same as Larkin's – Boyd-Mason's average should be reversed with that of T. P. Cowling" . . . wonder if he's the grandson of Four-eyes Cowling?'

'Highly unlikely – unless there's a cricketing strain on the boy's grandmother's side.'

' "A. N. D. Weston's bowling average of 17.43 has been omitted altogether, and the number of runs scored off L. G. Palmer's bowling should be one hundred less than the total given." ' Caldicott looked up. 'There's something wrong here, Charters.'

'There's a great deal wrong, Caldicott! I've never come across such slapdashery.'

'I wasn't talking about that. Johnson did stand down as captain, having smashed his wrist, but the chap who took over wasn't called Orton or anything like it.'

'You're right, Caldicott,' said Charters, beginning to take an interest at last. 'Name of a racecourse, that was it. Ascot.'

'Braintree. As for this fellow with the 17.43 bowling average – I'll swear there was no one of that name in last year's team.'

'Yes – who was that again?'

'Weston A. N. D.'

'Orton and Weston,' said Charters thoughtfully. 'They sound like a couple of wireless comedians.'

'Are you sure they weren't? Their names positively don't appear on the school fixtures list, yet there's something familiar about them. Orton and Weston.'

Charters was beginning to see light. 'N. Orton, A. N. D. Weston – Norton and Weston. Norton and West!'

'That lemonade factory in Oldham we keep hearing about!'

'Caldicott, this is another of Jock Beevers' teasers. That letter is in code – give it here!' Charters reached over and snatched it from him.

'Really, Charters, you might give a fellow a chance,' Caldicott began indignantly. Suddenly Charters froze, put a finger to his lips and pointed. In the gap under the front door they could see something moving. Charters tiptoed across and threw the door wide. Cecil St Clair stood there, holding a gun. He took a final bite out of an apple and tossed the core into the garden.

'By the way, I am quite an authority on codes. Allow me,' said St Clair, reaching forward and taking the letter. Charters put his hands up and retreated before the gun. 'Now I am

121

very surprised at you, gentlemen, to have left your old friend's home in such a state. It is not very nice, you know.'

'Do you dare suggest we're responsible for this, St Clair? More your line of country, I'd have thought,' said Charters.

'No. I should have been tidier.'

'How did you find this place, St Clair, and what do you want here?' Caldicott demanded, refusing to be intimidated by the gun.

'It is not difficult to trace the addresses of prominent persons, you know. I recommend a volume called Who's Who. As to why I am here, I think you know very well we are looking for the same thing. The crock of gold.'

'Then you're out of luck, old chum. This isn't the end of the rainbow either.'

'As to that, I believe you are wrong.' He produced a flashy, crocodile-skin pocket-book and tucked the letter inside it. 'Can you follow the instructions in this letter?'

'No. It's complete double Dutch,' said Charters defiantly.

'Permit me to say I don't believe you.'

'Then you'll have to do the other thing, won't you,' said Caldicott.

'Have you ever been shot in the kneecap, Mr Caldicott? It is a very painful experience, by the way. However, let me go on to say that for me, violence is the method of last resort. I make a proposal. Co-operate with me fully and we'll split the gold fifty-fifty.'

Charters snorted. 'You don't really believe that El Dorado tale about a sunken U-boat, do you, St Clair?'

'I say, careless talk, old chap,' said Caldicott. 'He may have less gen on the subject than he pretends.'

'The submarine was the *City of Hamburg*. Her commander was Captain Kühlner. The cargo was gold bullion worth perhaps twenty millions of pounds at present values, destined for South America,' St Clair recited wearily. '*Hamburg* was intercepted by a United States anti-submarine patrol on 12th of April 1945, escaped but was badly damaged and later scuttled. Her crew was picked up by the Americans. Captain Kühlner was repatriated at the end of the war but subsequently arrested for illegally possessing a gold ingot.'

Caldicott still wasn't convinced. 'If you know so much about the saga, why don't you know where the U-boat is sunk?'

'My dear Caldicott, until only recently nobody knew where

the U-boat is sunk. Captain Kühlner is dead. Colonel Beevers and Colonel Pokrovski had only half the information each.'

'How is that possible?' Charters asked.

'That is how the bargain was made. In exchange for Kühlner's freedom, Beevers should have the longitudinal bearing and Pokrovski the latitudinal, so that neither could trace the gold without the other. They made the arrangement that when they should have enough money to finance a dredging operation they should put their two pieces of information together – don't you know, like the two halves of a banknote. But then, you see, Colonel Pokrovski suddenly relinquished his half to Colonel Beevers.'

'Why?' Caldicott asked.

'Shall we say, he was persuaded.'

'By whom?'

'By whom do you think, Caldicott?' said Charters, his eye on the gun. 'I believe now I know who you are, St Clair, as you style yourself. I shall be very surprised if you're not the son of Captain Kühlner.'

'But you see you are wrong. I am the son of Colonel Pokrovski.'

'Nice try, Charters,' Caldicott smirked.

'Near enough, I thought.'

'You see, I used to do some buying and selling in Moscow, of a kind that was not quite legal,' St Clair continued.

'Black market,' said Charters.

'I was about to be arrested, and you know, I would certainly have been executed. That was not very nice. And so we explained the problem to Colonel Beevers who smuggled me out of the country.'

'And your old dad coughed up his half of the secret,' said Caldicott. 'Did you kill Colonel Beevers?'

'Why should I do that when he alone knew where to find the golden submarine? No, on the contrary – I hoped he would live into his dotage and then spill the beans. I am afraid I was rather a nuisance to him.'

'Pestered him, I suppose – and after he'd saved your miserable life,' said Caldicott contemptuously.

'I wanted and still want no more than the Pokrovski half of the gold. I have searched high and low for this document, which I knew must exist – I am most grateful to you.' St Clair put his pocket book with Jock's letter down on a table.

'Now I shall ask you to perform one more service and decipher the code.'

'Do it yourself, St Clair,' said Charters.

'If necessary I shall, but you can save me hours of labour. By the way, I can be very persuasive. Which knee, Mr Caldicott?' St Clair pointed the gun at him. 'You see, I give you a choice.'

The front door was flung open and Margaret dashed in. Oblivious of St Clair, she burst out, 'The little bitch gave me the slip but I've got a nice offer of a pre-lunch sherry from . . .' She took in the full cast and stopped as suddenly as she'd started.

'By the way, you are only just in time, Mrs Mottram. The floor show is about to commence,' said St Clair, turning towards here. 'If you would sit . . .'

St Clair's attention had been momentarily distracted by Margaret's entrance. Charters saw his chance, raised his stick and brought it crashing down on St Clair's outstretched arm.

'Get the letter, Charters,' Caldicott shouted, grabbing the gun as it fell at his feet. But before Charters could reach it, St Clair seized it, leaped behind Margaret and took hold of her arms.

'Shoot by all means, my dear Caldicott,' said St Clair, retreating to the door with Margaret as a shield. In the doorway he let her go and ran for it.

'There goes our murderer, Caldicott,' said Charters as they watched the fleeing figure from the front door.

'Time to put Inspector Snow in the picture, I think. Margaret, where would you say the nearest phone is?'

'The same place as the free sherry.'

'Hello, what's to do?' said Charters as they passed by the churchyard on their way to the vicarage. A cluster of villagers had gathered at one end and seemed to be staring down into an open grave.

'Mothers' Union meeting breaking up, I shouldn't wonder,' said Caldicott.

The Reverend Adam Lamb detached himself from the group and hurried down the path towards them. 'Ah, Vicar, we were just on our way to see you,' said Charters. 'I wonder if we could use your phone.'

'Sorry. I should think the line's going to be busy for some considerable time,' said Lamb and continued on his way.

Puzzled, the three moved closer to the source of interest.

They found themselves staring down at the body of St Clair, blood still oozing from his back where he'd been stabbed. His empty crocodile-skin pocket-book lay discarded on a pile of earth. Charters and Caldicott slowly removed their hats.

'Any more theories, old chap?' said Caldicott.

CHAPTER 13

In the Club library, silence was broken only by an occasional gentle snore. Charters dozed fitfully in one armchair; Caldicott was fast asleep in another. Before weariness had overcome them, they had been trying, with the aid of memory and Wisden's Cricketer's Almanack, to crack Jock Beevers' code. But a substantial lunch, followed by generous brandies and fat cigars, had been their undoing.

Caldicott surfaced first, yawned and picked up Wisden, his notebook and a fountain pen from a table at his elbow. 'I'll tell you what, Charters.' Charters stirred and grunted. 'We might get on better with the school year-book.'

'What?' Charters mumbled.

'School year-book. Which Jock's letter claimed didn't reconcile with Wisden.'

Charters woke up properly. 'Yes, but Jock's letter also mentioned one N. Orton as substitute captain – when, as we've confirmed from Wisden, the captain was Lingfield.'

'Braintree.'

'Plus the non-existent bowling average of the non-existent A. N. D. Weston. All he was doing, in his Jock-like elaborate way, was drawing our attention to that wretched lemonade factory.'

'Norton and West – I know that, Charters. But what about all that other stuff about so-and-so's innings total and such-and-such's batting average? What else was he trying to tell us?'

'Obviously the figures, if we could remember them, form a cipher.'

'One equals A, two equals B?'

'Nothing as simple as that, knowing Jock. If we still had the letter that would help.' Charters picked up his copy of *The Times* and went back to the crossword, prepared to wash his hands of Jock's games.

'So should the school year-book. Otherwise why mention it? If Jock wanted us to fiddle about with the batting averages to decode his message, why didn't he just say it was Wisden that was wrong?'

Charters' pen halted in mid-clue. 'Because that would have been an absurdity, old man. Wisden is never wrong.'

'Then he *must* want us to refer to the school year-book.'

'Very well. Do you have a copy?'

''Fraid not. It only goes to overseas old boys these days, unless one specifically applies for it.'

'Which you failed to do.'

'What about you?'

'No – I was never sent a reminder. Yes, Barstow?'

The Club porter tiptoed over and whispered into Charters' ear the unwelcome news that Inspector Snow was once again on the premises and asking to see them. Charters looked pained. A few minutes later, Charters and Caldicott exited, with furtive speed, via the area steps and the tradesmen's entrance.

'Did you observe the state of that still-room, Caldicott?' said Charters as they scuttled away down the street to the sound of the siren on Snow's departing car. 'I shall write to the kitchen committee.'

'I shouldn't do that, old boy. They'll want to know what we were doing below stairs.'

'You really think this is wise, Caldicott?' Charters asked, as they bounced through the London suburbs, crouched in the back of a very small minicab. They had decided to track the school year-book to its source, experience of the inspector's investigative techniques encouraging them to combine prudence with research.

'We could go by train if you prefer, but I warn you it means changing at Bletchley.'

'I was referring to our avoiding friend Snow in this fashion. We've got to face him sooner or later.'

'But preferably later rather than sooner. When we've unravelled Jock's latest brain-teaser.'

'You were all for facing the music earlier, until St Clair was found dead.'

Caldicott glanced warningly at the driver and murmured, 'I say – pas devant le domestique.'

'Oh, that's all right. They barely speak English, these minicab drivers. Famous for it.'

'Yes, I was forgetting that.'

'There's something else you're forgetting, Caldicott. Now that we're in a position to name the murderer, we have a duty to do so.'

'You mean the girl who's been calling herself Jenny?'

'I'm now convinced that she's the *real* Jenny.'

127

'Then I'm even more convinced that she didn't do it, old man. Jenny is after the will – so that she can destroy it and inherit from the previous will. Agreed?'

'Agreed,' said Charters, oblivious of the driver's keen interest in their conversation. 'Which gives her ample cause to kill Helen Appleyard who was her co-beneficiary.'

'Why? Why not simply join forces with Helen Appleyard, find the new will together, destroy it and split Jock's fortune down the middle?'

The driver seemed to agree with this, but Charters wasn't sure. 'You don't take human greed into account, Caldicott. With Helen Appleyard dead she becomes sole beneficiary.'

Neither Caldicott nor the driver were convinced. 'Are you sure?' Caldicott asked for them both.

'Positive. Does this fellow know where he's going?'

'I sincerely hope so.' Caldicott leaned forward and bellowed, 'Take road through Bletchley. Got that? Bletchley road.' The driver nodded, impatient for them to get back to the story. 'Wait a minute, Charters, you're wrong. If that will was assumed to be a genuine one, then half Jock's fortune goes to Jenny and the other half to Helen Appleyard. She having subsequently popped her clogs, her share become part of her own estate and goes to her next of kin.'

'Quite. Her husband.'

'Gregory.'

'There you are then.'

'What do you mean, there I am?' asked Caldicott, exasperated. The driver, unnoticed by his passengers, was so absorbed that he drove straight through a red traffic light, missing another car by inches.

'Jenny Beevers killed Helen Appleyard so that she wouldn't inherit. She then killed Helen Appleyard's husband so that *he* wouldn't inherit,' Charters explained.

'But what good does that do her? The money still doesn't revert to her. It goes to Gregory's old mum or his sister or the Sunshine Home for Retired Ne-er-do-wells.'

'Yes, I confess I hadn't thought of that.'

'As for her motive for killing St Clair, it's even more non-existent. Jenny was only after the will; St Clair was after far bigger stakes.'

'The submarine gold,' said Charters. The minicab lurched wildly and almost mounted the pavement. 'I say, do be careful, driver. It doesn't necessarily follow, Caldicott. Just supposing she *wasn't* after the new will. Supposing nobody was after the will. The whole pack and parcel of them – Jenny Beevers, Helen Appleyard, Gregory, St Clair, Josh Darrell – all in their different fashions could have been after the submerged gold.'

'If that's so, old lad, then Jock's message, even if it doesn't lead us to the gold, will almost certainly lead us to the murderer.' The minicab driver screeched on his brakes, over-turned a litter bin and almost wrote off his passengers and his car.

Inspector Snow finished snooping round Margaret Mottram's house and returned to the kitchen, satisfied that Charters and Caldicott were not lurking in the linen cupboard or hiding under the bed. 'I seem to be drawing a lot of blanks today, Mrs Mottram.'

'I'm afraid you do,' said Margaret, carrying on with her washing-up.

Snow picked up a glass she had just rinsed and began to dry it. 'Any particular reason, would you say?'

'Perhaps you're not looking in the right places.'

'No, I mean any particular reason why they're avoiding me?'

'Why should they avoid you, Inspector?'

Snow held the glass up to the light, breathed on it and polished it again with the tea towel. 'That's what I'm asking. Three murders and they've been on the scene of every one of them. That could be the reason.'

'I was on the scene of two and I'm not avoiding you.'

'No, well they need someone to report back what kind of mood I'm in, don't they?'

'What kind of mood *are* you in?'

'Not a sunny one, Mrs Mottram. They can go so far with me – and they've now gone just as far as they're going.'

Snatches of the old school song reached out from the chapel to greet Charters and Caldicott as they strolled up the drive. Passing boys respectfully raised their caps. A smatter of applause rippled round the cricket ground. Charters and Caldicott paused.

'Well played, sir! Well played indeed!' Charters leaned on his umbrella, quite happy to stay and watch the next couple of overs.

'Come along, old chap. Business first,' said Caldicott reluctantly.

The library was overcrowded and chaotically disorganised. Charters and Caldicott tracked down the bursar and recruited his help in finding the school year-book.

'Properly speaking, of course, these volumes belong with all our memorabilia in the new school archive annexe,' said the bursar, perching precariously on top of some library steps and reaching out for the relevant volume. 'Alas, it has yet to leave the drawing board.'

'Other claims on your purse, I expect,' said Caldicott uneasily.

'Many,' said the bursar, never one to let slip a fund-raising opportunity. 'Perhaps the appeal didn't reach you?'

'I believe it did but in fact we'd already heavily subscribed to the Pavilion Fund,' said Charters.

'Perhaps next year.' Caldicott took the year-book from the bursar and began to compare the figures from Wisden in his notebook with those on the appropriate page.

'Next year we'll be having a special drive for the science side. They badly need a computer.'

'A computer – for the stinks lab? What the devil for?' asked Charters.

'I expect you were on the classics side,' said the bursar, searching his mind for another area of need.

'A little Latin and less Greek,' said Caldicott. 'See what you make of this, Charters.' He passed over his notes and the year-book.

'The language laboratory is still woefully under-equipped.'

'Really? Pity I threw out my old French grammar.'

'A new word processor is what is needed – when we can find a benefactor.'

Caldicott side-stepped neatly. 'Someone who wholesales the things, that's what you want. I'll put the word round the Club.'

Charters looked up from his figures. 'I take it these notes you made from Wisden are accurate, Caldicott?'

'If you remember, Charters, you insisted on double-checking them.'

'Then there is not an iota of difference between the details in the school year-book and the corresponding details in Wisden.'

'Naturally,' said the bursar. 'They come from the same source.'

'I'm afraid we're on a fool's errand and have been wasting your time, Bursar.'

'We'd been led to believe that the school year-book cricket section contained a number of errors,' said Caldicott.

'Had you indeed?' said the bursar, showing interest in their mission for the first time. 'Not, by any chance, by the late Beevers, J. H. L., sometime of School House?'

'How on earth . . .?' Caldicott began.

The bursar turned to Charters. 'I knew he was a contemporary of yours from the obituary you kindly sent to the year-book. Tell me, shortly before he died, was he completely in possession of his, ah . . .?'

'Faculties? His mind was as razor-sharp as ever, Bursar. Why do you ask?'

'I had a strange letter from him drawing my attention to the year-book's alleged omission of an old boys' charity match from last year's cricket reports.'

Charters looked puzzled. 'I remember no old boys' charity match.'

'There wasn't one.'

'Do you still have that letter, Bursar,' asked Caldicott.

'I'm afraid not. Filing space is at a premium until we have the money to expand our limited office space.' The bursar crammed the school year-book back into the shelves.

'No matter,' said Charters. 'Unless Jock's brought us here on a wild goose chase, Caldicott, this must be our latest clue.'

'So the whole point of directing us to the year-book was to lead us to the bursar. Charity match? Why charity match?'

'We're meant to apply our thought processes. I'm getting rather tired of this game, Caldicott.'

'*Charity* match. Perhaps he wants us to see that the Beevers' fortune, when we've done what he asks us to do, goes to some particular charity.'

The bursar pricked up his ears. 'The Beevers' fortune! You've had sight of the will, then?'

'Er – briefly,' said Charters.

'Is it too much to hope he remembered the school?'

'Oh, indeed he did!' said Caldicott.

The bursar beamed. 'How very generous. And the – er – nature of the bequest, dare one ask?'

'His entire collection of Edgar Wallace books.'

'Can I be of any assistance, madam?' said Grimes, officiously intercepting Margaret as she made her way across the lobby of Viceroy Mansions.

'No, thank you.'

'Only he's not back yet, madam.'

'Yes he is. He's just telephoned.' Margaret stepped into the lift and slammed the door in Grimes's face.

'My mistake, madam. I must have been on my security rounds,' Grimes called grovellingly after the ascending lift. As soon as Margaret was out of sight, he went back to his cubby-hole and picked up the phone.

Margaret found Charters and Caldicott bickering and, silently prescribing her usual treatment, set to work with the gin bottle.

'no, I'm sorry, Caldicott, I've had quite enough of this,' said Charters, whose visit to his alma mater had failed to revive his flagging interest in amateur detection.

'Oh, don't be a dog in the manger, Charters. You *like* solving posers and so on.'

'*The Times* crossword is poser enough for me. You know perfectly well what will happen if we make this expedition to Oldham.'

'You make it sound like the unknown,' said Margaret, distributing large gin-and-tonics.

Charters thanked her. 'It *is* the unknown. Cloth caps, clogs and tripe. And when we *do* present ourselves at this Norton and West place, there's bound to be one more blasted concealed message from Jock Beevers saying now go to Timbuktu or my first is in apple but not in orange. I tell you I'm sick to death of it.'

'Don't you want to know why he invented that charity match, old fellow?'

'No I do not,' said Charters firmly. 'All this dashing hither and thither doesn't suit me. Besides, you know what tomorrow is?'

'First day of the Test,' said Margaret.

'Well done! I thought you had little interest in cricket, Mrs Mottram.'

'I haven't. I asked Caldicott to take me to Wimbledon.'

'Impossible, dear lady. We shall be glued to the wireless all day.'

'We can do better than that, old man,' said Caldicott. 'Why not come to Oldham and see the Test Match first hand?'

'But the Test Match is at Old Trafford, old man. As any fool knows.'

'Oldham is near Old Trafford.'

'No, no. Manchester is near Old Trafford.'

'But Oldham is near Manchester,' said Caldicott, exasperated. 'Really, Charters, for someone so widely travelled you know very little about the North. It's a mere tram ride away.'

'Really? But where should we stay?'

'How would I know? The Railway Arms, I suppose.'

Margaret, who had been standing at the window looking down into the street during this interchange, interrupted, 'Why don't you discuss that in the car?'

'We don't have a car,' said Caldicott.

'I have a car.'

'You mean you'd lend it to us? That's noble of you, Margaret.'

'Not on your nelly. I want to do some girl friday recruiting in Leeds.'

'Is that near Manchester?'

'A mere tram ride away. Shall we go – like now?'

'But see here, I haven't so much as a toothbrush with me,' Charters objected.

'They do have toothbrushes in Lancashire, Charters,' said Caldicott.

'I should think they also have them in the New Scotland Yard lock-up,' said Margaret impatiently. 'Is there a back way out of these flats, Caldicott?'

'What?' Caldicott joined her at the window and looked down. 'Oh, my golly.' Inspector Snow was just entering the block. 'Hello, he's got his sergeant with him this time.'

'What does that signify?' Charters asked.

'It signifies that if you don't leave now, you won't be leaving until you've told him everything he needs to know,' said Margaret.

CHAPTER 14

Caldicott pushed up the trapdoor, peered cautiously out and turned back to signal the all-clear to Charters and Margaret. The three of them climbed through and, crouching down to avoid being seen, picked their way gingerly across the rooftop and down the fire escape to the railings at street level. Only a gate stood between them, Margaret's car, Watford and the North and they scurried towards it. The gate was locked and Grimes stood on the other side of it, smirking.

'*Good* evening, sir, Mr Charters, sir, madam.'

Caldicott glared at him through the bars. 'This is a fire escape, Grimes.'

'It most certainly is, Mr Caldicott. Any conflagration at this moment in time, or was you taking a short cut?'

'It's locked, Grimes.'

'I know, sir. It's a constant what's-it-called – dilemma, for me, this gate is. Do I keep it locked, thus creating a safety hazard style of thing, or do I leave it open and encourage the criminal element?' Grimes folded his arms, prepared to debate the issue all night. 'Either way, if the dog-dirt hits the fan, excuse me madam, it comes back to me.'

'Let me out, Grimes.'

'More than my job's worth, Mr Caldicott.'

'Doesn't he have superiors you can report him to, Caldicott?' Charters demanded.

'Do I not, Mr Charters. And if they thought I was letting the residents use the emergency exit for their own convenience I'd be for the high jump. I kid you not.'

'You'll be for the high jump, laddie, if you don't unlock this gate. I kid *you* not,' Caldicott raged, shaking the spearhead railings.

'It's the security angle that bothers them, see, sir. Only with my bad back I can't do my rounds as often as I'd like to.'

'Give him a fiver for some liniment,' Margaret muttered, fearing the imminent arrival of Snow.

'Take more than that, Madam. Only I'm going to a private osteopath now, see, and honestly, what he has the nerve to charge, it ought to be exposed.'

Caldicott produced his wallet and took out a £10 note. 'The key, Grimes.'

'Not sure if I have it on me, tell the truth.'

'Give me a tenner, Charters, there's a good fellow.' Charters took out his own wallet.

'Very kind of you, sir. Only I expect you have your own reasons for coming out down the fire escape, so it's a case of I do you a favour and you do me one style of thing.' Grimes unlocked the gate and took a tenner each off Charters and Caldicott as they passed through, with the aplomb of a steward at Lord's.

'Thank you Grimes.'

'Thank you, Mr Caldicott.'

Free at last, Margaret and Charters were eager to be off but Caldicott lingered. 'And Grimes, I'm going away for a few days. When I get back I look forward to hearing all about your new job.'

'What job would that be, sir?'

'The job you'll be applying for in my absence. Will you break the news to the agents or shall I?'

Grimes shrugged philosophically and pocketed the money.

Charters, Caldicott and Margaret crammed themselves into Margaret's vintage open-topped MG and headed up the M1 with as much speed as they could reconcile with the law. As they passed a police lay-by, a patrolman made a note of the car's number and reached for his radio.

Grimes let Inspector Snow and Sergeant Tipper into Caldicott's flat and stood outside, his ear pressed to the door until Snow, displaying psychic powers, said conversationally, 'All right, Mr Grimes, I shan't need you any more.'

The inspector had been pacing the living-room, deep in thought. 'You see, it doesn't make sense,' he said finally to Tipper.

'What's that, guv?'

'You are Helen Appleyard, looking for whatever it is you're looking for. I'm the girl calling herself Jenny Beevers. I say calling herself – it could still turn out she *is* Jenny Beevers and that's why they're shielding her. I let myself in with the key I nicked downstairs – now you found that chip of nail varnish by the front door, correct?'

'One point two metres into the living-room, guv.'

'So that's where the struggle must have started.' Snow positioned himself to re-enact the scene as it might have happened. 'I let myself in, you come forward to stop me getting any further, and I force you all the way back to the bedroom without knocking anything down or even rucking the carpet.' Snow shook his head. 'It's not possible.'

'Oh, I don't know, guv. If you took me by surprise?'

'If *I* took *you* by surprise, yes, but you see we're talking about two slips of young women, by all accounts about the same height and the same weight. They'd have been all over the shop. No, I'll tell you what – she was propelled across this room by a man.'

'Our friend?'

'If we could prove it.'

'How did he get in?'

'He didn't come in with Jenny so-called Beevers, because she was seen by number thirty-two coming along the corridor by herself. Maybe Helen Appleyard let her in. The short answer is, I don't know.' Snow looked at his watch. 'You'd better be ringing in, hadn't you?' While Tipper dialled, Snow looked disapprovingly at a set of carelessly stacked encyclopaedias. 'Just look at that. How can anyone live with that kind of mess?'

'They leave it all to the charwoman in that class, don't they, guv? . . . Sergeant Tipper here. Anything?'

Unable to bear the sight, Inspector Snow began to straighten the volumes. As he did so, a tiny object fell from one of them. He closed his hand on it.

'They're on their way north, with that Mrs Mottram,' Tipper reported.

'She's a sensible woman. If they're going where I think they're going, let's hope she keeps them out of mischief till we get there. I thought you'd been over this room with a vacuum cleaner?' Snow opened his hand and showed Tipper a small blazer button. 'Lodged down the spine of that volume there.'

'Must have flown through the air while they were struggling.'

'Very likely.' Snow took an envelope from Caldicott's desk, dropped the button into it and held out the flap to Tipper. 'Just lick that, would you? It *still* doesn't make sense but I'll tell you what, Sergeant Tipper. We've nabbed him.'

Margaret deposited Charters and Caldicott at a sprawling, concrete, neon-lit hotel that might have sprung up as a conference venue on any ringroad of any town. As they checked in, they noted with distaste the muzak, the garish furnishing and the lop-sided noticeboard directing computer games salesmen to the Oak Suite and meat traders' reception guests to the Princess Room. The hotel operated a do-it-yourself system of customer service and Charters and Caldicott had to carry their own suitcases, bought and filled with socks, shaving-soap and other emergency rations, on the journey north. While they waited for the lift to take them to their anonymous rooms, they looked down at the matching cases at their feet, then at each other. Uncertainly, they switched the cases over.

Two substantial figures seated in the lobby had noted their arrival. When the lift doors had closed on Charters and Caldicott, one of Josh Darrell's minders put down his newspaper and headed for the house phones.

After enduring a Surf 'n Turf dinner in the Cape Cod Restaurant, Charters and Caldicott decided to call it a day. Five minutes later, Charters, fuming with impatience as he waited for someone to answer his phone call to reception, turned to find Caldicott had come into his room. 'Why can't I get room service?'

'Did you dial 526?'

'I haven't dialled anything.'

'Then you won't get room service.' Charters began to dial. 'And that gets you a recorded message advising that for the convenience of guests there *isn't* any room service at this hour, but for your further convenience please make use of your mini-bar.'

Charters banged down the phone. 'What the blazes is a mini-bar.'

'This contraption,' said Caldicott, opening the door. 'Mine's empty so I thought I'd join you for a nightcap.'

Charters relaxed a little. 'Large brandy and soda for me, if you please, old fellow.' Caldicott held up a miniature bottle of brandy daintily. 'Confounded place. And have you seen the size of the soap tablets they give you? It's more like Lilliput.'

'Well, what's our programme for tomorrow, old man?' asked Caldicott, mixing Charters' drink on the plastic oak-finish desk-cum-dressing table.

'Play commences at eleven-thirty. Norton and West presumably start business at nine. I propose we get there on the dot.'

'Yes, but what do we do when we get there?'

'Only one thing *to* do. Re-introduce ourselves to Gordon Wrigley and hope to bluff him into telling us what we want to know. Whatever that may be.'

'When we did that before, at Josh Darrell's house-party, we made complete twerps of ourselves.' Caldicott passed Charters his drink.

'Yes, well this time better leave the talking to me. No offence, old fellow.'

'None taken,' said Caldicott huffily, peering into the mini-bar. 'However, there's no reason to suppose your wits are sharper than – I say! I've given you the only brandy!'

'Chin chin,' said Charters, downing it in one.

Charters and Caldicott fiddled uncomfortably with their shirt collars as they picked their way between stacks of lemonade crates. Caldicott glanced up and drew Charters' attention to a large sign that read, 'Norton and West Mineral Waters. Mfrs of Birdade. "First for Thirst since 1891".' A grimace of acute embarrassment crossed their faces as they remembered their previous encounter with Gordon Wrigley. It seemed he didn't need a slogan after all.

The factory's enquiry office housed a commissionaire doing his football pools and a receptionist chatting to a friend on the switchboard. Neither paid any attention to Charters and Caldicott.

'No, I wouldn't mind, Sharon, but I don't even like fried bread,' the receptionist was saying. 'All right, so you don't expect a cordon blue meal when there's only the one gas ring, but you'd think he'd 've made some kind of effort, wouldn't you? So I said, ooh, for goodness sake, Brian, where's your tin-opener?' Charters had had enough of this. He banged peremptorily on the old-fashioned bell. 'Just a minute, Sharon. Can I help you?'

'Mr Caldicott and Mr Charters to see Mr Wrigley.'

'Did you have an appointment?'

'I think he'll see us. We met at a house party.'

'Mr Who, did you say?'

'Caldicott and Charters.'

'Charters and Caldicott,' said Caldicott.

'Sharon. There's a Mr Charters and a Mr Caldicott to see Mr Wrigley . . . No, but they say they know him – they met at a party.' The receptionist turned back to Charters and Caldicott. 'She's just off to see if he's in.'

'Damned uncomfortable, these ready-made shirts, don't you find, Caldicott?' said Charters, tugging at his collar. The receptionist glanced up curiously from painting her nails.

'Yes. It could be that they have different sizes in the North,' said Caldicott, running his fingers inside the collar of his own shirt, as if to take up the slack.

'Very likely. This sixteen-and-a-half collar feels like a fifteen-and-a-half.'

'My fifteen-and-a-half feels like a sixteen-and-a-half.'

The switchboard buzzed. 'Yes, Sharon? And you don't know when he'll be back? . . . All right – oh, and I'll tell you the rest of the saga at lunchtime.' The receptionist glanced up to relay the information that Mr Wrigley was down in London at the present.

'We may as well go to the fountainhead, since we're here, Caldicott,' said Charters. 'Mr Norton or Mr West?'

'I'm afraid Mr West's dead at the moment. And I don't think Mr Norton'll see you, if you don't have an appointment.'

'We'll leave that to the judgement of others, shall we?'

The receptionist sighed and plugged into another extension. 'Debra? No, dead loss – I might as well have stayed in and washed my hair. I'll tell you the gory details later. Listen, there's two gentlemen asking for Mr Norton. Mr Charters and Mr Caldicott.' She turned to Charters. 'Could you give me some idea of what it's in connection with?'

'It's a private matter.'

'Wait,' said Caldicott. 'Say it's to do with the affairs of the late Colonel Beevers of Hong Kong.'

'They say it's about a Colonel Beevers from Hong Kong. *I* don't know, Debra, do I?' The receptionist lowered her voice. 'No, definitely not reps. She's seeing if he'll see you,' she said to Charters and Caldicott.

'I have a question for you, Caldicott,' said Charters as they waited.

'Fire away.'

'What colour's your toothbrush?'

'My bathroom toothbrush or my travelling toothbrush?'

'The toothbrush you acquired last evening along with shirt, socks, etc.'

'Oh, *that* toothbrush. Green.'

'I thought as much. That green toothbrush is mine, Caldicott. Yours is red.'

Caldicott stared at him. 'I do believe you're right, Charters. You realise what we've done, don't you? We've got one another's suitcases.'

'Hence this wretched fifteen-and-a-half collar. You would insist on changing the suitcases round, Caldicott – the fact is that they were right in the first place. We'll have to go back to the hotel and change.'

'And miss the first overs? Can't we do it somewhere else, old man?'

'I move with the times as much as the next man, Caldicott, but unlike some cricket supporters I draw the line at removing my shirt outside the pavilion at Old Trafford.'

The switchboard came to life again. 'Yes, Debra? Really? Wonders will never cease. Mr Norton will see you now. Stanley,' the receptionist called to the commissionaire, 'could you take these two gentlemen to the boardroom?'

Surprised at the success of their manoeuvre, Charters and Caldicott followed Stanley upstairs and along a covered footbridge that linked two factory buildings. A row of windows gave out onto a cobbled courtyard and as they passed one of them, Caldicott murmured, 'Hello,' and nudged Charters. Josh Darrell's Jaguar and his minders were waiting in the yard below. As the pair looked down, Darrell himself came out of the directors' entrance and headed briskly for the car.

'Now what in the name of thunder is Josh Darrell doing here?' said Caldicott.

'Having an audience with Gordon Wrigley, I imagine.'

'Unlikely, old man.'

'Come, Caldicott – you don't really believe that yarn about Wrigley being in London, do you?'

'Not for a minute. Equally I find it hard to swallow that a little fish like Wrigley wouldn't have come out to see a big fish like Darrell into his car instead of glowering down at him from that office window as if hoping looks could kill.' Charters followed Caldicott's glance across and saw Wrigley standing at a window opposite, wearing just such an expression. As they watched, he raised a hand to his chin. One of the cuff buttons on his blazer was missing.

The panelled boardroom was lined with portraits of bearded directors from the past. Charters and Caldicott made a tour of them while they waited for Norton. 'Who does that remind you of?' asked Caldicott, pausing in front of one.

'W. G. Grace, of course. I wonder who'll win the toss?'

They'd just reached the portrait of the present managing director, Jacob Norton, every inch the Yorkshire industrialist, when the doors of the boardroom were pushed open and a young nurse wheeled in the man himself: an old, haggard-looking travesty of the portrait.

Norton dismissed his nurse brusquely. 'Buzz off – I'll ring when I want you. And shut them doors – this is private business.'

Charters and Caldicott introduced themselves. 'Good of you to see us, Mr Norton,' said Caldicott, getting the interview off to a civilised start.

Norton stared at them. 'Bloody hell. Have they put the retirement age up, or what?'

Norton's opening gambit threw them off balance. 'Come again?' said Caldicott blankly.

'I say I thought they'd have pensioned you off – CID, Special Branch or whatever you call yourselves.'

The penny dropped. Caldicott would have set the record straight but Charters interrupted him with uncharacteristic foolhardiness. 'Seniority is not an asset to be discarded lightly, Mr Norton, as you yourself would agree,' he said smoothly.

'Oh, aye, there's nobody can tell *me* when to retire. I'll go when I'm good and ready. Well, do I get cautioned or what?'

To Caldicott's dismay, Charters continued with this dangerous deception. 'We'd just like to ask you a few informal questions, Mr Norton. No need for your notebook.' Caldicott glowered at being cast in the Tipper role.

'Ask all the questions you please. Whether you get any answers or not, we'll have to see.'

'Now, you know why we're here, of course?'

'I've a good idea. You'll never prove owt.'

Charters knew a promising lead when he saw one, and gave Caldicott a smug glance. 'You think not?'

'Not while I'm alive. After I'm dead's another matter – but there'd be no point then, would there? You can't prosecute a corpse.'

Caldicott decided to join in the game of bluff, a move which filled Charters, in his turn, with misgiving. 'Perhaps

141

not, Mr Norton – but there are others involved in the business, aren't there?'

'Not criminally, there aren't,' said Norton sharply. 'Now you keep my family out of this, do you hear?'

Charters raised an eyebrow at Caldicott. 'We'll do our best to accommodate you, Mr Norton, but *you* must do your best to help *us*. Now, given anything to *charity* lately?'

Norton laughed bitterly. 'That's not where it's all gone – unless you call my bookmakers charity.'

'I see,' said Charters, baffled.

'When were you last in Hong Kong, Mr Norton?' asked Caldicott cunningly.

Norton looked down at his blanket-covered legs. 'Me? Don't talk so daft.'

'Someone representing your company, then. Gordon Wrigley, perhaps?'

'Never mind Hong Kong and never mind Gordon Wrigley. I've told you – I won't have my family involved.'

'Family?' asked Charters.

'I suppose you'd call him that. He is my son-in-law, after all. Though it's not him I'm worried about.'

Caldicott, all at sea, broke with custom and tried the straightforward approach. 'Who *are* you worried about?'

'Who do you think? Not you two, I can tell you that much.'

Charters stepped in. 'We're not here to cause anxiety, Mr Norton. We're here to clear up certain matters.'

'Well you seem to be going a funny way about it. My secretary said you mentioned this Colonel Beevers chap. What's it got to do with him?'

'Do you know he's dead?' Caldicott asked.

''Course I know he's dead. He died while our Gordon was out there, didn't he?'

'Quite,' said Caldicott. 'Exactly,' said Charters. Neither had the slightest idea what he was talking about.

'What are you two looking at me like that for, the pair of you? Do you really think I sent Gordon Wrigley all that way to commit a murder – just to keep this business quiet?'

'It's possible,' said Caldicott cautiously.

'Pigs might fly – that's possible. Any road, it wasn't Beevers I should have been worried about – it was who Beevers was dealing with this end. So why didn't I just send my son-in-law down to London to bump off Josh Darrell and save myself the air fares?'

'Why indeed?' said Charters, reminded, for some reason, of being lost in a real old London pea-souper.

'I wish I *had* done now, after what's happened,' Norton fretted. 'But I'll tell you why, if you want to know.' He groped under his blanket and brought out a bottle of pills. 'You see these? Twelve of these with a glass of whisky and I'm a dead body. *That's* my way out if it comes to it.'

Charters was heartily sick of corpses. 'There's no need for melodramatic gestures, Mr Norton. Just answer our questions frankly and there's no reason why what you tell us should go beyond this room.'

Norton couldn't believe his ears. 'You what?'

Caldicott tried to save the situation. 'What my colleague means is that you won't be involved. In – er – subsequent proceedings.'

'I won't be involved?'

'Firm promise.'

'Then what are you *doing* here?'

Caldicott looked at Charters. 'Never mind that for the present, Mr Norton,' said Charters uneasily. 'Just put your cards on the table, there's a good chap.'

'I'll put my cards on the table when you produce a warrant to see them. Well, have you got a warrant?'

'Er, not at the moment, no,' said Caldicott.

'Have you got *anything* to prove you are who you say you are?' Charters and Caldicott coughed awkwardly. 'Or any identity at all? Come on, I'm waiting.'

Caldicott shuffled forward sheepishly. 'My card.' Charters also presented his.

'I bloody thought so! You're no more police than I'm King Kong.' He spun his chair round and wheeled himself furiously towards the bell push in the wall.

'Cast your mind back, Mr Norton. We never *claimed* to be policemen.'

'A misunderstanding, Mr Norton,' said Charters.

'Pure assumption on your part.'

Norton's nurse raced into the boardroom and whisked him out, just in time to save him from bursting a blood vessel.

CHAPTER 15

'This really is absurd, old man,' said Caldicott as the pair strode purposefully through the lobby of their hotel. 'It isn't as if wearing the wrong shirts would cripple us for life.'

'It would spoil my day, Caldicott. Besides which, it's extremely bad for the circulation and furthermore we look ridiculous.'

'We could take our ties off.'

Charters stepped into the lift. 'Caldicott, I have not gone open-necked to a cricket match since I was at prep school. I don't propose to relax my standards now – even if we *are* in the North.' He jabbed irritably at the lift button. Before the doors could close completely, two enormous hams of hands came between them and forced them open again. Josh Darrell's minders joined them in the lift. Deaf to all pleas and protests, they bundled them out at a strange floor, frog-marched them ignominiously down the corridor and propelled them through a door.

Darrell looked round as they entered, waved to them and carried on with his phone call. Charters and Caldicott, ruffled and furious, straightened their ties and flexed twisted wrists while Darrell read out some rigmarole of a formula. 'Does that sound like a beverage to you or does it sound like a bomb?' he finished, pocketing his notes. 'I guess it's this synthesised burdock ingredient that's been eluding us. Listen, I have a meeting right now. We'll talk later.' Darrell hung up and, ever the polite host, gave Charters and Caldicott his full attention. 'Good of you to drop by. May I offer you something? Coffee?'

Caldicott bristled with rage. 'You may offer us, Darrell, an explanation.'

'It's gone beyond that, Caldicott,' said Charters. 'An action for heavy damages may lie. I don't know whether you know anything about English civil law, Darrell, but wrongful imprisonment is a very serious matter.'

The television was on in the corner. Darrell turned the sound down before saying, 'Maybe we'll settle out of court. I don't aim to keep you long, gentlemen.'

'I should jolly hope not. We have a most important engagement,' said Caldicott.

'You've just come back from one. Your busy morning.'

Charters glowered. "Evidently you know we've been to see Jacob Norton.'

'I was with him when you called.'

'You may as well know, Darrell, that he made a full and frank confession.'

Darrell smiled. 'I don't think so. I'll give you a piece of advice, Charters. Never play poker.'

His telephone rang again. While Darrell dealt with the call, Caldicott nudged the affronted Charters and nodded towards the silent television screen. The BBC had started its Test Match coverage. The pair edged closer and watched, riveted, the opening balls of the game.

'Fine, send it up.' Darrell turned back to Charters and Caldicott. 'How much did old Norton really tell you?'

'Rather more than you think,' said Caldicott abstractedly, his eyes glued to the set.

'You know he's been swindling his own company for years – playing the horses and rigging the books to cover his losses?'

'We gathered something of the sort, yes,' said Charters, equally inattentive. 'Run, man, run.'

'How the hell he's gotten away with it I wish I knew – I'd sell the secret. His daughter's a major shareholder and *she* never guessed. Maybe having a crooked accountant for a son-in-law helped. I guess Wrigley fixed the books in exchange for a slice of the action. If young Wrigley hadn't confided in your buddy Jock Beevers about what was going on, the old man might have taken his secret to the grave as the saying is. But, he *did* tell Beevers and Beevers told me and I guess he told you so here we are.'

'Here we are,' said Caldicott, wincing at a dropped catch. 'So, let's hear it.'

Caldicott brightened. 'You'd like the sound up?'

'*Your* game I'm interested in, not Association cricket.' Charters rolled his eyes heavenward in horror at the gaffe.

'I say, you could have waited till the end of the over,' Caldicott protested as Darrell switched the set off.

'What was your pitch with the old man? Blackmail?'

'Do we look like blackmailers?' Charters demanded, outraged.

'Maybe a nicer word is persuasion. Now I know what *I* persuaded him to do. What I need you to tell me is what *you* persuaded him to do.' Someone knocked at the door. Darrell checked through the security spyhole before opening it. A tiny page-boy, sweating under the weight of a two-dozen-bottle crate of Birdade, staggered in escorted by Darrell's minders. Darrell tipped the boy and dismissed him. 'You fellows had better go and get yourselves something to eat. We'll be checking out in an hour.' The minders withdrew.

Darrell took a card out of the crate. ' "With the compliments of Norton and West." That's style. That – is – style. Jesus will you look at that? They don't even gift-wrap it. Not so much as a ribbon! I tell you, if I were a Jap I'd take this as an insult! My God, no wonder they never cracked the Far East.'

'By the Far East I imagine you mean Hong Kong,' said Caldicott, his interest reviving.

'I think you know where I mean. Fellows, I'm still waiting for my answer. What kind of deal did you do with Jacob Norton?'

'Just call the manager, would you, Caldicott, and complain that two of his guests are being held against their will.'

'Oh, come on! You guys have owed me an explanation ever since you weaselled your way into my house with Margaret Mottram. How *is* Margaret, by the way?'

'In tip-top form,' said Caldicott, replying civilly to a polite question. 'She'll be here presently.'

'So she's in this, too. I figured she had to be. Smart girl.' Darrell took a bottle of Birdade from the crate and opened it with the opener from his mini-bar. 'Why don't we drink a toast to Margaret?'

'In that stuff?' asked Caldicott, appalled.

'Have you ever tasted it?'

'Certainly not,' said Charters.

Darrell poured a little into a glass. 'Try it.'

Charters took a sip. 'Disgusting.'

Caldicott followed suit. 'It's even fouler than Zazz.'

'I agree, but the Chinese lap it up.'

'I thought the Chinese lapped up Zazz. At funerals and so on.'

'At funerals period. That's our problem. It's so much associated with death in their minds, they won't drink it at any other time. But Birdade! Wow! It could replace tea! If Norton and West knew anything about marketing, they could be worth millions. Billions. You mean Jock never wrote you about this?'

Caldicott shook his head. 'He never touched on business.'

'Business is not our forte,' said Charters.

Darrell stared at them incredulously. 'He didn't advise you to buy out Norton and West, then wait for a windfall takeover bid from Zazz?'

'Had he left any such instructions we should have passed them on to our solicitors,' said Charters with quiet dignity.

'Do you know, I believe you?' And all this time I've been assuming we were after the same thing. Hey!' Darrell went impulsively to his mini-bar. 'How would you fellows like a *real* drink?'

Charters looked at his watch. 'I think not. We have to be cutting along.'

'Maybe it is a little early.' Darrell poured himself a glass of Birdade instead. 'How wrong can you be? Every time you brought up Jock Beevers' name I thought you were fishing to find out how far I'd gotten in our negotiations before he died.'

'Your negotiations with Norton and West?' Caldicott asked, astonished. 'What had that to do with Jock?'

'Family connections with Norton.'

'Really?' said Charters.

'Plus, with all his Chinese trade contacts, he was my intermediary. For a while. Then Gordon Wrigley flew out in a hurry to Hong Kong and suddenly Jock Beevers *stopped* being my intermediary. Tried to play down the whole thing, said he'd misjudged the market, Norton and West would never sell, we'd never get a licence to ship to the Chinese in bulk, anything he could think of to turn me off. I suspected a double-cross.'

Charters came loyally to his old friend's support. 'On Wrigley's part. Hardly on Jock's. Not the type.'

'They were both the type. Know what the wheeze was? Sell out Norton and West not to Zazz, but privately to Jock Beevers. A paper transaction. No money changes hands.'

'I don't follow,' said Caldicott.

'Stock Exchange mumbo-jumbo. Bulls and bears,' said Charters.

'In a pig's ear! It's Norton's swindling we're talking about. Here's the idea. Sell the outfit to Jock – he writes off the discrepancies as bad debts, then comes to Zazz with a new set of books. Zazz buys the cleaned-up property, Jock and Wrigley split the proceeds, and everyone's happy.'

'Did Jock Beevers tell you this personally?' asked Charters, not wholly convinced.

'Uh-uh. Jock died on me. I had it from Helen Appleyard. She'd listened in to the whole conversation – I gather over-hearing valuable information was her hobby.'

'I wouldn't put much credence on what that little Jezebel told you, Darrell,' said Charters.

'She was on the ball. I checked it out. I also found out why old man Norton sent Wrigley to negotiate with Jock. He lives in terror of his daughter – Wrigley's wife – finding out he's a common thief. Apple of his eye, I guess.'

'That must have been why he was in such a state when he mistook us for detectives,' said Caldicott.

Darrell chuckled. 'You'd better blame me for that. I'd been working on the old son-of-a-gun for weeks but he just wouldn't crack. Offers, bigger offers, threats, nothing. Then you two jokers were announced and I just couldn't resist it. I said, OK, Jake, this is it. Either you see reason or I'll tell Charters and Caldicott of the Fraud Squad they can get all the evidence they need from your daughter. He saw reason.'

Charters grunted. 'Pretty shabby trick.'

'So you achieved a takeover by blackmail. That's going to make quite a paragraph in the Zazz Corporation annual report, I must say,' said Caldicott scornfully.

'Who said anything about a takeover? I got the hundred-year-old secret formula for Birdade – that's all I needed. Now how about that drink?'

Cricket beckoned. Charters shook his head. 'I think you've detained us long enough, Darrell.'

'Thanks for your time, gentlemen. I have what I want – I hope you get whatever it is you want. Satisfy my curiosity – did you two happen to kill St Clair?'

'Don't be absurd!'

'I only asked. You always seem to be around where there's bodies. Good health!' Darrell raised his glass of Birdade, drained it down – and crashed to the floor. Charters and Caldicott stared down at him in silent amazement, then at each other. 'Are you keeping count of all these, Charters?'

'This is ridiculous.' Charters knelt by Darrell's body and felt his pulse. 'He's still breathing.'

Caldicott picked up the open Birdade bottle and sniffed it. 'Shouldn't this smell of bitter almonds, or something, old chap? It has such an awful pong of its own it's difficult to judge whether it's poisoned or not.'

'Of course it's poisoned, man! Ring for a doctor.'

Caldicott found the hotel directory and began to flick through its pages. 'Dining, dry cleaning, doctor. See medical services.'

'Do get on with it, Caldicott.'

Caldicott rang Medical Services. 'Recorded message. In case of emergency dial 999, otherwise kindly leave room number on answering machine.'

'Nine nine nine, then. Quickly!'

Caldicott dialled it, first absent-mindedly thanking the recorded message for its help.

'When this reaches Inspector Snow's ears, Caldicott, he'll have our guts for garters.'

'Hello, Emergency?' said Caldicott, finding himself connected with a human voice at last. 'How odd. Oh, I *see*. Thanks awfully.' He put the receiver down. 'That was the coffee shop. Apparently for an outside number you first have to dial nine.'

'Then do so and hurry,' said Charters, making an ineffectual attempt at artificial respiration.

Caldicott dialled once more. 'Recorded message. All outside lines are engaged. Please dial later.'

'For heaven's sake!' Charters exploded.

'Should I ring room service, do you think?'

'Don't be ridiculous, Caldicott. Get the manager. At least there's little doubt who our murderer is.'

'Little doubt who he is,' Caldicott agreed, tracking down and ringing the manager's number. 'And little doubt why he did it. No reply.'

'Keep on trying,' said Charters, standing up. 'I'll go downstairs to reception.'

'Don't let Darrell's minders know what's happened, whatever you do.'

Charters nodded and opened the door. Gordon Wrigley stood on the threshold confronting him with a gun.

'You've just saved me the trouble of forcing the door,' said Wrigley, coming in, shutting the door and putting up the chain. 'Put that phone down.'

Caldicott protested, 'Yes but look here, this man is . . .'

'Seriously asleep,' said Wrigley. 'There's not enough in the whole crate to kill him, let alone in one bottle.' He knelt by the unconscious form of Josh Darrell, rolled him over roughly and took the Birdade formula from the wallet in his back pocket.

'What do you think you're doing, Wrigley?' Charters demanded.

'Recovering family property.'

'Ah, your precious formula,' said Caldicott. 'I wouldn't have thought you needed all those hieroglyphics for making your particular brand of mouthwash. Simply take a bucket of paint-stripper and add used bathwater to taste.'

'I thought it was your favourite drink. What was that slogan you dreamed up?'

'Name your poison – Birdade.'

'Very funny.' Wrigley glanced at Charters who was feeling Darrell's pulse. 'He'll have a nasty headache, that's all.'

'And you, laddie, will go to bed with a very nasty headache when Darrell's bodyguards have finished with you,' said Caldicott.

'They've got three jumboburgers apiece to wade through first. By the time they're back from the coffee shop we'll be gone.'

'I should jolly well hope so. We should have been at Old Trafford half an hour ago,' said Caldicott.

'You can forget that. You're coming to my place.'

'What do you want of us, Wrigley? You've got your blasted formula – what else are you after?' asked Charters.

'Colonel Beevers' last will.'

Charters gaped at him. 'The will? What's that to you?'

'Plain as a pikestaff,' said Caldicott. 'He's after the gold too and believes the will reveals its whereabouts.'

'Yes, you're just the kind of public-school twits who would swallow that kind of romantic codswallop, aren't you? Cricket, British Empire, clubs in St James's, Army and Navy Stores.'

'Nothing wrong with any of those institutions, Wrigley,' said Charters, drawing himself upright.

'And a nice adventure yarn to read over your toast and gentlemen's relish. Submarine gold! Is that why that twit St Clair was following you about?'

'How did you know he was?' asked Caldicott.

'Because I was following *him*. Now, that letter he got off you . . .'

'You killed him for that, did you?'

150

'I didn't even know the letter existed. It was the will I was after. I thought he'd found it. That's what we were all looking for, after all, wasn't it?'

'Some of us with scant regard for other people's property,' said Charters.

Wrigley ignored him. 'The letter's in code, isn't it? All that gibberish about public-school cricket matches – it tells you where the will is?'

Caldicott tried to look poker-faced. 'It may do. We never had the chance to study it.'

'Well, I'm going to give you the chance – and make sure you take it because I want that will.'

'So much so that you've committed one murder after another in your pursuit of it,' said Charters.

'But why, Wrigley?' Caldicott asked, puzzled. 'If you don't believe the gold yarn, what can there possibly be in it for you?'

'That's my business. Now, you're going to walk out of here ahead of me into the lift, through the lobby and into a cab. If you try anything, I'm going to shoot you. All right?'

'Come along, Charters, we may as well resign ourselves to the fact that we're not going to reach Old Trafford before the lunch interval.'

'Can you give us a moment before we go?' Charters asked.

'For what?'

'We'd like to change our shirts.'

'Move.'

The taxi dropped them outside a substantial, stone-built suburban house. While Wrigley looked on, his gun hidden, Charters and Caldicott meticulously divided the fare between them.

'And the, er, service?' Caldicott murmured discreetly.

'Oh, the tip. Let me have twenty pence, will you, Wrigley? Come along – frankly, I don't see why we're having to pay the fare in the first place.'

Burdened with his gun, Wrigley produced the change with difficulty. Charters and Caldicott were taken at gunpoint into the house and through to the drawing-room where french windows opened onto a long garden.

'Sit down. Meg, my wife, has the letter. She's been having a crack at decoding it. I'll get her.' Wrigley went to the french windows and called out.

They could see a young woman down the far end of the

garden dead-heading roses. 'Meg, you're wanted,' Wrigley called again and she turned and walked slowly down the long path to the house. Charters and Caldicott joined Wrigley at the window, shielding their eyes against the blinding sun, seeing the approaching figure only as a silhouette. Meg had almost reached them before they recognised her. It was the so-called Jenny Beevers. She gave them a rueful, almost apologetic smile.

CHAPTER 16

A sufficiency of girl fridays recruited, Margaret drove back across the Pennines, happily unaware that Charters and Caldicott were risking anything more dangerous than a bump on the head from a gloriously-stroked cricket ball. She checked into the hotel and, when the house phone and the paging service failed to produce either Caldicott or Charters, she shrugged philosophically, picked up her overnight case and headed for the lift.

Inspector Snow and Sergeant Tipper came into the hotel as the loudspeaker was fruitlessly calling for the missing pair. They exchanged worried glances and Snow, spotting Margaret across the lobby, murmured, 'If she's let her two boy-friends slip the leash we've got trouble.'

'Rather a fetching little watercolour, Caldicott,' said Charters, his back turned pointedly on Wrigley and his wife.

Caldicott examined the picture closely. 'Quite nice. Scotland, would you say?'

'Yorkshire Dales,' said the fake Jenny. 'A poor thing, but mine own.'

'I don't think it can be,' said Caldicott icily. 'It's signed Meg Wrigley.'

Charters turned to face her with his scorn. 'Perhaps one of your many pseudonyms.'

Meg was contrite. 'I'm sorry. You have every reason to be angry.'

'Angry? Why should we be angry?' Caldicott asked. 'Total stranger takes the name of our best friend's daughter, tricks us into affording her protection and shelter, all but gets us arrested, in short, makes total Charlies of us — what is there to be angry about?'

'I truly am sorry. I wish there were something I could do to make it up to you *and* Margaret.'

Charters frowned unforgivingly. 'There is, my girl. Explain yourself.'

'Never mind that,' said Wrigley. 'Get the letter.'

Meg ignored him, eager to rehabilitate herself in Charters' and Caldicott's eyes. 'I'm as close a friend of Jenny's as you were of her father's. We were at school together in Switzerland.'

'Very likely,' said Caldicott.

'It's true!'

'How do you expect us to swallow that?' asked Charters. 'We don't even have proof that the girl is still alive.'

'Oh, she's alive all right – just. You know her father threw her out? She went to San Francisco and began drifting across America. One day she was driving to some commune or other with a bunch she'd got mixed up with, all of them high as kites – they met a truck coming the other way. Three of them died instantly. Jenny wasn't so lucky. She's been living for the past year in a private sanatorium in upstate New York, almost completely paralysed.'

Caldicott shook his head sadly. 'Poor girl,' Charters murmured.

'All right – we've had the two minutes' silence,' said Wrigley. 'Now let's have that letter.'

Meg turned to him. 'Do you really think they're going to show us where the will is hidden when they don't even know why Jenny wants us to have it, why I deceived them, how this whole nightmare started?'

'Your wife has a point there, Wrigley,' said Caldicott.

'How much *do* you know?' asked Meg.

Charters and Caldicott answered simultaneously: 'A great deal,' and 'Not a lot.'

Charters nodded to Caldicott to continue. 'Only what we've learned from Darrell.'

Charters felt this didn't do them justice. 'Plus what we've deduced ourselves.'

'It started in Hong Kong,' said Meg. 'Dad had given me the money to take myself off on a kind of flying world cruise while I sorted out what to do about my failing marriage.'

'They don't need to know about that,' said Wrigley.

'I wish I'd known it wasn't his to give, then none of this would have happened.'

'You didn't know because you didn't want to know. Daddy could do no wrong! The sun shone out of his backside!'

Charters glared. 'That's enough of that, Wrigley!'

'Jenny's father took me out to dinner. He told me how popular Birdade had become with the Chinese, just from the few crates we were exporting to Hong Kong. He was convinced there was an enormous market for us, just waiting to be tapped.'

'Shrewd fellow, Jock. Knew how many beans make five,' said Caldicott.

'Well, I wasn't much interested at first. We're such a tiny company we don't have the capacity to expand on that scale. But then he mentioned the Zazz Corporation and how *they* were trying to break into China. He thought Josh Darrell would leap at the idea of taking us over. And so then I *was* interested. I cabled Dad – not knowing, of course, that he lived in terror of an outsider examining the books. My husband arrived on the next plane.'

'With the object of blocking Jock's bright idea by hook or by crook,' said Caldicott.

'Or murder,' said Charters grimly.

Meg looked shamefaced. 'There was no murder. I'm afraid I had to pretend it wasn't a straightforward heart attack for the same reason I pretended I was being followed. So you would take me under your wing.'

'Yes, we rather fell for that, didn't we?' said Caldicott.

'Never mind going on,' said Wrigley. 'The old man'll be home any minute. Are you going to get that letter or shall I?'

Meg stood up. 'Is there anything you'd like. Coffee?'

'This isn't a café.'

'There *is* one thing you might rustle up, since you ask,' said Caldicott, brightening. 'Mrs Mottram's pigskin suitcase.'

Margaret repaired to the semi-darkness of the Wild West bar to recruit her strength with a gin and tonic before setting out in search of Charters and Caldicott.

'May I join you, Mrs Mottram?' Inspector Snow materialised beside her, flicked imaginary dust off the adjacent saddle-shaped stool and sat down.

Margaret managed to hide her surprise. 'We must stop meeting like this, Inspector. Would you like a drink?'

'Not while I'm on duty. Oh, go on then. A Virgin Mary while I'm waiting.'

The barman looked blank. 'That's a Bloody Mary without the vodka,' Margaret translated. 'And I'll have a gin and tonic without the tonic. Waiting for what?'

'My opposite number to arrive with a warrant. It's all got to be done by the book, you know.'

'Of course it has,' said Margaret, suppressing a smile.

155

'So where are they? Your wandering boys.'

'Watching the Test Match, if I know them. They're not in the hotel.'

'I only hope they *are* watching the Test Match, out of harm's way. They were over at Norton and West earlier this morning, I know that much.'

'You have your spies everywhere.'

'No, I don't. Sergeant Tipper's just checked with their receptionist. She said they'd been and gone.' Snow began to arrange a dish of olives on sticks in a sunburst pattern. 'Which is one load off my mind, I must say. That's not far off a maniac they're tangling with.'

'Gordon Wrigley?'

Snow looked surprised. 'How did you work that out? Intuition?'

'Something like that. How did you work it out? Inspiration?'

'Perspiration.' Even the mention of the word made Snow reach for a cocktail napkin and wipe his hands. 'I'm a meticulous man, Mrs Mottram.'

'So I've noticed.' Margaret pointed to one of the olives. 'Shouldn't that be at nine o'clock?'

Snow made the necessary adjustment to the straying olive. 'Matching fingerprints, breaking alibis, comparing statements, collating descriptions, putting hairs and fag-ends and buttons in plastic envelopes, comparing pictures of Mrs Wrigley with descriptions of a young lady seen leaving your house with a pigskin suitcase.'

'Oh, my pigskin suitcase!' said Margaret, her voice unnaturally high. 'It's all right, Inspector, I don't want to prefer charges.'

'Checking, double-checking, treble-checking – hard slog, that's what detective work's all about, Mrs Mottram, not chasing round the country like, well, like . . .'

'Blue-arsed flies,' said Margaret, to save him the embarrassment. 'Still, it's a hobby for them, isn't it?'

'Playing Sherlock Holmes at their age is a riskier hobby than hang-gliding, Mrs Mottram.'

'Would you say Sherlock Holmes? I think they're both Dr Watsons.'

'That's even riskier. They're very old friends of yours, aren't they?'

'Caldicott is,' said Margaret, with a reminiscent smile. 'I think Charters simply tolerates me.'

'You don't know how near you came to having to identifying the pair of them on a mortuary slab.'

Margaret shivered.

Charters completed his protracted and careful study of Jock Beevers' letter and handed it to Caldicott with a significant grunt and a meaningful look. Caldicott glanced blankly through the letter and returned it.

'Now look here, Wrigley, you're quite right,' said Charters. 'This letter should lead us to the will.'

'What?' said Caldicott, slow to take his cue. Then he remembered Charters's grimaces. 'Oh, absolutely. You see, it's in code.'

Wrigley sighed. 'You don't say.'

'However, that will is meant to be in our trust,' said Charters, 'Mrs Wrigley, if we're to place it in your hands, I'm afraid we shall require a fuller explanation than you have volunteered so far.'

'Hear jolly hear,' said Caldicott. 'Now you said this started as Jenny's idea. Does that mean she asked you to find the will?'

'Find it and destroy it – so that the previous will would become valid.'

'Whereupon, so a little bird tells me, she and Helen Appleyard would have carved up the estate between them. Well that seems incentive enough.'

'that *wasn't* the incentive. She was only thinking of me.'

'Brings tears to your eyes, doesn't it?' said Wrigley. 'You've done *her* enough favours.'

Meg followed what seemed to be normal practice and ignored him. 'After Colonel Beevers' funeral I flew to New York to see Jenny. They's been close to one another once and I thought she'd need a shoulder to cry on. By now, Gordon had told me the trouble my father was in if Josh Darrell took us over. I poured out the whole story to Jenny and she had what seemed, up there in the Adirondack Mountains, a wonderfully simple idea.'

'Impersonate her, destroy new will, produce old will, presumably in her possession,' Caldicott summed up. 'Then what?'

Wrigley answered him. 'The same stroke I'd already meant

to pull with Beevers. Buy Norton and West out of what's coming to her, straighten out the books, sell out to Zass, and we'd all be laughing.'

'But how could the poor girl lying in hospital all those thousands of miles away know where the new will might possibly be?' asked Charters.

'Helen Appleyard,' said Meg.

Charters snorted. 'Scheming baggage.'

'Helen kept her in touch with everything that was going on, particularly the fact that Colonel Beevers had sent the only draft of his new will off to England so that "no one could throw a spanner in the works," as he put it. Helen thought, so therefore Jenny thought, that it must have come to you.'

'It did,' said Wrigley.

'But not as directly as you would have liked,' said Caldicott.

'Helen Appleyard was livid,' Meg continued. 'She wrote that she'd a good mind to track down the will and burn it. I suppose that's what put the idea into Jenny's head.'

'The trouble was, it also put the idea into her own stupid head,' said Wrigley. 'If the silly bitch had kept her nose out of it, she could be sitting at home in Hong Kong waiting for a million quid to drop into her lap.'

Caldicott turned his back on Wrigley and his coarseness. 'So you came back to England primed as Jenny Beevers, with Jenny's papers, plus cock-and-bull yarn for my consumption about wanting to see Jock Beevers' diaries. But your nerve failed, so you thought you'd resort to burglary.'

'I suppose my nerve did fail. You see, on one of my visits to Viceroy Mansions, while I was screwing up the courage to go in and ask for you, I saw someone I recognised coming out. I'd seen her at the funeral.'

'Helen Appleyard. Fresh from greasing Grimes's itchy palm, I suppose.'

'I assumed that she must have been to see you. Why, I didn't bother to think – it never occurred to me that she must be after the will, too. I thought that as a friend of Colonel Beevers you must be a friend of hers, too.'

'Hardly likely.'

'Her returning like that upset everything. If she *had* spoken to you, if she *had* told you that Jenny Beevers was in a nursing home three thousand miles away, and then I arrived at your door pretending to be Jenny . . .'

'You'd have been in the soup sooner rather than later,' Caldicott finished for her. 'But hang on, according to Grimes, admittedly not a reliable witness, that's precisely what you *did* do.'

'I had to double-check that you were out, though he'd already told me you were never in on the first Friday of the month.'

'I'm amazed he doesn't announce my movements on the Residents' Association bulletin board,' said Caldicott crossly.

'You know how I got the key. This time Gordon was waiting for me outside. He went up to your flat first.'

'Yes. I've been puzzling about that.'

'I must say there's one thing I've been puzzling over, Mrs Mottram,' said Inspector Snow, consulting his notebook.

'Aren't I supposed to say that?'

'Come again?'

' "But there's one thing I don't understand, Inspector. If the 3.17 from Bodmin was running forty minutes late that day, how could the murderer have hidden in the library before the butler came in with the sherry tray at 6.30?" '

Snow discreetly but firmly moved Margaret's gin glass out of her reach. 'You read a lot of detective stories, do you?'

'All the time.'

'Then tell me this. Wrigley's wife wasn't a party to any of these murders, I'm convinced of that. He was alone with Helen Appleyard when he killed her.'

'I'm sure you're right. She steals pigskin suitcases but wouldn't stoop to murder.'

'Then why did Wrigley go up to Mr Caldicott's flat ahead of her? Obviously to check there was nobody on the premises – a cleaning-lady, say – before she let herself in with the key she'd just pocketed. But why make a double-act of it? Why couldn't she have just marched up and rung the doorbell herself, and if anyone answered,claimed she was selling encyclopedias?'

'Oh, that's easy-peasy,' said Margaret, rocking back dangerously on her bar stool. 'If Mrs-Duggins-what-does *had* answered the door she'd have got a good look at her. Now, if she didn't get her hands on that will – which indeed she didn't – and had to fall back on passing herself off as Jenny

Beevers – which indeed she did – she couldn't run the risk of Mrs-Duggins-what-does blurting out, "That ain't no Miss Jenny Beevers, Mr Caldicott – that's the lady what came round selling encyclopedias".'

Snow nodded slowly. 'That fits.'

'Now I'll give *you* one. You keep saying she let herself into the flat *after* the murder.'

'That's right. She was seen hanging about near the lift, nervously fiddling with a key. Evidently she thought she'd somehow missed Wrigley – that place is a maze of corridors – so she took a chance and let herself in.'

Margaret shivered. 'And found him standing over the body.'

'Yes.'

'Then who let *him* in?'

'Helen Appleyard.'

'But for Pete's sake, *why*? Helen Appleyard wasn't supposed to be in the flat. Why the hell would she answer the door?'

'Mrs Mottram. Do you remember when I called on you the other day and you looked through your little spyhole and decided not to open the door?'

'I was in the loo, if you want to know,' said Margaret defiantly.

'I sent the car away and waited. Five minutes later you peeped out to see if I'd gone. As you know, I hadn't.'

'As *you* know, I came out to put out the milk bottles.'

'You came out *with* the milk bottles, yes. Come on, Mrs Mottram. It's human nature. Helen Appleyard waited, had to reassure herself, opened the door a crack, and saw Wrigley still standing there. He must have heard a movement in the flat – like the chink of milk bottles.'

Margaret stretched across and retrieved her glass. 'All right, I'll give you that round, Inspector. But you still don't know *why* he killed her, do you?'

'I don't have to know why, Mrs Mottram. I expect he'll tell us, in the fullness of time.'

Wrigley was unwittingly in the process of clearing up that aspect at that very moment. 'Panic, sheer blind panic. She was wetting her knickers.'

Charters frowned. 'No need for that kind of talk.'

'I can understand what the sight of you would induce a

nasty turn in anyone, Wrigley, but why panic?' asked Caldicott. 'What did Helen Appleyard have to fear from you?'

'Everything. She knew all there was to know about the scheme I hatched with Jock Beevers out in Hong Kong. If she was interested in selling that information to Josh Darrell, as I thought she was, then very likely I'd be interested in stopping her.'

'You say "if". You can't be sure if Darrell was wise to your little plot or no.' Caldicott turned bitterly on Meg. 'So our role in that foul house party of his, when we thought we were investigating a murder, was merely to pick up any crumbs he might drop about your tinpot little pop factory.'

'I'm afraid so.'

'I'll have you know,' said Charters, 'that was the most disagreeable weekend we've spent since we were snowed up in a Scottish temperance hotel in the bad winter of '47.'

'Not since – inclusive of. However, water under the bridge, old chap. So Helen Appleyard panicked?'

'I bundled her back into the flat,' said Wrigley. 'She wouldn't listen to reason, just went on struggling. Her hand closed on a knife of some sort on the desk. She tried to lunge it into me. I twisted her arm round and she stuck it into herself. Finito. It was her or me.'

'Self defence and no witnesses,' said Caldicott scornfully.

Charters turned to Meg. 'Then you arrived on the scene?'

Meg looked a little sick. 'I was horrified.'

'But not so horrified that you didn't calmly proceed to change handbags.'

'That was my idea,' said Wrigley. 'If Helen Appleyard was in London, Gregory had to be with her. She would have told him about Meg catching her coming out of Viceroy Mansions. As soon as he knew she was dead, he'd be on to us. So. His wife isn't dead but her pal Jenny Beevers is.'

'But *he* must have known, even though no one else did, that it couldn't possibly be Jenny,' said Caldicott.

'Right. He'd guess it was someone posing as Jenny – someone after the will for her own reasons. Helen Appleyard surprises her, there's a row, she kills her, panics and takes off.' Wrigley shrugged. 'All right, so he was bound to rumble it sooner or later, but it did give us a bit of time to play with while we looked for the will. Once we'd got it, easy enough to prove it's all been a terrible mix-up by finding the real Jenny Beevers alive if not kicking in New York.'

'I'd have given anything to have brought Helen Appleyard back to life, too,' said Meg sadly. 'But as it wasn't possible, I couldn't see what harm we were doing – apart from causing a little confusion.'

Caldicott snorted. 'A little confusion! One Jenny Beevers lying dead in my flat, a second Jenny Beevers lying in a nursing home bed in New York, a third Jenny Beevers getting us mixed up in one unpleasantness after another!'

'And you really believe it was self-defence, do you?' asked Charters.

Meg met his eyes squarely. 'I have to. The alternative to believing it is not believing it.'

'How does he account for Gregory's death?'

'An accident.'

'It was,' said Wrigley. '*I* didn't know he was going to be at Josh Darrell's. As soon as he saw me he put two and two together. Figured I'd killed his wife and thought why shouldn't I pay for it.'

'Blackmail?'

'Attempted. He pulled a knife on me and unfortunately got the worst of it.'

'St Clair. Do you believe that was yet another accident?' Caldicott asked Meg.

'Look, all these people – Helen Appleyard, Gregory, St Clair – were criminals. Desperate with greed. They'd have killed either of you, both of you, just to get what they wanted. They'd have killed me; they'd have killed my husband.'

'If he hadn't killed them first.'

Meg had fine-tuned her moral judgement in the interests of self-preservation and there was nothing more to be said. Now that all aspects of the mystery had been cleared up, Charters was conscious again of the call of Old Trafford. Caldicott caught him surreptitiously consulting his watch and did the same himself. 'Yes, time is getting on, Charters, isn't it? I enjoyed our chat Wrigley, Mrs Wrigley, but now we really must be making tracks.'

'Perhaps you'd be kind enough to call us a taxi,' said Charters.

'The will,' said Wrigley.

Caldicott shook his head regretfully. 'I'm afraid after all we can't help you on that one.'

'Please!' Meg pleaded. 'Not for me, for Jenny and my father.'

Charters looked down his nose. 'One doesn't wish to be sanctimonious . . .'

'Well, dammit, I *do* wish to be sanctimonious,' said Caldicott. 'You got into all this to protect your father. Sooner or later he's going to learn that however far he may have strayed from the straight and narrow, his daughter has strayed a good deal further. Whatever you do now, you can't shield him from that.'

'As for poor Jenny,' said Charters. 'From what you tell us, she's regrettably beyond the help of worldly fortune.'

'But she isn't!' said Meg. 'With money there are operations she could have – a new clinic in Texas. But you know what these things cost over there.'

Caldicott wavered. 'What do you say, Charters?'

'What I say, Caldicott, is that provision for Jenny may safely be left with us. There are ample funds available and I'm sure it would be her father's wish. As to handing Jock Beevers' last will and testament over to this blackguard, I should sooner be roasted over a slow fire.'

'Hear hear! Shall we go, old man? We'll probably pick up a cab at the corner.'

Charters and Caldicott stood up defiantly and prepared to take their leave like ordinary guests. Wrigley picked up the gun that had been lying unregarded on a table.

Meg pressed her hands to her cheeks. 'Gordon – no!'

'Don't worry, my dear. I'm sure if precedent is anything to go by, the verdict will be self-defence,' said Caldicott.

'Sit down,' said Wrigley. 'You already have the will, don't you?'

'As we used to say at school, Wrigley, that's for us to know and you to find out,' said Charters.

'We went to different schools, Charters.' Wrigley raised his revolver and pressed the barrel to Charters' temple.

CHAPTER 17

Margaret changed into something suitable for watching cricket, summoned a taxi and set off for Old Trafford. A minute or two later her taxi stopped abruptly, made a speedy U-turn and dashed back to the hotel. Margaret, very agitated, hurried across the lobby to where Snow and Sergeant Tipper were going over some papers spread across a coffee table.

'Charters and Caldicott are with Gordon Wrigley.'

Snow leaped to his feet. 'The stupid old . . .! Where?'

'At his house. My cab driver took them there.'

'Is he sure it was Charters and Caldicott?'

'He remembers them vividly,' said Margaret laconically.

'I'm going to count to ten, then it's your turn,' said Wrigley to Caldicott, holding his gun to Charters' head.

'Gordon, you can't!' Meg pleaded.

'Look here, Wrigley! Charters doesn't know where the blasted will is.'

'Decent of you to bluff, old man,' said Charters gruffly. 'The secret dies with me, Wrigley. Caldicott knows nothing.'

Wrigley began to count – slowly. He'd got as far as nine when the drawing-room door burst open and Jacob Norton was wheeled in by his nurse. Regardless of the circumstances, Charters and Caldicott rose with automatic courtesy. Wrigley hurriedly hid the gun.

Norton glared at his unexpected guests. 'What are you two doing in my house?'

Meg kissed him, greatly relieved. 'Father, this is Mr Charters and Mr Caldicott. We met in Hong Kong – they were very old friends of Jenny's father.'

'Is that what they told you? It's not what they told me.'

'Told you what? I didn't know you'd even met,' said Wrigley.

'You don't have to know all my business, Gordon. Meg, what have they been saying to you?'

'Oh, just chewing the fat, don't you know,' said Caldicott reassuringly. 'About this morning, sir – I believe we may owe you an explanation.'

'You do that.'

'Possibly in private,' said Charters, a plan of escape occurring to him.

164

'We don't need to bother Mrs Wrigley with our tiresome business affairs,' said Caldicott.

'You can wheel me round the garden.' Norton turned to his nurse. 'Lunch in ten minutes.'

Powerless to stop them, Wrigley watched Charters and Caldicott push Norton's chair through the french windows and down the garden path, Jock Beevers' letter safely in their charge once more.

Always the appreciative guest, Caldicott glanced about him. 'Wonderful show of roses you have.'

'Betty Uprichards, I belive,' said Charters.

The party came to a halt at the far end of the garden beside a door set into the wall. 'This'll do,' said Norton. 'We're out of earshot now.'

'And eyeshot, too, which is more to the point,' said Caldicott. 'That door, Mr Norton. Does it lead to the outside world?'

'Never mind that. Come on, let's have it then! What's your game, the pair of you?'

'Cricket, sir. We've already missed the first morning's play.' Charters opened the door and peered out. 'A most convenient alley.'

'Sorry to desert you, Mr Norton. I'm sure your nurse will be along in a jiffy. Good morning.' Caldicott joined Charters in a hasty retreat through the door.

Wrigley looked round as Norton's nurse brought in his lunch tray. 'He's still in the garden. You'd better go and fetch him.' He turned to his wife. 'Come on, Meg.'

'Where are we going?'

'The same place they're going.'

'It's no use, Gordon. It's all over.'

'I'll be the judge of that.' Their car, Wrigley at the wheel and a set-faced Meg beside him, sped out of the drive seconds before a police car carrying Margaret, Snow and Tipper drew up outside the house.

Charters and Caldicott took a fast bus back to their hotel and hurried up to Charters' room. As soon as they were inside, they tugged open their shirt collars and let out simultaneous sighs of relief. Caldicott shed his jacket and picked up the phone. It was time to bring Inspector Snow up to date with developments. While he waited for London to answer, he peeled off his braces and began to unbutton his shirt.

While Charters undressed, he heard Caldicott, in the surprising absence of both Snow and Tipper, prepare to bring enlightenment into the life of a very junior, unknown police-officer. The constable refused the part allotted to him. 'He says they know who the murderer is too,' Caldicott reported in a hurt manner as he accepted Charters' shirt in exchange for his own. 'Are we talking about the same chap?' asked Caldicott, still hoping to surprise Scotland Yard. 'Oh, very well. One was only trying to do one's duty as a citizen.' He hung up in a huff. 'Says Inspector Snow has everything in hand and will we please keep our noses out of it.'

'Impertinent little pipsqueak! You got his name, did you?'

'Well, I'm glad we've got that sorted out,' said Charters, fingering his collar with relief as they got out of the lift.

'So am I, Charters, much more satisfactory.'

'You know, these reach-me-down shirts are really quite comfortable.' Charters dropped his key at the reception desk on the way out. Venables, the clubman, paused in the middle of signing himself in and watched their departure for Old Trafford with a smile.

Charters and Caldicott were fortunate enough to find seats in front of the pavilion. As they settled themselves in, score-cards at the ready and hats adjusted against the sun, an English fielder welcomed them with a spectacular catch. They applauded the returning batsman, recorded his innings on their cards and sat back contentedly. Unexpectedly, a frown flickered across Caldicott's face. 'I'll tell you something that's been puzzling me on and off, Charters. Why are we here?'

'Why are we here, Caldicott? We're here to see England take another three wickets before tea on present form.'

'That goes without saying, Charters. What I meant was, why did we come north in the first place? Why did we go to Norton and West?'

Charters looked at him with concern. 'I know a good deal has happened, old chap, but surely you remember – we were directed there by Jock's letter.' He dug it out. 'There, you see. For Johnson read N. Orton – Norton – then A. N. D. Weston. And West. One of his confounded clues, like his fictitious charity match and the non-existent Old Corinthians.'

'Yes, I know that, Charters – but *why*? Why did he send us to Norton and West?'

'Why? Isn't it obvious why? If we *hadn't* gone to Norton and West, we should never have recovered Jock's letter, nor pinned down Wrigley as the murderer.'

'But Jock wasn't to know that Wrigley would have his letter – much less that he would have taken it from St Clair's body. I repeat, Charters, why are we here?'

The next batsman was walking to the wicket but Charters was staring at the letter. 'I begin to wonder, Caldicott. I begin to wonder.' They dutifully watched the next over and joined in the smattering of applause; then Charters returned to his study of Jock's letter. 'Norton and West,' he muttered, frowning.

Caldicott's attention had wandered to the neighbouring public stand where a nun sat engrossed in her Bible. 'Now that's a sight one doesn't often come across at a Test Match.'

Charters allowed himself a perfunctory glance. 'You'd think, having come here, she'd pay attention to the game. Norton and West. Do you know what I'm beginning to think, Caldicott?'

'You too, old man!'

'What?'

'Pay attention to the game. The over's begun.'

Charters did as he was told.

Gordon Wrigley, a tense Meg in tow, paid for entry at the turnstile and began to search the ground for Charters and Caldicott. Hot on their heels came Snow, Tipper and Margaret who were all admitted free on Snow's pass and at once split up to track down Wrigley. Inevitably, Venables had beaten them all to Old Trafford. Holding a cool drink and sporting a pair of expensive binoculars, he strolled to the front of the pavilion balcony and looked down benignly upon Charters and Caldicott. Perfectly oblivious of all this activity, they were applauding the end of another over.

'That was leg before, if you want my opinion, Caldicott,' said Charters.

'Oh, I don't know, Charters. Benefit of the doubt, what? Mark you, a couple more degrees of spin on that ball and you may well have had a case. You were saying?'

Charters stared at him in sudden excitement. 'A couple more degrees!'

'No – that's what *I* was saying. What you were saying was something about Norton and West.'

'But that's it, Caldicott! When Jock referred us to N. Orton and Weston he didn't mean Norton and West!'

'No?'

'No!' Charters flourished the letter. 'That's what was beginning to dawn on me, and now it's perfectly evident. It was the nearest he dared get to spelling out North West.'

Caldicott looked at him blankly. 'North West?'

'North West.'

'How do you make that out?'

Charters thrust the letter at him 'See!'

'Hold on, old chap. The over's starting.'

Charters and Caldicott settled back to enjoy the new over while assorted search-parties scoured the ground for them and each other. Margaret had actually reached the members' enclosure but her attempt to saunter casually inside was foiled by an alert steward. On the balcony, Venables applauded the fall of another wicket and peered down at Charters and Caldicott through his binoculars.

'Now, see what you make of this, Caldicott,' said Charters, picking the letter up off his lap.

'Half a jiff, old chap, must keep the scorecard up to date.'

'Never mind your scorecard for the moment, Caldicott. Where are those notes you made from Wisden when we made the comparison with the school year-book?'

Caldicott stared at him, astonished. 'Never mind my scorecard?'

'I said, for the moment. Just let me see those figures while their next man is padding up.'

Caldicott got out his notebook. 'What's this north-west business? I don't follow.'

Charters tapped the letter. 'This rigmarole about the batting order. Degrees, Caldicott. North-West. Degrees latitude north, degrees longitude west.'

'I'm beginning to twig this, Charters. So by changing round all these averages and so forth as instructed . . .'

'We get the chart references for Jock's U-boat of gold, or I'm a Dutchman. Now. "For R. H. L. Johnson as Captain read N. Orton." Write down North – "whose innings figures should be the same as Larkin's".' Caldicott obediently wrote twenty-one. '"Boyd-Mason's average should be reversed with that of T. P. Cowling."' Caldicott wrote down 69.93 then glanced up, prepared to discuss this remarkable figure, but Charters' mind was not on cricket. 'Then the non-existent Weston – put down West – and his non-existent bowling average of 17.43. And finally, "Number of runs scored off L. G. Palmer should be 100 less than the total given".'

Caldicott painstakingly subtracted one hundred. 'Nine-O-six. Is that it?'

Charters looked at Caldicott's figures. 'Yes. 21 degrees 69.93 north. No, that's impossible.'

'Why? Is it in the middle of Greenland?'

'No, it isn't anywhere, Caldicott. It's simply not possible.'

'Why not?'

Charters sighed. 'You never did that advanced map reading course in the army, did you? Take it from me, old fellow – that can't be a bearing. It's like saying the time is 2.26 and 93 seconds.'

'Nearer half-past, actually,' said Caldicott, consulting his watch.

'As for the longitudinal reading – far too high.'

'Oh, I don't know. Bear in mind the school had a very good batting side last year.'

'It simply isn't a chart reference, Caldicott,' said Charters, exasperated. 'And a moment ago I was so sure I had it.'

'Supposing we juggle the figures around a bit more?'

'We can juggle them till hell freezes over, Caldicott – there are simply too many digits. Besides, this next paragraph about the fictitious Old Corinthians being 131 for three not out in their first innings. How does that fit in?'

'Search me, old fellow.'

'It doesn't make sense.' Charters frowned over the letter. 'Or does it?'

Margaret had discovered a tunnel that led into the members' enclosure and appeared to be wholly unguarded. Primly buttoning up her jacket as she passed a sign saying 'No bare torsos', she slunk through and up into the enclosure, tiptoeing past a row of dozing colonel-types. One of them opened an eye blearily. 'Good God! It's a woman!'

'He's not wrong,' said Margaret with a wink as she was escorted back past him by a pair of stewards.

Caldicott had given up playing navigators and was attending to the game but Charters, still closely observed by Venables, continued to worry over the letter. 'Corinthians,' he muttered to himself.

'Good show.' Caldicott gave Charters a bemused glance. 'I say, you missed a fine save there, old chap.'

'Corinthians!' Charters leaped to his feet and made off across the pavilion enclosure, deaf to Caldicott's scandalised, 'I say! Watch out,Charters, you're walking behind the bowler's arm!'

As Caldicott watched in amazement, Charters approached the railings, raised his hat to the nun who was still reading her Bible, said something to her and returned holding her Bible and leafing feverishly through its pages.

'What the blazes are you up to, Charters?' Caldicott demanded. 'You'll have us thrown out.'

'corinthians, Caldicott! Corinthians first innings – or, One Corinthians. One-three-one for three or, if you run the figures together, thirteen thirteen. One Corinthians, chapter thirteen verse thirteen.' Charters stabbed his finger at the open page and read, '"And now abideth faith, hope, charity; these three; and the greatest of these is charity".'

Caldicott gasped. 'Charity! By Jove, Charters, our visit to the old school! The only purpose of which was to inform us, via the bursar, about an old boys' charity match which never took place!'

'Yes. One had deduced that while you were gawping at the cricket.'

'One does not gawp, Charters, when Botham is bowling. One concentrates.'

'Yes, I withdraw that remark, I do beg your pardon, Caldicott. I was pre-occupied. *These three* – just supposing. Give me your notebook again.'

'You're missing some awfully good cricket, you know, Charters,' said Caldicott wistfully, handing it over.

Having failed to effect an entrance into the members' enclosure itself, Margaret descended the steps of the adjoining public stand. Looking for Charters and Caldicott through the railings she was spotted by Venables who raised his hat and drew her attention to where the pair were sitting some distance away. Margaret, not quite recognising Venables, nonetheless smiled her thanks and waved at Charters and Caldicott to try and attract their attention.

'Faith, hope and charity, *these three*, Caldicott. That's the significant word,' said Charters, oblivious of Margaret.

'I thought the significant word was charity. The greatest of these is charity.'

'Indeed, but he has already drawn our attention to charity, though for what reason we know not. But *these three*. Suppose we divide those numbers we had *by* three. We now get 07 23.31 north, 58 13.02 west. This could very well be the precise position we're looking for.'

'Really? Where is it?'

'How the devil should I know?'

Margaret abandoned subtle measures, put her fingers to her mouth and gave a piercing whistle. Startled, Charters and Caldicott spun round to see who on earth could be making such an infernal racket. Identifying Margaret, they gave hideously embarrassed smiles. 'Thank God she didn't get into the members' enclosure,' Caldicott muttered. 'Ignore her, Charters.' Wearing glassy grins that disowned her, they turned their attention back to the match.

Margaret, seeing them peering around nervously a moment later, threatened to whistle again. For all that it was the middle of the over, they were galvanised into action. Crouching down so as not to spoil anyone's view of the cricket they made a scuttling run across the enclosure in the manner of Groucho Marx. 'I say, Margaret, you're causing a distraction,' said Caldicott, squatting beside the railings.

'They'll be even more of a distraction if Wrigley finds you. He's scouring the ground for you.'

'Never fear. There's little he can do,' said Charters.

'Don't be too sure, Charters,' said Caldicott. 'A man who'll commit murder probably shows scant respect for the conventions of cricket.'

Charters wasn't convinced.

'And Inspector Snow agrees,' said Margaret urgently.

'Is he here, too? You know, I think we *had* better make ourselves scarce, Charters. Let's watch from the bar – neither Wrigley nor Snow will find us there.'

'Why shouldn't they?' asked Margaret.

'Not members,' said Charters.

'Boom-boom. I walked right into that one, didn't I?'

'You might just return this to Sister over there,' said Charters, handing Margaret the Bible.

'Really, I knew you supported England but I didn't know you prayed for them,' said Margaret. As she turned to hand the nun the Bible, she recognised Wrigley, Meg still in tow, at the top of the public stand. At the same time, Wrigley spotted Charters and Caldicott and, dragging Meg with him, headed round to the back of the members' enclosure.

'Get the hell out of here,' said Margaret. 'I'll see if I can find Inspector Snow.'

Venables, having watched all this activity with detached interest, turned away, his glass empty.

CHAPTER 18

Wrigley shoved aside the steward who tried to stop him getting into the members' enclosure and, deaf to Meg's pleading, began to search frenziedly along the rows of seats. Charters and Caldicott watched from their vantage point in the bar as he came nearer and nearer. When discovery seemed imminent, they abandoned their positions, fled from the enclosure through the tunnel Margaret had discovered earlier and hurried into the scoreboard building. High amongst the statistics of batting and bowling, first Charters' head then Caldicott's appeared, framed in two small windows. By ill luck, Wrigley spotted them and tried to argue his way past another officious steward. Snow arrived at the entrance to the members' enclosure, Tipper and Margaret at his heels. 'Get that man! He's armed!' Wrigley made a dash for it, scattering spectators to left and right.

Charters and Caldicott, observing the scene from high above, exchanged embarrassed looks across the record of the day's play and withdrew their heads. Caldicott took a fiver out of his wallet and handed it to the scorekeeper. 'Thanks awfully, old son. Do have a large drink in the tea interval.' He gave a last glance out at the ground and said to Charters, 'I do believe the blighter's got away.'

'Not for long – and he certainly won't bother *us* again.'

On their way back to the members' enclosure, Charters and Caldicott passed the open door of the press room. Charters glanced casually inside. 'Hold on, Caldicott. Let's just drop in here for a minute.'

The cricket correspondents, engaged in watching play from the verandah or typing up their reports, ignored the new arrivals. Charters went over to a large table scattered with newspapers, old Wisdens and, among other reference books, one that had particularly attracted his attention: a battered Times Atlas. 'You were asking, before we were so rudely interrupted, for the precise location of that chart reference I worked out – if it really is a chart reference. We'll know soon enough.'

'Whether it is or where it is?'

'Either or both. If it leads us to the rain forests of Borneo, we're on the wrong trail again.' Charters checked the notes he'd made on the back of Jock Beevers' letter and turned the pages of the atlas. 'Fifty-eight west, seven north – this region, I fancy.'

Caldicott looked over his shoulder. 'Brazil? Possible.'

'No. Much further west and much further north. Somewhere about here.' Charters jabbed at the map.

'But that's in the sea!'

'Of course it's in the sea, Caldicott. Where else would you expect to find a submarine?'

One or two of the correspondents glanced up curiously at this.

'But how do we know that's where the submarine *did* scuttle itself?' asked Caldicott, examining the map as if expecting to find a symbol indicating the actual wreck.

'We don't – that's the trouble. The position *seems* likely enough but it could be a coincidence. If only we had one more clue to tell us we're on the right track.'

'Charters, look here, old man,' said Caldicott, almost reverently.

'I'm afraid this small type defeats my glasses.'

'Then take them off and use them as a magnifying glass.'

Charters followed this suggestion and peered closely at the blurred outline of the Guyanan coast. Finally he focused the lens over one place-name – Charity.

Charters and Caldicott beamed at each other and shook hands. 'The largest of Scotch and sodas, Caldicott,' said Charters as they turned to leave the press room. Wrigley stood in the doorway. To the astonishment of the cricket correspondents, he was pointing his gun at Charters.

'You've already had your count of ten, Charters,' said Wrigley, positioning himself to fire.

'Gordon, no! No more!' Meg burst in and seized his arm. In the struggle that followed, the gun went off. Snow, Tipper and a constable rushed in as Wrigley threw Meg to the ground and dashed for the verandah. The police made as if to follow but stopped abruptly when Wrigley turned the gun on them.

'Don't do anything stupid, Wrigley,' said Snow. 'Drop the gun on the deck and walk forward.' Margaret came softly into the room and put her arm round Meg. 'Just drop it, Wrigley. Come on, lad, you can't do anything now. Just drop the gun and . . .' Another shot rang out. Meg buried her face in Margaret's shoulder. The sergeant ran to Wrigley lying on the ground but Snow stayed where he was, shaking his head. The cricket correspondents had all jumped to their feet – except for one particularly cool customer who picked up his phone, dialled and asked for the news desk.

Charters and Caldicott exchanged what they thought to be worldly glances and turned again to the door. As they passed Meg, Caldicott patted her shoulder and Charters coughed sympathetically. 'I'd say that stiff drink was still in order, wouldn't you, Charters?' asked Caldicott.

'Mr Charters, Mr Caldicott,' Snow called after them. 'You won't be going far, will you?'

'Not until close of play, Inspector,' said Caldicott. As Snow joined them, he went on more quietly, 'We can take it he's dead?'

'Not a pretty sight. Still, look on the bright side – no trial. That does mean your statements can be a little less, shall we say, detailed than they might otherwise have been. We don't want to waste police time, do we?'

'Good Lord, no, that would never do,' said Caldicott.

'What will happen to Wrigley's wife, Inspector?' asked Charters.

'Not a lot, I shouldn't think, Mr Charters. What happens to us all? I suppose there *are* peripheral charges I could make, but once we start on that game we never know where to stop, do we? Mr Caldicott?'

'Indeed no. Thank you, Inspector Snow.'

'I trust we may be able to help you again one day, Inspector,' said Charters, civilly. Snow shuddered and closed his eyes.

'Two extremely large Scotch and sodas,' Caldicott ordered, but before the words were out of his mouth the drinks were put before them. They followed the barman's glance down the bar and saw Venables drinking by himself at the far end. He raised his glass to them and they, with reluctant good manners, raised theirs in return.

'What the blue blazes is he doing here?' Charters muttered.

'God knows, said Caldicott through a fixed grin.

'If he claims to be the official keeper of the Ashes or any such nonsense, I shall have it out with him.'

Caldicott turned away from Venables and was confronted by the even more unwelcome sight of Margaret, Meg close behind. 'You can't come in here!' Caldicott hissed, hideously embarrassed.

175

'There, Meg, I said you should wear a tie,' said Margaret. 'She's all in. Brandy.'

'He would refuse to serve us!' Caldicott belatedly remembered what Meg had been through. 'I say, are you all right? You've had a frightful, er, experience.'

'Don't worry about me. I've known ever since Helen's death that it would have to end something like this. I just wanted to apologise to you both for all the trouble I've caused. And to thank you.'

'Think nothing of it,' said Charters, taking her arm. 'Now if you'll allow me to show you the way . . .'

Margaret stayed put. 'What about that medicinal brandy?'

'Oh dear, this is very difficult.'

'And I'll have a medicinal gin and tonic.'

'Look here,' said Caldicott. 'Why don't we go across and have a nice drink in the Ladies' Lounge?'

'Can't. You're not ladies and we're not members.'

'Pity. We could have been your guests.'

'That's all right. We can be your guests.'

'Ah, but you see, this is members only,' said Charters.

'Vive la différence.'

Charters and Caldicott exchanged desperate glances and peered furtively about them. Deeply disapproving glowers met them on all sides. Only Venables seemed to find the situation amusing.

'Well, my dear, I don't know what your arrangements are,' said Charters pointedly to Meg.

'Oh, look after Father as best I can. He's still got Josh Darrell to worry about, remember. And I suppose I'd better write to Jenny in New York about the plot that failed.'

'Quite. I meant your immediate arrangements.'

The barman finished making a phone call and gave Charters and Caldicott a meaningful cough. They sidled over and listened to his whispered message. Before rejoining Margaret and Meg, they exchanged a few discreet words of their own.

'The stewards are on their way,' said Charters. 'Now look here, Mrs Mottram, we don't want a scene.'

'Speak for yourself.'

Charters ignored her and said to Meg, 'Jock Beevers' will. Jenny has the original one, I believe.'

'Yes. And you have the later one.'

'No. There is no later one,' said Caldicott. 'Isn't that so, Charters?'

'Positively,' said Charters, grasping Meg's elbow again. 'And now . . .'

Meg resisted. 'But there is. We all know there is.'

'Misunderstanding,' said Caldicott.

'Jock was thinking of changing his will but in the event he never got round to it,' said Charters, putting the lie they'd agreed upon as succinctly as he could. 'You may be sure that if the will in Jenny's possession goes for probate, no one will come forward to challenge it.'

Meg was overcome. 'I don't know how to thank you.'

'By leaving instantly.'

'Home-time, ducks,' said Margaret, apparently capitulating. 'You need sleep and I need my pigskin suitcase.'

'Goodbye and good luck,' said Caldicott.

Charters and Caldicott heaved heartfelt sighs of relief as Margaret took Meg out. 'Large ones, I think,' said Caldicott, turning back to the bar. Charters nudged him. Glancing round, he found that Margaret had returned. 'Now look here, Mottram!'

'You're taking me out to dinner tonight, that goes without saying. I just want to make it clear that one subject is banned.'

'Yes, I know you hate cricket.'

'I wasn't thinking about cricket. I was thinking about the murders. So we'll just get it over with now, shall we?'

'Mrs Mottram, I really must ask you to leave,' said Charters as two stewards came into the bar.

'I'll leave when I have the answer to one question. In a sentence, how did you know it was Wrigley?'

'Not in a sentence, dear lady, in a word. Deduction.'

'What a coincidence. That's how Inspector Snow worked it out.'

Caldicott took her arm. 'Yes, well tonight you can tell us how you worked it out, clever britches.'

'Oh, no – no shop-talk, remember.' Margaret smiled at the two hovering stewards. 'Shan't keep you a jiff, ducks. Anyway, it was just a routine blinding flash. I was driving over the Pennines this morning when out of the blue I suddenly remembered something. You know that weekend with Josh Darrell?'

Caldicott gave the stewards an embarrassed grin. 'Don't remind me.'

'I overheard him on the phone to Wrigley, telling him that

you two had turned up and wanting to know who you were. And it was quite plain that Wrigley already *knew* you were there.'

'So he did,' said Caldicott, temporarily forgetting his social difficulties in his interest. 'And only one person could have told him. His wife – our little cuckoo in the nest.'

'Plain as a pikestaff, isn't it,' said Charters. 'Goodbye, Mrs Mottram.'

'Show Mrs Mottram to her taxi, would you?' said Caldicott to the stewards. 'It's a pity you didn't have that blinding flash earlier, Mottram. Your inspirational tardiness has cost us a full morning's cricket.'

'Still, never mind, so long as you know how it ends. It's like detective stories, isn't it?' With a naughty wink at the scandalised pair, Margaret linked arms with the stewards and departed.

'Large ones, barman,' said Charters. He nodded towards Venables. 'I suppose we've got to buy that fellow a drink?'

'Can't be avoided, old chap. He bought us one. And whatever that gentleman is having,' said Caldicott, completing the order.

Venables reacted with exaggerated surprise to the arrival of a full glass, then raised his drink in thanks. Charters and Caldicott, raised theirs in return and Venables moved along the bar towards them. Charters and Caldicott, with reluctant civility, shuffled forward to meet him half-way.

'Saluté,' said Venables.

'Your health, Venables,' said Charters.

'Cheers,' said Caldicott.

'An eventful day,' said Venables.

Charters nodded. 'Very. What's the score?'

'One hundred and fourteen. No more wickets since your hasty departure from the members' enclosure, you'll be relieved to hear.'

'Nothing to be relieved about. England needs those wickets, Venables,' said Caldicott.

'What do *you* know about our hasty departure, Venables? Are you spying on us again?' Charters demanded.

'Observing. I am an observer.'

'Ha! Your official title, I suppose.'

'No. My official title, such as it is, is Special Investigator for the Treasury.'

'The Treasury,' said Caldicott, surprised. 'What – tax and so forth?'

'Gold and so forth.'

Charters and Caldicott exchanged uneasy glances. 'Oh, that,' said Charters.

'That. Any, er, news at all. Of its whereabouts?'

'I don't see what that is to you, Venables. *Or* the confounded Treasury.'

'Quite,' said Caldicott. 'Britannia may rule the waves and all that but I don't think that extends to possession of a German U-boat sunk thirty years ago off the coast of never mind where.'

'That's one view,' said Venables blandly. 'Another view is that Colonel Beevers was a serving officer when knowledge of the U-boat came into his possession. Any submarine gold, then – it could be argued – would be government property.'

A prolonged round of applause from the ground distracted Charters. 'Someone out, by the sound of it.'

'Or a thundering good six,' said Caldicott.

'We really should be witness to these excitements, wouldn't you agree,' said Venables, leading the way outside.

'This Treasury of yours . . .' said Charters when, drinks in hand, they'd established themselves in front of the pavilion.

'I wouldn't say one's Treasury, Caldicott,' said Venables, beginning to fill his pipe.

'Charters,' said Charters.

'As the case may be. One's paymaster.'

'If this gold *should* be recovered, would the authors of its recovery have a say in what was done with it?'

'All those millions, what?' said Caldicott, his eyes lighting up. 'Hospitals? Lads' clubs? Cricket grounds for deprived areas? I say, we could set up a trust fund.'

'I'm afraid not. The Treasury is to cash what blotting paper is to ink. It simply – absorbs.'

Charters and Caldicott grunted their disappointment and looked at each other. Caldicott raised an inquiring eyebrow and Charters nodded in agreement.

'Do you have a match, Charters?' Venables asked, his pipe filled.

'No, he's Charters,' said Caldicott. 'I have a lighter.'

'Never light a pipe with a petrol lighter. Bad for the tobacco. Allow me.' Charters folded Jock Beevers' letter into a spill, lit it from the lighter and handed it to Venables.

'Sorry to disappoint you,' said Venables between puffs. 'So you thought that sunken gold would go to a good cause?'

'Had we found out where it was,' said Caldicott mendaciously.

'To *charity*, perhaps?'

Charters and Caldicott gave Venables a sharp glance but a splendid piece of cricket distracted them. 'Good show!' said Caldicott, rising to his feet.

'Well played, Charters applauded, standing beside him.

Venables blew out the flames of the folded letter and put the charred remains complacently into his wallet unnoticed.

Charters and Caldicott, beaming with pleasure, continued to clap the fall of another wicket. Venables, the gold and the murders were alike forgotten in their enjoyment of the only really important thing in life.

For a complete list of books available from Penguin in the United States, write to Dept. DG, Penguin Books, 299 Murray Hill Parkway, East Rutherford, New Jersey 07073.